This Game

Other books by Carol Westron

The South Coast Crime Series
The Terminal Velocity of Cats (Mia Trent)

About the Children (Tyler)

Karma and the Singing Frogs (Mia Trent)

The Fragility of Poppies

Victorian Murder Mysteries
Strangers and Angels

Children's Picture Books
Adi and the Dream Train

Adi Rides the Night Mare

Adi and The Ghost Train (a Christmas Story)

This Game of Ghosts

Carol Westron

I'll go with you then, since you must play this game of ghosts.
 Siegfried Sassoon

Copyright © 2020 Carol Westron

Carol Westron has asserted her right under the Copyright, Designs and Patents Act, 1988 to be identified as the author of this work.

This book is sold subject to the condition that it shall not, by way of trade or otherwise, be lent, resold, hired out, or otherwise circulated without the publisher's prior consent in any form of binding, cover other than that in which it is published and without similar condition including this condition being imposed on the subsequent purchaser.

All characters and events in this publication, other than those clearly in the public domain, are fictitious and any resemblance to actual persons, living or dead, is purely coincidental.

ISBN 9798608257490

First published in the UK 2020 by Pentangle Press.

Dedication

To my brilliant beta readers: Lesley Talbot, Jo Halsall and Dot Marshall-Gent.

Thank you!

Acknowledgements

The annual Easter folk music concerts at Ferneham Hall, Fareham, were always a delight and made me aware of so many great musicians and inspiring songs, including my favourite band, the magnificent Show of Hands.

Thanks to Jack Halsall for producing another gloriously unique and thought-provoking photograph for the book cover.

My gratitude to Peter Westron for his help with proof reading and the book lay-out.

Thanks to Christine Hammacott of The Art of Communication for her help and support.

As always, my love to my family, Peter, Jo, Jack & Adam, Paul, Claire, Oliver & Henry, Alan, Lyndsey, Thomas, Tabitha & Pippa. Thank you for being there for me.

Easter 2011

Chapter 1 Good Friday

It's seven years since Matt and I split up, but still I hate coming home to an empty house, especially after dark. I'm edgy as I drive the narrow country roads. The glare of my headlights turns the fresh shades of April to acid green.

I tell myself to get over it. Single women must learn to live alone. I've had it easy so far, but one day Allie and baby Ben will move out. Then I'll always come home to an empty house. I guess Matt foresaw this when he insisted I had a top-grade security system installed. The lights activate the moment I turn into my driveway.

There's a figure sitting on the floor in the shelter of my open porch. I see a face in the shadows. My heart lurches. It's Simon's face, the way he looked in the weeks before he died. I stare deeper and know my mind's playing tricks on me. This is no ghost. It's Matt. Simon, our son, was always the image of his dad.

Matt clambers to his feet and hurries towards the car. Past fears are outed by a more desperate one. I release the central locking and scramble out. "What's wrong? Allie? Ben?"

He's beside me in two strides. "No! Nothing like that. I didn't mean to scare you. I'm sorry, Honey."

This quells my worst panic, but I'm still frightened. The tempestuous, disjointed speech is so unlike Matt's usual control. I remember Simon and a cold claw sears through me. "Are you ill, Matt?"

"No!... At least... no, I'm not sick."

"Let's go inside. I'll make coffee."

"Don't forget the car."

I lean in and turn off the engine. The noise that warns I've left the lights on starts its caterwaul and I retreat in clumsy confusion. Matt silences it, then retrieves the keys and picks up my bag from the front passenger seat. As he locks the car I wonder why I don't resent it when Matt takes control. Perhaps it's because he does it so quietly, or maybe it's just habit, thirty years of marriage isn't easily overcome.

"Where's Allie and Ben?" he asks as I open the front door.

"Out." I try to keep my disapproval from showing. Allie and her dad find enough reasons to quarrel without me stirring things. Allie had been cross when I'd told her I couldn't baby-sit this weekend. Sometimes I find it a difficult balancing act, between supporting a single-parent, student daughter and letting her push her responsibilities onto me whenever it suits her.

I lead the way into the kitchen and put the kettle on. Matt perches on a stool at the breakfast bar. Questions bubble in my mind but I damp them down and wait for Matt to tell me why he's here. He removes his glasses and rubs his eyes, which gives me a chance to look him over without meeting his gaze. I think he looks tired and strained, but that's the way I remember him. What's new is the network of fine lines around his mouth and eyes and the feathering of grey in his brown hair. In his mid-fifties he's beginning to look like the grandfather he is.

"Are you okay?" I ask.

"Aye." He puts his glasses back on and smiles at me, a shadow of his usual grin. "I didn't mean to scare you. I should have phoned, not just turned up. I'm sorry."

His voice still holds a hint of the soft Northumberland accent that wound itself around my heart half a lifetime ago.

"That's okay. Have you been out there long?"

He glances at his watch. "An hour or so, I guess. I was thinking and kind of lost track of time." He shivers. "It's cold for Easter."

I hand him a mug of coffee. "You're lucky I left the Ferneham Hall early, otherwise you could have been there for another two hours."

"You were at the Folk Festival? Wasn't it any good?"

So he's not ready to tell me what's wrong with him. Apparently we have to do a prologue of the polite trivia that poses as communication between us nowadays.

"Not my sort of thing tonight," I explain. "Some middle-aged, look-how-cool-we-are group shouting political propaganda. Four of their songs were enough for me."

"I know who you mean. They're supposed to be cutting edge folk-rock."

"That's what Terry said. I told him I felt like I was stuck between the folk-rock and a hard place."

When I'd made this comment to Terry, after the first bellowed number, he'd frowned at me blankly. Matt grins, then asks, "Where does it come from? That saying about being trapped between a rock and a hard place?"

"I don't know. Why?"

"Just thought it summed up where I'd got to." He shrugs, as impatient of self-pity as he's always been of sympathy. "Sorry. I've had a funny sort of day."

"What sort of funny day?"

Another shrug.

I'm fed up with faffing. In the past three years, since Allie stopped going to stay with him, Matt has dropped in occasionally with Christmas and birthday presents, and last year, when my mum had a hip replacement, he phoned every day to check she was okay. At the moment no-one's ill and he's not acting like he's dropped round with an Easter present for Ben. This is obviously something very different, something bad.

"Matt, presumably you came here to tell me about your problem, so get on with it."

He catapults into speech, "When I got home this evening there was a woman in my house. She'd cooked dinner."

Call me old-fashioned, but that's hardly the sort of news a man rushes round to share with his ex-wife. The only unusual feature of Matt having a woman in his house was her ability and willingness to cook. When it comes to lovers he goes for ditsy blondes who prefer eating out. But Matt has never been insensitive and this stills the caustic comment that hovers on my tongue. "Who was she?"

"I don't know."

I sit down opposite him. "How about you tell me from the beginning?"

"I got home about six and I heard music... 'I love you because'... awful slushy stuff. There was this woman. She was acting like she'd got a right to be there."

"What was she like?"

"Ordinary. That's what made it so scary." He lapses into silence.

"How old was she?"

"I don't know. Pretty old and sort of frumpy. Grey hair and about as tall as me, and big..."

"You mean fat?" I struggle to keep my tone neutral. I don't like talking about body size, even though I've slimmed down a lot. When we'd split up I'd blamed my billowing weight for Matt's infidelity. It was only when I'd returned to some sort of sanity that I accepted that my obesity had been a symptom, not the disease.

"Not fat exactly, just solid. And she smelled of old-ladies' perfume."

"You said she was frumpy?"

"She had a frilly flowered apron and the sort of clothes old ladies in the village used to wear when I was a kid." He bites his lip. "She was wearing pink slippers, the sort with phoney fur round the top."

I almost giggle, a nervous reaction rather than amusement. I choke back my laughter and feel glad I did because Matt's voice trembles as he says, "It's crazy but that scared me worst of all."

I put my hand over his and feel his fingers shake.

"What happened then?"

"I asked who she was and how she'd got into my house and she said this really creepy thing." He swallows hard. "'You know who I am, Matthew. You must have known you couldn't keep me out forever.' It was scary and yet it felt totally unreal. Honey, I swear I don't know who she is."

I squeeze his hand. "Go on."

"She said she'd cooked me dinner. The whole house stunk of liver."

"But you hate liver!" I stop, appalled at how flippant this sounds.

Miraculously he takes it the way it's intended. "That's right," he says eagerly, "most people who know me know I don't eat red meat."

"Did you leave this woman still in your house?" If so, prompt action is required.

"No, she's gone."

He seems reluctant to elaborate so I move on to how she got in. Matt's never been lax with security. "Perhaps she's related to some girl you picked up. She must have got your door key from somewhere."

"I don't give my key to the women I sleep with." His response is breathtaking in its simplicity and its shamelessness.

"Fine. So how many people have got your keys?"

"Just you." My surprise must show, because he says, "Don't you remember? I sent you a new key and alarm code when I changed my security firm a few months ago."

"Yes, I remember that, but I didn't know I'd got the only spare key."

"Allie had one when she used to come and spend weekends with me, but she threw... gave hers back long ago."

"I see." Allie is our only surviving child and there are times I feel as if we lost her as well as Simon when he died eight years ago.

"Have you got a cleaner? Or a gardener? Somebody like that?"

"Only a window cleaner and he comes when I'm there. I do my own gardening and cleaning. It doesn't take a lot to keep the place straight."

"For you maybe." I look around my chaotic kitchen.

"It's different when you're living on your own." He picks up Ben's toy xylophone and absent mindedly plays a rippling tune.

"I've got your key. I'll show you, if you like." He must think I've lost his key and he's checking up.

"There's no need for that. I wasn't blaming you. I needed to talk it through. I'm sorry. There's no reason I should dump my problems on you."

"Who else should you dump on?"

Most people would regard this as absurd, but some things in my life are not negotiable. I've known Matt for thirty-five years, loved him, married him and had two children by him. Together we'd suffered a soul-wrenching loss. It wrecked our marriage, but I can't turn away when he's in need.

He shivers and rubs his hands across his face. "Thanks for saying that. It's so crazy. Like a nightmare. After she'd gone, I didn't know what to do or what to think. Then I realised I needed to see you."

"Why?" I ask the question against my better judgement.

"Because you're the most honest person I know, and the most sensible."

That isn't the view of most of my friends, family and acquaintances, at least not the sensible bit. I'm the sort of woman who always manages to push doors when I should pull, and keeps a strainer specifically for sieving cork out of the wine I've failed to open. On more than one occasion I've been known to lose my classroom. Although I maintain this is not my fault, the college's building policy means they erect new wings faster than I can track them down.

"Are you planning to tell the police?" I know the answer even as I ask.

"No way. Can you imagine me going into the cop shop and reporting that an old woman got into my house and cooked liver and onions?"

I see his point. "You need to change your locks as soon as possible." I try to live up to this new, practical image Matt's offering me.

"I know."

"Matt, you said 'after she'd gone,' but how did she go?"

"What do you mean 'how did she go'?" He sounds irritable.

"I assume you didn't sit down and munch your way through the liver with her?"

He shudders. "No!"

"What happened then?"

The look he gives me is a mixture of shifty and scared. This time I put both my hands over his and squeeze. "Tell me."

"She went into the kitchen and shut the door. I took a minute to go after her."

"Why?"

"I don't know why! I was bloody confused, and the smell of liver was making me feel sick. Then I went into the kitchen and she'd gone."

"But it's three miles to the nearest village and, wherever she parked, you'd see the car."

When we divorced he bought and converted a pair of farm cottages situated along an isolated track. It seems unlikely an elderly woman could have sprinted fast enough along the rough road to be out of sight before Matt looked. And it's even more improbable that she could easily scale the six foot fence that divides his property from the tangled woodland that borders that side of the farmer's fields.

Matt's voice is jagged. "That's not all. The food had gone as well. There wasn't even a dirty frying pan. Just the smell of liver stinking out the place. Do you think I'm going mad?"

Chapter 2

How the hell can I answer that? I've always been afraid that no-one can keep control of their emotions the way Matt does without something cracking, but I hadn't expected a breakdown. I'd thought it would be a stroke or heart attack... or cancer... the way it had been with my beautiful boy.

"I guess that gives me my answer." Matt cuts across my thoughts.

"What?... No! I wasn't thinking that. Matt, I don't know if you're having a breakdown. How can I tell? I've hardly seen you for the past three years."

"Fair enough." He stands up.

I can't let him leave like that. "Have you eaten?"

He shakes his head.

"Sit down again. I'll make you something."

"Thanks, but I need to go outside and grab a cigarette."

We'd both smoked when we were at University and we'd both given up before we started trying for a family. I wonder when Matt took it up again.

"Okay, but put your coat on."

"Aye Mum."

As easily as I'd slipped into the fussing mother role, he'd responded with the teasing reply that he, Simon and Allie had always given me. By his stricken look I know he too has plunged into the black hole of remembrance and pain.

"Stir fry suit you?"

"Fine, thanks." He's fumbling with the bolt on the kitchen door, his clumsiness a sign of how uptight he is.

I prepare a vegetable stir-fry. I don't know if Matt's turned totally vegetarian but he's never been keen on red meat. I remember Allie's complaints, not that her dad refused to cook her hamburgers when she stayed with him, but that he couldn't entirely conceal his distaste.

As I stir vegetables into the oil, I try to put the story into context using the guidelines of my own experience. It had taken four years from the diagnosis of Simon's leukaemia until his death. I'd gone through the last months of his life in a queer, trance-like state, doing all that was needed and yet cut off from everything.

After his death I'd fallen apart, mentally and physically. The scariest symptom of all had been a weird hallucination phase. I could see Simon in my peripheral vision and hear him in my outer listening range, but when I focused fully it was never him. For a split-second I'd relived that tonight when I'd seen Matt sitting in the shadows.

I can think of three possible explanations for Matt's weird visitor. One, he's going crazy; two, he's lying; three, someone's doing this to him. I can cut number two. Matt doesn't lie. Even in business he's got a reputation for telling it like it is. In our personal lives, I've sometimes wished I'd had a deceitful husband. I didn't want to know Matt was playing away from home, but my sister kept nagging at me and I was forced to confront him. I wish he'd made more effort to blag it but he didn't and I'd realised he was as sick of me as I was of myself.

He returns as I spoon egg-fried rice and stir-fry onto a plate.

"Matt, do you think someone set you up?"

"I wondered. But set me up for what? And why?"

"And who?" I finish in chorus. "I don't know but it seems odd to have a hallucination like that if it's not based on anyone you've met before."

"You're telling me." He pushes his laden plate away.

I move it firmly back in front of him. "Stop thinking about it and eat."

"Bossy," he murmurs.

"Only when it's for your own good."

That wins the first unforced smile I've seen from him all evening. He picks up his fork and dutifully tucks in.

"Are you enjoying the Folk Festival so far?" he asks.

So he wants to retreat to the impersonal? That's okay by me.

"It's been okay. Tomorrow should be good, it's Show of Hands."

"It's a long while since I've heard them live."

"You should try and get a ticket. They may still have a few single seats."

Immediately I wish I could bite my tongue out. If he's alone I don't want to rub it in. Still less do I need him telling me he prefers clubbing with his latest bimbo.

"Maybe I will if I get round to it." His casual response lets us both off the hook.

"Do you still play?" I'm referring to the guitar, rather than other games.

"No."

"But you were so good."

He shrugs. "Things aren't as much fun as you get older."

"True. Shall we have our coffee in the sitting room?"

He follows me through and settles into an armchair with a weary sigh. "Is the boyfriend keen on Folk Music?"

"His name is Terry." I struggle to keep irritation from showing in my voice. 'The boyfriend' makes it sound like I've set up a toy boy. Terry's fifty-four, only four years my junior, and in many ways he's more middle-aged than me.

"Yes, he likes Folk Music. He's got some friends arriving tomorrow to go to the rest of the Festival with us."

"That's cosy."

Whatever other snide remarks Matt's going to make about Terry are averted. We hear the front door open and, a moment later, Allie arrives in the sitting room.

"Hi Mum. I didn't expect you back yet." Her gaze slides past me to Matt and her dissatisfaction deepens. "Oh, hello Dad. What are you doing here?"

"He dropped by to talk a few things through," I say. "Where's Ben?"

"Ross is bringing him in. I didn't want to wake him and he's too heavy for me when he's asleep."

One shouldn't call one's only and much-loved daughter a liar but, in my head, I do. Allie's small and slender but she's strong enough to carry her twenty-month-old son anywhere she wishes without disturbing him. She'd assumed I'd still be out and Ross could stay over without me knowing. "He'd better bring Ben in then," I say.

She glares at me defiantly. "Ross is staying the night."

"Yes, I thought he would be." I keep my tone affable.

"You got a problem with that?"

"No." Allie knows that Ross staying over is accepted, but him moving in isn't.

"He's got no money even for food, Mum. That bitch takes every penny he earns."

I don't enquire why, if Ross is starving, Allie had thrown a tantrum because I couldn't baby-sit while they went to the cinema, but I do say, "That bitch is his wife and she's got three small children to bring up by herself."

Allie gives Matt a spiteful look. "You mean it's all right for rich married men to screw round but not others?"

I see Matt's expression and speak before he says something we'll all regret. "Allie, whatever happened in our relationship, your dad never begrudged either of us anything. When we split up, he'd have willingly gone without to make sure we had everything we could possibly want."

"But he didn't have to go without, did he?"

I keep my voice soft, but by now I'm very angry, "I don't think your dad can be blamed because Ross is less successful and hard-working than him."

I look past her to the figure hovering in the hall. "Good evening, Ross. You'd better take Ben up. We don't want him waking. If you're hungry there's plenty of food for you to cook."

"No, thanks. I'm fine. Good evening, Mr Alder. It's great to see you again." Ross turns his bright beguiling smile on Matt. I know I'm an over-protective mother, but I haven't liked Ross ever since he started work at the college, long before Allie came into the mix.

He carries Ben up the stairs to bed and Allie follows them.

"Phew," says Matt.

I smile at him. "You know, I think your house may have a lot to recommend it, even with a loony woman dropping in."

"Does Allie really think because I was a bloody fool it's okay for her to do the same?"

"I'm not convinced thought comes into it, certainly not logical thought."

I know Allie wants to pay us back but I've never been certain why. I'm not sure she has worked it out herself. I think part of it is for focusing on Simon and having so little quality time left for her. But equally I think it's for us losing Simon, for being unable to hold back death. And afterwards we made such a mess of things, me deep in depression and Matt screwing any female who was up for it. It can't have been easy for a thirteen-year-old girl.

Matt removes his glasses and pinches the bridge of his nose, then rubs wearily at his forehead. "What a mess. I'm sorry, Honey."

"It's not your fault, at least not all of it." I supply him with paracetamol and a glass of water.

"Thanks. I gather she wants lover boy to move in here?"

"Yes. His wife threw him out and he's living in a bedsit."

"I suppose it'd make life easier for them."

"I don't particularly want to make life easier for them."

"You don't?"

I try to explain my position. I don't think I've become an ogre but the chances are I'd be the last to know. "When Allie got pregnant, I promised her I'd be on her side whatever she decided to do. I said if she chose an abortion I'd support her, but if she went through with the baby, I'd make sure they had a home and she'd get every chance to finish her degree. At no point did I say Ross could move in here."

"You don't like him?"

"No. Do you?"

"I haven't had a lot to do with him, but I'm kind of prejudiced, him being the bastard who knocked up my little girl."

That sums up my position as well. Ross is thirty-five, fifteen years older than Allie, although he appears younger and keeps himself in good shape with frequent visits to the college gym. I think he's a freeloader and suspect he hoped Allie's rich dad would subsidise their life together. Matt has always respected my opinion, especially concerning people. That's why I don't tell him how anxious I feel. I won't make more trouble between Matt and Allie.

I offer Matt a limited version of the truth as I see it. "I don't like tutors who hit on teenage students. And I don't think it makes it any better that he was calculating enough to wait until a few days after she'd left college. And it's made it hard for me at work, I've got Ross' young brother-in-law in my tutor group."

"That's awkward for you."

I shrug. "I can cope."

There's a disciplinary hearing scheduled next term to discuss aspects of Ross' behaviour but I'll cross that conflict-of-interest bridge when I come to it.

Matt refuses to drop the subject, "Ross seems so phoney."

"What do you expect? He's a drama teacher. But I agree, I can't stand guys who drip self-conscious, boyish charm."

He grins at me. "I'll remember that."

"Too late, you're long past boyish." I don't add that Matt's charm, and he's got plenty, has never been the self-conscious sort, nor does he turn it on and off at will. "How did you get here? I didn't see your car."

"I walked."

"But it's eight miles!"

"Aye. I'll get a taxi back."

I'm about to offer to drive him when the doorbell rings. Allie answers it. I hear her say, "She's in the kitchen but I don't think she's expecting you."

Terry enters. "Are you okay, Honey?" His eyes go to Matt and I see him thinking this is why I'd run out on him.

"Yes, I'm fine."

"I didn't realise you'd got company." His tone is hostile.

I think ruefully that I may have had company but this is definitely a crowd. "Terry, this is Matt."

"Hello." Neither of them smiles or offers to shake hands.

Matt stands up. "I'd better go, Honey. I'll phone for a taxi and wait for it outside."

They make a curious contrast. Terry is tall, at least six-foot-three. He has dark hair and eyes, strong features, tanned skin and a ready smile that displays his excellent teeth. At five-foot-ten, Matt is only an inch taller than I am and he's never been the sort to turn heads in the street, although many people have warmed to his soft voice and quiet charm. Few people would guess it's Matt who's the successful businessman, while Terry's a Social Worker.

"Let me know if there's anything I can do, Matt."

"Thanks Honey." He smiles acknowledgement, but it isn't his warm smile, it's the sort that puts the world on the other side of a glass wall.

As the door shuts behind him, Terry demands, "What did he want?"

"He'd had an intruder and he wanted to make sure I'd got his key safe." The quarter-truth falls glibly from my tongue.

"Oh I see. I thought for a minute you'd fixed up to meet him this evening."

I'm tempted to tell him to sod off, but I say, "No. I wasn't expecting him."

He smiles and pulls me towards him, hands sliding up my tee-shirt and fumbling at the fastening of my bra.

"Terry, not here. Allie and Ross are still up."

"Let's go to bed then."

So what do I want? I could tell him I'm too tired and send him home to his small Portsmouth house. He won't like it but I know he'll go. But I'm on the brink of that dark and lonely place I never want to travel through again, and, more than anything, I don't want to be alone.

Chapter 3 Easter Saturday

I know Allie has been stirring when my sister phones early the next morning before Terry and I have got up.

"Honey, it's me."

"Jackie? What's wrong?" My first thoughts fly to Mum.

"Nothing. I wanted to check you're okay."

"Of course I am. Why shouldn't I be?"

"It's a while since we had a chat."

"Jackie, cut the garbage. You don't phone at eight in the morning unless there's something wrong, or you think I'm about to do something you'll disapprove of. Has Allie been in touch?"

"She did ring through a few minutes ago to ask whether I could baby-sit tonight."

"I see." On the whole I can probably see a lot more than my sister wants me to, and can put it into the context of fifty-five years of sibling love and sibling rivalry.

"Actually, Honey, I wanted to warn you that Mum's not very well."

Mum and Jackie both still live in the village where we were born and she sees Mum almost every day. "What's wrong?" I assure myself if Mum had been really ill she'd have told me. We phone each other constantly. But, since Simon, people treat me as if I'm too fragile to cope with the big things in life.

"She gets lonely. As her hearing gets worse she feels more isolated."

"I'll go and see her as soon as possible. In fact I could nip round this morning."

There's a moment's silence, then Jackie says, "She'll be out until lunchtime. She's going to a WI Coffee

Morning." She sounds defensive, aware she's been sussed.

At seventy-six my mum is bright and brisk and, since her hip replacement, she's remarkably fit. Simon's death had hit her hard, even worse than the loss of our dad ten years ago, but she'd done more than anyone to get me through. Despite everything she's still very fond of Matt. Suddenly I long to see her.

"I'll bring Ben over to visit her soon," I say and ring off.

Neither Jackie nor I had actually mentioned Matt and yet his spectre hung between us as vengefully as Banquo's blood-caked ghost. It's been like that since she'd pushed me into confronting him and showing 'proper pride.'

Worry about Matt is with me, as it has been all night, lurking in the shadows of my mind. I'm afraid there's something badly wrong with him and I feel helpless because I no longer have any right to interfere.

Terry is nibbling my shoulder. I roll away from him, get up and go into the en suite to take a shower. As I stand under the warm water I realise my hands are lingering on my bum and thighs, stroking, softly, sensuously, as if the caress came from someone else. I look down at my boobs, and move my fingers to slowly trace around their soft pale orbs. They're still quite sexy although nowadays they need a good bra to face the world. I move downwards to my belly with its cracked-glaze effect of stretch marks; six stone doesn't disappear without leaving its signature. My legs aren't bad, at least the calves are still acceptable, and my ankles and feet are slender and shapely, although around the anklebone a few small veins are a visible reminder of the years of flab. The door opens and I snatch my hands away, flustered and guilty as if I'd been caught in some secret perversion.

Terry pads in and says, "Room for a little one?" Without waiting for an answer he steps in beside me. He cups my boobs with his hands and kneads them.

"Don't do that!" I step away as he bends forward to kiss my nipples. The spray of warm water catches him full in the face and makes him splutter.

"Sorry," I say. "Not this morning."

He grabs a towel and dries his face, then scowls at me. "What is it? Time of the month or time of life?"

"That's an offensive thing to say." Usually I can't be bothered to quarrel with Terry but when I do stand up to him he backs down fast.

"Sorry, Honey. It's just I want you at your best to meet my friends."

"I will be." I leave the shower. "I've got things to do this morning. I'll see you there this afternoon." Back in my bedroom, I dress in jeans and tee-shirt, grab my jacket and bag and go downstairs before Terry has finished in the en suite.

In the kitchen Allie is spooning cereal into Ben. They both look heavy-eyed so I guess it's been another long, teething night. I assume Ross is still in bed. There's little of the New Man in his attitude to childcare.

"Good morning darling." I say to Ben and tickle him as I pass his high-chair. "Morning, Snitch," I say to my daughter. I put the kettle on and make toast.

She gives me a wary look but doesn't deny the unspoken charge. "Sorry."

"You should be. What goes round comes round."

"I don't know what you mean."

"You can stir things up and tell tales on me all you like, and it won't stop me from loving you or looking out for you and Ben. But every time you do stuff like that, you lose a bit of my trust."

"I'm sorry." This time I think she means it.

I take advantage of her repentance to ram the real message home. "We all make mistakes and we all do stupid things. God knows your dad and I have mucked up big time. But he's still your dad and he deserves you should treat him with respect. And he was my husband for thirty years. If he's in trouble I can't turn my back."

"Is Dad in trouble?"

"I don't know, but I think he may be." I hand her a mug of coffee. "Do you want me to take Ben out for the morning?"

Now deeply repentant, she hugs me. "Thanks Mum. You're wonderful."

"It's the best butter," I comment, which clearly confuses her as I'm smearing low-fat spread onto my toast. "Alice in Wonderland, the Mad Hatter's Tea Party."

"Oh I see." She adopts the soothing tone she uses to humour my quotation habit.

As soon as Ben and I are clear of the house I pull into a passing place and take out my mobile. He answers on the third ring, "Matt Alder."

"Hi, Matt. It's me. I wanted to check you're okay."

"Thanks for ringing, Honey." His voice warms from its initial crispness. "I'm fine. No more loony visions. Sorry I was a nuisance."

"You're not a nuisance. Let me know if you need anything… or anyone to talk to."

"Thanks. Maybe we could go out for a meal. It would be nice to catch up."

The formality of that offer chills me but I say, "I'd like that. Bye."

Ben falls asleep before we get to the park, so I put him in his buggy and head into our small local town to do some retail therapy. I'm a size eighteen, enormous by the standards of the fashion magazines, but a lot better than the twenty-six I'd been when life was at its worst.

I try on a deep purple top and realise vibrant colours don't suit me since my dark hair has turned grey. On impulse I get out my mobile, ring my wonderful hairdresser and blurt out my request. Miracles do happen. Tara's had a cancellation and can do me straight away. I buy the purple top and, getting thoroughly carried away, a scarlet silk nightdress with lace straps; then I hurry to her small salon.

Tara's enthusiastic about my new dark-haired, spiky look. She's been my hairdresser for years and used to come to the house when I couldn't make it past my drive without panicking. As she finishes the low-lights she says, "The first few times you see yourself in the mirror you won't recognise yourself."

She's wrong. I look at my reflection and know myself for the first time in years.

As I walk along Waterlooville Precinct, to my surprise I see Ross in heated discussion with a middle-aged woman, which is a polite way of saying she's shrieking abuse at him. She's short and plump, with a tight, low-cut jumper and very high heels and Ross looks distinctly uncomfortable. I step into a shop doorway and keep my back turned until Ross walks away. I wonder who she is and why she's so angry.

It's eleven-twenty when I reach my car. Determinedly I rouse Ben and sing to keep him awake as we drive home, otherwise he won't sleep tonight. Like most men who are forced to socialise when they'd rather be sleeping, Ben's grumpy and doesn't seem to notice my new look.

It's otherwise with Allie. "Wow! You look brilliant, Mum."

I hug her, grateful for the compliment. Encouraged by her praise, I put on my new purple top and team it with a calf-length, brown skirt.

For years after Simon died, I'd worn black trousers and long-sleeved tops even on the hottest day. I'd not been wearing mourning, at least not Queen Victoria style. But I'd hated myself. I'd loathed my blubber body. I stare in the mirror and wonder if I'm doing this for Terry or for Matt. I dismiss the doubts. I'm doing this for me.

I feel shy as I go downstairs but Allie says all manner of nice things.

"I've got to try and look good for Terry," I explain. "He's got some old university friends coming down for the weekend and he wants me to impress them."

"Are you really keen on Terry?"

Now that's a question I find hard to answer. Terry had been an important part of my healing process. Before we met I'd believed no man would ever fancy me again and, in the five months we've been together, he's made me feel good about myself. But lately I've noticed a controlling element creeping into his attitude.

"Terry and I have had some good times but I don't plan to make a permanent commitment to anyone again, apart from you and Ben."

To my surprise she smiles with an understanding she's never shown before. "I know what you mean. In the end your kids are what really matters, aren't they?"

I hug her and don't explain that's what I find so hard to forgive in Ross. He hardly ever bothers to see his other children nowadays.

I have a bright idea. "If Aunt Jackie's coming over to baby-sit tonight, we could invite Nanna as well. She could stay over and enjoy Easter Day with Ben."

"That would be great. Do you want to phone Nanna or should I?"

I glance at my watch. "Could you do it please? Terry will strop if I'm late."

Fareham is a small town not far from Portsmouth and the most direct way from my village is to use the lanes, which suits me, I prefer lanes to the motorway.

I'm almost there when my mobile rings. I swear, thinking it's Terry nagging me to be on time. The lane is narrow and by the time I pull into a passing place the call has switched to my answer phone. It's listed as coming from Matt's landline.

I listen to the message. There are no words, just the sound of laboured breathing. I phone the landline, but it gives the engaged signal and his mobile rings until it hits the answer phone. I'm shaking as I turn the car round and race to Matt's house.

Everything's closed and silent but his car is on the drive. After his visit yesterday I'd checked his key was safe, and, without reasoning why, I'd slipped it onto my keyring. I don't want to intrude, so I ring the bell and knock on the front door. There's no answer. With trembling hands I unlock and open the door. "Matt? Matt, are you there?"

I go through the house swiftly, room by room. I find him upstairs, lying on his bedroom floor, wet and naked, his face a mask of blood.

Chapter 4

Fighting panic, I go down on my knees beside him. His breathing seems okay and I wonder if I should turn him into the recovery position or whether that will do more damage. A large towel is lying beside him on the floor, and I use it to carefully wipe his face. There's a deep gash on his forehead that has also split his eyebrow. "Matt, can you hear me?"

He groans. Slowly his eyes open, but they don't seem to be focusing.

"Matt, it's Honey."

"Honey?" His hand goes to his forehead. "My head hurts."

"I'm not surprised. What happened?"

"I fell."

I register the sound of running water and go into the en suite to turn off the shower. I grab a clean bath sheet and return to Matt. "I'll call an ambulance." I pick up the phone that's still lying close beside him on the floor.

"No, I'm okay."

I'm not convinced but I put the phone back on its stand and steady him as he struggles to sit up. It's a bright spring day but he's shivering. I wrap him in the bath sheet and dry him with no more embarrassment than I'd have felt doing the same task for Ben. I help him to hoist himself up onto the bed and cover him with the duvet.

The doorbell rings. I go downstairs and put the security chain on before I answer it. "Good morning, Fairhaven Security." The man shows me his ID. "Your alarm's been going off in our depot for fifteen minutes."

"I'm sorry, I forgot about the alarm. My husband... my ex-husband had a fall and I was in a hurry. He'd told me about the alarm being silent and going off at your offices, but I... look what do I have to do to cancel it?"

"I'll need some proof of your identity."

Flustered, I look around for my bag. My relief when I find it is disproportionate, triggered by the suspicion in his voice. My driving licence is the old-fashioned paper kind but my college ID bears my picture. I unlatch the door-chain and open the door fully then give it to him. He examines my ID and hands it back to me, then checks a list he's holding. "That's fine, you're listed as a keyholder. Now, if you could give me the code number to confirm it's really okay."

For a moment my mind is blank. Then I remember, when Matt sent it to me I'd resolved to keep it handy so I put it in the side pocket of my purse. I look there and don't find it. Fighting down panic, I undertake an archaeological expedition to the bottom of my handbag, and find Matt's letter.

I repeat the code to the man, who checks it and rings through to his office to cancel the alarm. "That's not a secure place to keep the code you know."

"I'll change it," I say obediently, although I think it's a very secure place, so secret it's a miracle I'd found it.

I see the security man out but, before I can go upstairs, the doorbell rings. Absurdly cautious, I put the chain on again before opening it. The security man says, "Sorry to disturb you again. Could you tell Mr Alder that he can change his security code any time he wants. It's usual to do so after a call out."

"I'll tell him." I give a perfunctory smile, shut the door and run upstairs to check on Matt.

For reasons best known to himself, he's attempted to get up. He's sitting on the edge of the bed, white and shaking. The cut on his forehead is bleeding again. "What are you doing?" I run to steady him.

"I wanted to... check you were... okay."

"Very heroic. Unfortunately, Sir Galahad, you can't even protect yourself."

There's a moment's pause then he mutters, "Lancelot... not Galahad."

"What?"

"Lancelot... he was the one... who screwed around."

"And screwed up," I say unkindly.

"Aye... that too."

I ease him back onto the pillows.

"Feel sick," he whispers.

I fetch a bowl. "You need to go to hospital."

"I know. Could you help me get some clothes on?"

Fair enough. No-one wants to go naked to A&E. I find joggers and shirt and help him put them on. "I'm sorry, Matt. I'll have to call an ambulance. I can't get you down the stairs and out to my car."

As we wait for the ambulance, I ask, "Do you feel well enough to tell me what happened? Did you slip in the shower?"

He doesn't answer. His face has a strangely shuttered look. "Matt, what happened?"

"You won't believe me... no-one would."

"Try me."

"She was here."

I stare at him. "The woman?"

"I was in the shower and I heard a noise in the bedroom. I grabbed a towel and went to see what it was and it was her. She said, 'However much you try, you can't wash away the guilt.'" He shudders.

"Very Lady Macbeth. What happened then?"

"I tried to get to the phone to dial 999 but she held onto me. She was stronger than I expected. She pushed me and I fell. The rest is hazy. I sort of remember crawling to the phone and trying to ring you... You don't believe me, do you?"

"I'm sure you're not lying but there are things I don't understand."

"Like who she is and why she's doing this?"

"Yes. But I meant how did she get in?"

"Presumably the same way as yesterday," snaps Matt.

"Yes, that time too. The point is the security guy arrived fast enough when I came in. This strange woman doesn't just have a key, she knows your code as well."

I hadn't thought it possible for Matt to lose more colour, but he does. Then he grabs the bowl and throws up.

I'm relieved that the ambulance comes so quickly. As I run downstairs and wrench open the door I have a fleeting sense that something's wrong but banish it, focusing on explaining what has happened and accompanying Matt in the ambulance.

At the hospital Matt's put in the fast track, because of his head injury. I'm surprised when he names me as his next-of-kin, but I don't argue. His dad lives in a care home in Northumberland and Allie doesn't need this responsibility.

While we wait in an A&E cubicle, he says, "Like old times, isn't it?"

I smile at him. "I was thinking that."

When we were students Matt used to play rugby for the University team. He was more lightly built than most of his team-mates but fast and bloody-minded. It wasn't surprising he spent a lot of time in Casualty. I always went to watch his games, which entailed accompanying him on his trips to hospital.

It has always enthralled me that Matt approached everything with twice as much energy and commitment than anybody else. It wasn't just sport; he'd loved music too. We'd attended a small folk club every Sunday night. It had many professional performers but Matt was often invited to take a turn on stage.

My sister said I was an idiot to believe a guy like Matt could be faithful to me. I felt sorry for her because her own teenage marriage had self-destructed after a few months.

In the run-up to Finals Matt had asked me to marry him. I'd been shaken by Jackie's marital disaster and suggested we should wait. In reply he'd said something strange, 'I'll wait forever for you, Honey. I need you. You're the only person in the world I feel totally safe with.'

And so I'd married him. Despite everything Jackie said then, or has said since, I know he was faithful to me for the next quarter-century.

The first years after Uni were hard work but fun. I'd taught English in Adult Education, which kept us afloat while Matt set up his business. He used his charm and technical knowledge to develop a company that arranged events with faked exotic scenarios and recorded them, afterwards supplying copies on video tape to his clients. At that time it was original enough to take off. The play school end of the business was lucrative and I still cherish the tapes of Allie in Wonderland and Simon amongst the dinosaurs. Of course, technology has advanced a lot nowadays and everyone is more sophisticated, but Matt has managed to stay ahead of the game.

Ten years into our marriage we had enough money for me to quit work and start our family. We had to try for five years before Allie came along and I'd had a difficult pregnancy. Grateful to have our beautiful little girl, we'd accepted that she was likely to be an only child, but when we tried again I fell pregnant straight away with Simon and had very little trouble carrying him. Allie had been delicate, the sort of child who always got ear infections and colds, but Simon was a robust, happy-go-lucky boy. Allie was nine and Simon seven when I returned to part-time teaching. Two months later Simon's cancer was diagnosed. He died four days after his eleventh birthday.

"I'm sorry, Honey." I blink back to the present and realise Matt's looking worried.

"I didn't mean to upset you... to bring back bad memories... If hanging round here's too much for you, I'll be fine by myself."

This is getting positively insulting. What happened to the image of the most sensible, sanest person, he was offering me yesterday? I glare at him. "It's not me that's seeing liver-cooking she-devils all over my house."

Immediately, I hate myself for being so nasty. "I'm sorry. I didn't mean to snap. But when you treat me like I'm about to fall apart, I'm scared I'm turning into a gibbering wreck again. I'm not like that any more."

"I guess I'm the one who's cracking up this time."

I hate to see him so vulnerable. "Matt, this woman may be real. She could have got the door key and code from somewhere. Perhaps she works for the security firm or something like that. Loony stalkers can be amazingly inventive."

"That's great. Best-case scenario: I'm being stalked by a lunatic with hideous taste in clothes, who has access to my security system." Nevertheless he does seem comforted. "I'm sorry, Honey. I hope I haven't buggered up your afternoon." He smiles at me. "You're looking gorgeous and I love what you've done to your hair."

It's then I remember Terry. It's after three. I'm over two hours late. I'm amazed he hasn't phoned me. I search my bag and find no mobile. I must have left it in the car after Matt phoned. If Terry's contacted Allie she'll think I've had an accident.

"Matt, have you got a phone?"

It's a stupid question and deserves his sarcastic response, "Get real, I haven't even got any underwear."

"I'll be right back. I've got to let Allie know I'm okay."

I hurry out and locate the public phones.

Allie picks up on the second ring. "Hello?"

At the sound of her sharp voice I know she's heard about my non-appearance.

"Darling, it's me. I'm fine."

"Mum, where are you? Have you had an accident?"

"No. I'm sorry. I didn't mean to frighten you. Did Terry phone?"

"Yes, at twenty-past-one and two o'clock and again at two-thirty. Where are you?"

"I'm at the hospital..."

"Mum!"

"I'm okay. Your dad had a fall and knocked himself silly for a while."

"Dad? But how did you know? Mum, what's going on?"

"Nothing's going on. Dad phoned my mobile, so I went round to check on him. I left my mobile in my car and it's still at your dad's place, so I was out of touch."

"Why's your car still at Dad's place?"

"Because I went with him in the ambulance."

"Ambulance! How badly is he hurt?"

It's good to hear her sounding worried about Matt. "He's got concussion and a cut on his forehead. They have to play safe with head injuries, but I'm sure he'll be fine."

"How are you planning to get home?"

"I don't know. Taxi I guess."

"I'll come and get you."

"Are you sure?" It occurs to me that asking for help can be a sign of strength, not weakness. "I'd appreciate it, love."

"No problem. I'll see you soon."

"Hang on. Can you give me Terry's mobile number? It's on the phone pad."

Allie does so and I ring through. Terry's phone is turned to answer service. I leave a grovelling apology, ring off and hurry back to Matt.

"The doctor says the scans are clear and I can go home."

"Are you sure?" I'd expected them to keep him in hospital overnight.

"Of course I'm sure." There's a snappish note in his voice that sets off warning sirens. I'm certain there's something he's not telling me.

I mutter an excuse and slip out of the cubicle to find someone who'll give me a straight story. I encounter the nurse who has been looking after Matt.

"I wondered if there's anything I ought to know?" I say, fishing for all I'm worth. "My husband is okay to leave, isn't he?"

She looks surprised. "As the doctor told your husband everything seems satisfactory. We're short of beds and, as he's got proper care at home, he's been discharged. But you need to keep a close eye on him.

All the information is in the Head Injuries pamphlet I gave your husband."

"He hasn't shown me that. Matt hates being fussed over."

She flips a white card from the stand behind her and holds it out to me. "This is all you need to know. He needs checking on regularly for the next two days, especially tonight. Make sure he's focusing and not disorientated, but don't worry if he's sick. Take him straight home to bed. Give him plenty of fluids and keep a close eye on him."

"Thank you." I tuck the card into my handbag and return to Matt.

"It's no good, you've been sussed."

"What?" He squints up at me and it's clear he's got a savage headache.

"The nurse told me you've got to be looked after for the next two days."

"She had no business to. Nurses aren't supposed to talk about their patients."

"You can't have it both ways. You claimed me as your next-of-kin and forgot to add the ex to wife, so don't moan when they give me instructions for looking after you."

"It's a fuss about nothing. If you'll lend me the taxi fare I'll be fine."

I know if I refuse to let him have the money he'll simply call for a taxi and pay when he gets home, except of course he hasn't got a door key. When I think of Matt's front door I have a feeling I've forgotten something important, an elusive memory of something I've seen. But this isn't the moment to think it through. The key on my ring means, in this fight, I have the upper hand. I could turn this into a power play but I don't want to fight with Matt.

Whoever wins the argument, ultimately both of us will lose.

"I don't think that's an option, Matt. If you insist on going home, I'll have to stay there with you, but I'd rather not."

"I understand that. I wouldn't ask you to. You're busy." It's clear he's thinking about Terry and the Folk Festival.

"I don't want to be away from home because this is Ben's first Easter since he discovered chocolate. That's why I think you should come home with me."

There's a brooding silence, then he says, "Wouldn't Allie mind?"

"I don't think so. She sounded worried about you when I phoned. Come on. She'll be here soon to drive us home."

I think he's glad to have the decision made for him. He clambers slowly from the bed and walks with me to the main exit. He moves in a shaky shuffle that makes him appear suddenly old and frail. Allie looks shocked when she sees him and accepts without question that he's coming home with us.

Allie has already made up the bed in the spare room ready for her Nanna's visit, and I get Matt straight into it. I've just got him sorted when she returns with two hot water bottles, both with cartoon character covers. "Here Dad, I saw you shivering."

"Thanks love." He seems overwhelmed by her small gesture of care.

His gratitude makes Allie shy and she disappears again.

Matt looks preoccupied and I wonder if he's feeling sick, but then he says, "Honey, there's something else I've remembered about that woman."

"What's that?"

"She had a Northumberland accent. Quite a strong one."

It seems to me he's building his fantasy. "Try to rest now." I rearrange his pillows.

Matt moves and the hot water bottle makes a peculiar noise. "What the hell?"

"That's Pingu," I explain.

He squints painfully down at the penguin in question, which is lying beside him. "Of course it is," he says.

"It makes that noise if you press it in a certain place."

"Of course it does." He laughs, albeit shakily. "I think I'll just lie here very still."

"That's probably best," I agree.

He rummages in the bed and produces the other bottle. Its cover is a bright pink pig, with black beady eyes and an evil expression. I expect him to ask what sort of noise it makes but he repeats, "Very, very still," and puts it back with exaggerated care.

Chapter 5

I don't like Terry. This thought thrusts itself into my conscious mind a short way through the concert and I feel irritated. Show of Hands is my favourite folk-rock band and I don't want to be distracted from the music to think this through. There are many times that would be more appropriate, like when I'm attending a College Curriculum Meeting or cleaning the bathroom.

It's no good, despite my best efforts I can't shelve it. Reluctantly I tackle my discovery. What's brought this on? The obvious answer is Matt's re-entry into the centre of my life. But that's old ground. What Matt and I had together was special but it's over and there's no way back.

It had been hard to step back into the world alone but, in the last two years, I'd realised it was no use waiting for another perfect love affair. If I planned to have sex with anyone again, I had to go for it, and, as long as the relationship was with someone I liked and respected, it was fine. Which brings me back to where I started. I don't like Terry. And I'm running pretty low on respect too.

I sneak a look sideways. I'm at the end of the row and he's next to me, but his body is slanting towards his guests. His face has its usual blandness, that non-committal expression I think of as the social worker's mask. But, as he looks along the line at his old friends, I spot something else, a kind of placatory eagerness. I recall the look of anxious pride on his face as he'd introduced me to them. Brief greetings were all we'd had time for because I'd arrived two minutes before the show. With a sinking feeling I realise his vulnerability means I can't call a halt to our relationship until the old pals leave on Tuesday. To spoil this for Terry would be unkind.

If there's nothing I can do for the next three days, I can concentrate on the concert. That's good timing. They are just starting 'I Promise You', Steve Knightley's lyrical love song, in which he promises the listener a series of delicate delights once they have endured the bitterness of winter. I first heard this song after Matt and I had parted and yet it's Matt's voice that lilts within my mind.

In the interval I chicken out and spend a long time lurking in the Ladies, which is pretty antisocial considering the limited number of cubicles in Ferneham Hall. Eventually I creep out and brace myself to join Terry and his guests. They remain unaware of my approach. Terry's friend, Jez, is talking loudly about the sort of music he admires. Apparently if it doesn't blast you out of your seat it's not worth going for. Nicola suggests that, when I rejoin them, they go off for a meal and don't bother about sitting through the second half of the concert.

My bright pink top and flowered maxi-skirt wouldn't usually rank as camouflage, but this time I strike lucky because I'm standing by a stall that sells ethnic clothes. I blend into the background and sneak away, making for the outer door. If I creep in just as the second half starts, they won't be able to make me miss the rest of the concert. They may go off to dinner without me but that's okay. I took a taxi here and I can take a taxi home.

"So you're one of the antisocial brigade as well?" The voice comes out of the darkness and makes me jump. "Sorry, I didn't mean to startle you. I keep forgetting this fancy dress acts as camouflage in the dark."

He steps into the light and I recognise Edward, another of Terry's friends. He's an accountant and he's married to Nicola. Like all of the visitors, he's dressed in black, although his well-cut suit and silk shirt are more suited to a funeral than a Folk Festival.

"I feel like I'm auditioning for a part in a gangster movie," he complains.

I can't imagine him as a gangster. From the little I've seen, his wife strikes me as the tough one of the pair. "I suppose some people like reliving old times," I say.

"I'm not sure what the hell we're doing here. It's only Jez who's kept up with folk festivals. And because we used to dress in black when we were at university, thirty years ago, doesn't mean we have to carry on. Jez has heard rumours this is likely to be the last folk festival in this hall. Next year they'll probably insist we go under canvas in a muddy field."

"Tents are too hard on the knees when you get to our age," I agree.

"Now with me it's my back." He smiles apologetically. "I'm sorry. You must think I do nothing but moan."

"I suppose it's a symptom of middle-age."

"Moaning?"

"Sort of. When you're young you don't tell people you've only just met about the bits of you that are stiffening up."

How the hell could I have said that? I feel myself blush, then I see Edward's startled look and giggle. "I didn't mean that the way it came out." One thing about me, I'm not a quitter, and I can always make bad worse.

His laughter surprises me. I hadn't expected any of Terry's friends to have a sense of humour. "You're one hell of a girl! I never thought Terry would have the bottle to get a woman like you."

That dries up my amusement and he sees it immediately. "Sorry. I didn't mean to offend you. You know Terry a lot better than we do nowadays."

"You haven't offended me." What he's done is set a new explosion of thought cascading through my brain, which is irritating when the second half of the concert is about to begin.

He must see me glance at my watch. "We'd better get back in. I'm sorry, you haven't had time for your cigarette."

So that's what he meant by antisocial habits.

"I don't smoke. I came out for a breath of fresh air."

"And ended up with me polluting the atmosphere instead."

"It's not a problem."

"You're more tolerant than Nicola."

"That's different. If you're married to someone you worry about their health."

"You reckon?"

"Are you enjoying the concert?" I'm curious to see if he's running with the crowd.

"Yes, it's good. Apart from the seats. They're doing my back in."

"I'm not sure the others are enjoying it." Through the glass doors, I can see them waiting in the foyer. If I go in with Edward, I won't be able to sneak past them for the second half.

"No, Jez likes the sort of stuff that shatters your eardrums."

"I think they're planning to leave early."

"And you don't want to?"

I shake my head.

"Then say so," says Edward. "Dig your heels in."

"But they're Terry's guests."

"Then they can show some manners. Take it from one who knows, let your partner call all the shots and they'll trample over you. But I guess you know that. Terry said you'd already been married and divorced."

I open my mouth to defend Matt, who with all his faults has never been the trampling type, then I keep quiet as it strikes me how much Edward has given away about his own marriage.

"So there you are!" Nicola strides towards us, obviously put out. She's a tall, dark-haired woman, good-looking but her manner is arrogant. She glares at her husband. "Now you've finished polluting the atmosphere we can go."

"Yes, they're about to start," I say and move towards the concert hall.

"We've decided to cut the rest and go for supper," says Terry, which makes me angry. He bought the ticket as my birthday gift and he knows this is the one concert I really want to hear.

I smile sweetly. "That's fine. You go. I'll stay until the end."

"But you can't!" protests Terry. "I want you to get to know my friends."

"There's still tomorrow and Monday."

"Actually there's all next week," says Nicola. "We've decided to stay on."

The word 'Bugger!' rings stridently in my mind. "That's nice," I say.

"But how will you get home, Honey?" Terry hasn't given up his attempt to make me comply.

"Taxi."

"I don't like you taking taxis alone at night."

I open my mouth to point out it's not his business to like or dislike anything I do.

"She doesn't need to. I'll stay. I'm enjoying the concert." Edward smiles at me. "And afterwards I'll be happy to see you home."

"I suppose we'll all have to stay if you want to," snaps Nicola, "but I warn you, Edward, don't expect sympathy when you moan about your back."

"Don't worry, Edward, I'll sympathise," I say, and Nicola turns her glare onto me.

I listen to most of the second part of the concert, although I spend a few moments' pondering about Edward's statement that I was one hell of a girl. It's a long while since I regarded myself as anything but dreary and this new image is one I like.

Terry's sulking and has turned pointedly away from me. Surreptitiously I look along the row. Terry, then Edward, who's arching his back as if it's hurting him, then Nicola, who's glaring at him in a mixture of triumph and admonishment.

Beside Nicola there's Jez, whose real name is Jeremy. He seems to dabble in a lot of things, including the management side of popular music, although, I suspect not with the success his boastful manner claims. He's wearing a black tee-shirt emblazoned with names of groups and classic festivals. Terry told me that, when they were students, it was Jez who attracted all the girls. If that's true, time has been crueller to him than most. He's got receding hair worn in a greasy ponytail, a nasty little beard and a large beer gut.

Jez's wife, Deirdre, is sitting on the other side of him. I hadn't realised it was possible for anyone to look so totally like a Deirdre, but to my mind she does. Deirdre of the Sorrows, or at least of a severe depressive state. She's thin and brittle looking, with limp brown hair and dreary, shapeless clothes, so drab she's almost invisible.

Lastly, at the end by the wall, there's Graham, Edward and Nicola's son. I'd guess he's in his mid-twenties. He's brown-haired and ordinary looking, tall, thin and quiet. In many ways he seems younger than his age, especially when his mother lectures him, but in other ways he seems older. I think that's because, when he does speak, his manner is abrupt and yet pedantic and because he's dressed in strangely old-fashioned clothes. I'd smiled and greeted him when we were introduced but he'd flushed and muttered an answer and refused to meet my eyes.

As the concert draws to an end I bend to get the Festival programme from my bag. A movement attracts my attention and, looking along the row, I see Nicola has got her shoe off and is running her foot up Jez's leg. I'm amazed at her dexterity. I guess she's the sort of woman who works out to a strict schedule.

I almost up-end my bag and only recover it by an undignified scrabble. I straighten up and join in with the chorus of 'Arrogance, Ignorance and Greed', Steve Knightley's commentary on the banking industry. Nicola's sitting stiffly upright, looking offended. She glares at the rest of our party and Graham stops singing immediately. Terry stops as well and gives her a placatory smile. It's going to be a very long week before I can ditch him.

I nearly drop my bag again. I'd forgotten how slippery the silk is. It's a genuine Sixties bag, although I'd bought it in a jumble sale in the Seventies. I'd dug it out of my cupboard this afternoon to match my Retro look. I prefer to carry it as a clutch bag but Matt put a handle on it for me, for the times it gets out of control. This is one of those times and I fish it out carefully from the inside of the bag. I smile when I remember Matt fashioning it out of the remains of the chain he'd bought to fix inside the door of our first, very grotty, Portsmouth bedsit. Matt's always been security-minded, especially where my safety is concerned.

As I run the metal links through my fingers the sensation triggers the memory that's been lurking in my mind. I'm sure I put the chain on Matt's front door before I opened it to the security man a second time and we'd spoken without me removing it. But when I'd run down to admit the paramedics, I'd flung the door open without impediment. Had there been someone lurking in the house? Someone who'd opened it to sneak out while we had been upstairs?

Chapter 6

After the concert we have a drink in the bar. Jez keeps disappearing to talk to people, or maybe to demonstrate how popular he is. He's greeted by a group of guys of the same generation. Judging by their clothes they've all attended the same festivals for the past thirty years. With my new perception I see Nicola watches him with proprietary smugness, but Deirdre seems indifferent.

Nicola's black trousers and jumper look new and designer label. In contrast, I think Deirdre must have aimed for the ageing hippie look. If so she's hit the target with room to spare. She's wearing a floppy lace dress and lots of beads and a tasselled shawl that keeps getting entangled with things and dipping its ends in strangers' drinks.

Abruptly Nicola turns her attention back to me. "Tell us about yourself. It was quite a shock, hearing Terry had got a girl at last."

I glance up at Terry, who's standing beside me, his arm around my waist. I wish he'd wipe that 'look what I've got' expression off his face.

I get my wish. Nicola continues with all the sensitivity of a charging rhinoceros, "We all thought he must be queer, the way he never had a woman in his life."

The words are as unpleasant as the condescending smile that accompanies them. I feel a ripple of tension running through the group. Perhaps the others are more sensitive than I'd thought.

"No," I say, "you don't have to worry about that."

"So what exactly happened to you this afternoon?" demands Nicola. I feel as if I've been summoned to the headmistress' study to account for my behaviour.

"My ex-husband had a fall and I've got a key to his house. I had to sort things out." I limit the information to basics, the way I'd have done when I was fourteen and been caught out in some misdeed.

"How badly hurt is he?" I think Terry is trying to sound concerned but I'm pretty sure he's still sulking about my late arrival.

"He's got a nasty concussion."

While we're on the subject I might as well make it clear how buggered up Terry's plans are liable to be for the next few days. It's better to do it in public. If he makes a scene it will embarrass him a lot more than me because these are his friends not mine.

"The doctor said Matt needed a lot of care, so he's back at my house." I try for a light note, "My sister and mum are baby-sitting him along with my grandson."

Terry's grip on my waist grows tense. Perhaps I was wrong and he is going to make a fuss. "That's typical of Honey, always a soft touch. That's why I have to stop people imposing on her."

On the other hand, perhaps it's me that's going to make that scene.

"You've got a grandson? How lovely," says Deirdre.

I smile at her. "Yes, he is."

"Honey is a funny sort of name for a middle-aged woman," says Nicola, which I think is rude.

"It's short for Honor," I say.

"Oh like Honor Blackman. A lot of women name their children after television stars." Nicola's tone makes it clear she regards this as pathetically lower class.

I wonder if anyone has ever stood up to her before. I achieve a patronising smile. "Maybe your friends do that, but my mother called me after my grandmother."

Nicola flushes and returns to the attack. "Do you do anything? I mean apart from being a mother and grandmother?"

"I can't think of any role more worthwhile, but yes, I teach."

"Oh, some arty subject, I presume." I guess my new colourful image has had the desired effect.

"English Literature, but I do play with the odd bit of textile art." This is a grandiloquent way of describing my dabblings.

"I'm Head of Maths and Religious Studies at a Private School for Girls," she says.

"You know, that doesn't surprise me in the least."

I hear Edward's laugh, although it's turned hastily into a cough, but Nicola's too self-satisfied to notice the irony in my tone. "Of course it's a great pity we didn't have any daughters that I could educate there."

"Well whose fault's that?" snaps Edward.

I see Graham flush. He keeps his gaze on his shoes, not meeting anyone's eyes. Suddenly I don't find the situation amusing any more.

"Shall we go for supper and on to the late-night folk session at the hotel?" says Terry.

Nicola sniffs. "As long as it's not more of that anti-establishment propaganda."

That puzzles me. "But you weren't here for last night's group?"

"They could hardly have been more offensive than that group we heard tonight."

"Nicola's father's a banker," explains Edward.

"He's suffered terribly during this financial crisis," says Nicola. "People are so vindictive."

"People who've been robbed of everything tend to be a trifle cross," I agree. "That song is in the best tradition of the Broadsheet Ballads." I'm certain Nicola won't know about the political songs that were a popular source of news and social commentary in the eighteenth century. Nicola brings out the worst in me and I'm showing off. "Of course we're lucky to hear Show of Hands at a provincial venue. They appear regularly at the Albert Hall."

I give them a moment to process this, then say, "I'm sorry, I can't stay for supper. I've got to go home. My sister owns a flower shop and she opens on Easter Sunday morning."

"Please Honey. Just for a while." Terry sounds desperate.

It's mean to desert him, especially when I've just whetted the Killer Shark's appetite and sharpened up her teeth. And, in a perverse way, I'm having fun. "You can all come back to my place," I suggest. "If we're quick we can buy a few bottles on the way."

Surprisingly my suggestion goes down well, although I feel Jez saying, "Hey, cool, a rave," is unnecessarily juvenile.

"I can fit everyone in the people carrier," says Nicola. "Come on, Terry, we'll go and buy some drinks while Jez finishes talking to his friends."

"Honey, are you coming to the shops?" asks Terry.

"No. If you lend me your mobile I'll phone my sister and tell her to raid the freezer for sausage rolls." I want to warn her and mum about the coming invasion and to check on Matt.

Surprisingly, Jackie accepts the news quite cheerfully, even with pleasure. She assures me both Ben and Matt are fine and she won't have to rush off immediately. It seems like she's up for a party too.

"What are they like, these friends of Terry's?" she asks.

"Wait and see." Edward has just come out of the building and is standing within earshot. I key off and go to join him. "How's the back?"

"All right." It's clear this isn't true.

"Edward, this is the sympathy I promised you, but it's hard to administer when you're being heroic."

"Believe me, I'm no hero. It's just I'm not used to sympathy, especially over something they say is stress-related."

"Let me guess, Nicola believes the mind should be kept firmly in its place?"

"Yes. I'm sorry about the way she was with you. She likes to know about people."

I'm bored with the hypocrisy game and decide to change the rules. "Let's be honest, what she likes is to be in control."

He looks surprised but not offended. "Have you got us all sussed already?"

"No."

There's lots of things I don't know, including what's going on between Nicola and Jez. Is it a mild annual flirtation or a full-blown sexual liaison? Is Edward aware of it, whatever it is? Has Deirdre sussed it out? Dozy women can notice a lot about their husbands' little games. More than they're willing to admit, I know that better than anyone. And Graham? How does he feel about these middle-aged capers? And why are his parents so negative about him?

The last question is the thing that matters most and I'm still indignant enough to take Edward to task. "I think you hurt Graham, making it clear you wanted a daughter rather than a son."

Edward stares at me. "I didn't mean that! I always wanted us to have two or three kids, only Nicola hated being pregnant and she refused to have any more."

"Are you sure Graham realises that's what you meant?"

My respect for Edward increases when he thinks this through. "I'll make sure he understands. It's not easy getting it right with an only child, is it?"

"I guess not."

He looks surprised at my non-committal response. "You've only got one daughter, haven't you? That's what Terry said."

"We had a son. He died. Leukaemia." I push out the brittle words and hear them spike the softness of the night.

"Oh God! I'm sorry! I didn't know. Terry never said." Edward puts a gentle hand on my forearm. "What was his name? Your son?"

"Simon." As I say the word the jagged misery softens. Through Edward's simple question I feel as if I've found a friend. I smile at him.

He tries to return the smile but his face is tense with pain. He hobbles to a low wall and eases himself down.

"You should get some treatment for your back." I sit beside him.

"I had some aromatherapy massage last year and it helped."

"Didn't you keep it up?"

"No."

"Why not?"

"Nicola made it difficult."

"You should have a quiet word with my sister when you meet her at my place. She does some aromatherapy work alongside her florist's business."

"You're so kind."

That's a polite way of putting it. Matt used to say I was the most interfering woman he'd ever known. He used to call me Supermum. It's a long time since I summoned up the interest or energy to intervene in the lives of mere acquaintances.

Edward smiles at me. "Terry's a lucky guy." Then he drops a bombshell, "When's the wedding going to be?"

Chapter 7

"Wedding?" The way I squawk the word must be a total give away.

"Sorry, was I speaking out of turn?"

"What did Terry say about weddings?"

"Just that you and he were very much in love, but you'd been so badly hurt by your bastard husband it was taking time for you to get the courage to fully commit again. He said you'd probably get married in October, so we were to keep the weekends free."

Personally, I'd have thought it was polite to ask the bride before inviting the guests.

I open my mouth to blast Terry and his lies out of the water, when Edward says apologetically, "I shouldn't have mentioned it. Terry said you were shy about it. I guess he only told us to make Jez shut up."

"What do you mean? What was Jez saying?"

"The usual stuff. Winding Terry up. Terry's never been good with women and Jez likes to rub it in. When you didn't turn up this afternoon, Jez said Terry had invented you."

"Invented me?"

Edward looks embarrassed. "It doesn't matter. It was a long time ago."

"Then it won't matter if you tell me. If I'm a figment of anyone's imagination I have the right to know."

"Please, leave it."

"If you don't tell me I'll ask Terry."

That unlocks the information. "In the Third Year of Uni Terry pretended to have a girlfriend."

"Pretended? You mean he made one up?"

"Yes. He really went for it, disappeared off for weekends, got himself presents and said they came from her, even left a few bits of women's underwear in his room. He had us fooled, but in the end Jez and Nicola sussed him out." Even in the dim light of the car park I can see Edward is red-faced, as if the shame was his. "It was horrible when they confronted him. Like seeing someone stripped. Please, don't tell Terry you know."

"I won't." I'm appalled at what I've got into. I'd always suspected beneath Terry's smug façade, there lurked someone different, but I hadn't foreseen this. I feel sorry for him and a bit uneasy. I'll play along for a few days and extricate myself as gently as I can, but I'm not going to marry him to boost his image with his appalling friends.

There's one thing Edward said that rankles and can be sorted here and now. "You called my ex-husband a bastard. Whatever Terry told you, Matt's not a bastard. He's a good person, generous and kind, but circumstances got too tough for us."

"I'm sorry. I didn't mean to be out of order."

"That's okay." I backtrack to ask, "Were you all at university together?"

"Us three guys and Nicola. Jez met Deirdre much later. In fact we hardly know her. She's a lot younger than us. They've only been married a few years."

I imagine Nicola at university, queening it over her male followers. I've rarely met anyone I dislike as much as I do Nicola, although Jez is running a close second.

Graham comes out of the building and wanders across to join us.

"What are you doing?"

"Waiting for your mother and Terry to come back," says Edward. He stands up, suppressing a groan.

"Oh God, you're not whinging about your back again?" Like a pantomime demon, Jez follows Graham and barges his way into the conversation.

Deirdre drifts after him but is brought up short as her scarf snags on a bush.

"He always was a moaner," continues Jez. "I don't know how Nicky puts up with him. When he had that massage treatment, I said he only wanted to feel a woman's hands on his arse. It's tough if you're the sort of guy who has to pay for it."

No-one seems to know how to answer this. I look at Jez's bullying, leering face and lose my temper. "How's your leg, Jez?"

"What do you mean, my leg?" His tone is wary, ready to lurch into belligerence.

"When you needed it massaged in the middle of the concert, I thought maybe you were suffering from cramp. I guess you stiffened up." This time I speak with malice and forethought. I smile sweetly and look straight into his eyes.

He seems amazed at my temerity, then his temper flares and his dark eyes are hot with anger. "I reckon Terry's bitten off more than he can chew with you."

"Maybe Terry's more of a man than you are." This is too easy. I can't understand why Edward and Terry put up with his crap.

Graham gives a high-pitched giggle and Jez turns onto easier prey. "What's so funny, weirdo? You sound like a bloody schoolgirl. Or a bloody poof."

"Shut it, Jez!" snaps Edward. The situation I've been stirring is getting out of hand.

"God, you're protective! No wonder he's never grown up." Despite the provocative words, Jez backs away. He turns to his wife and snarls, "Why the hell are you lurking behind my back?"

She hurries forwards, eyes down, nervous hands clasping the shawl to her thin bosom. I wonder if he hits her. I feel guilty. I hope he doesn't take the anger I've provoked out on her when they're alone tonight.

I'm glad Terry and Nicola return before the silence becomes too oppressive. Terry puts down the carrier bags of booze he's carrying in order to kiss me. This full on, public embrace is unusual and I know he's doing it for the benefit of our audience. I damp down my irritation and fake my response. Then I break away, "Later darling." I'll deal with that promise when the time comes.

"You could have got everyone in the car, Edward," complains Nicola.

He doesn't argue, just gets out a remote and aims it at the large and expensive vehicle that's parked behind us. It's an excessive amount of car for a family of three.

Edward must read my mind. "Nicola uses it to take the girls in her RE group around to look at churches."

"Terry, you'd better sit in front to give me directions," Nicola commands.

Edward gives me a helpless look, mutely apologising that his wife hasn't offered me the front seat. I flash him a smile, to show I don't mind.

We pile in and I get the middle seat, between Edward and Graham, while Jez and Deirdre sit behind.

"It's hard on you not being able to drink," I say to Nicola.

"I always say there are more important things in life than getting drunk."

"Like being the boss," mutters Edward and I think this is one likeable worm who seems gearing up to turn.

Jackie's very good at things I'm useless at. I can do homely and welcoming but, given the same materials, she can make a house elegant. My sitting room looks much more spacious than usual, the way it was when Matt and I held parties regularly.

"What did you do with all the mess?" I whisper, as I kiss her cheek.

"I piled it in the small room Matt used as a study. Here's the key."

"Thank you." She'd chosen wisely. Not only is the room no longer used, it's also the only one with a lock. It was put on to keep the kids out when they were small and Matt didn't want them fiddling with his business files.

"How's Matt?"

"Okay. I've checked him every hour, the way you said. He's still got a bad headache but he's not in a coma or anything. Honey, I hope you know what you're doing."

"Of course I do." I speak with more assurance than I feel.

"I don't know how you can bear to have him here. I couldn't if it was me."

"I know." Jackie's far distant marriage is a bitter memory. Her long vanished ex had been unfaithful on their honeymoon and the few months they spent together had gone downhill from there.

I steer her back into the living room. "Let me introduce you to Terry's friends."

Soon everyone is supplied with food and drink and I hurry upstairs to check on Matt.

"You having a party?" he asks as I slip quietly into his room.

"Sort of. Did we wake you? Are we being too loud?"

"No, it's fine. I keep drifting asleep then jumping awake again, but your talking didn't wake me. I keep dreaming about that woman. I hear her whispering, 'You won't forget me,' and I see her standing in the shadows, watching me."

Instinctively I stare into the murky corners where the room's not lit by the muted bedside lamp. Of course, there's no-one there. "It's the concussion. Try not to worry. Is your headache still very bad?"

"Pretty bad but I'll be okay soon. I'll get out of your way tomorrow."

"You'll stay where you are until you're well. Do you need anything?"

"Could you pour me a drink please? Every time I move I feel peculiar."

I supply him with lemonade and help him to sit up to drink it. When he's lying down again, I say, "I'll come up again soon."

As I leave Matt's room I encounter Graham, lurking in the corridor. "What are you doing here?" The suspicion that he was eavesdropping adds sharpness to my tone.

"There was a queue for the cloakroom so your mother said to come up here."

The explanation is reasonable and maybe his furtive manner is due to shyness. I smile at him. "I didn't mean to snap. You startled me. I was just checking my husband... my ex-husband... was okay. I expect you heard me say he'd had a fall."

"Yes. I listened to you talking. You sounded so nice together. As if you liked each other. That's odd isn't it? I mean most married people don't sound like that."

I'm astounded by his naivety. "Graham, you shouldn't listen to private conversations." What I mean is, if he does he shouldn't own up to it.

"I have to. Otherwise I wouldn't know what they're doing."

"Do you mean your mum and dad?"

"No, her and him." The words are heavy with loathing. He giggles. "I liked it when you said that to him. You really got him going."

So Graham knows about his mum and Jez. His attitude to their relationship seems odd, but everything about Graham seems slightly out of step.

As we talk we're going down the stairs and, in a few seconds, we'll be back amongst the throng. I stop and sit down on the stairs and signal for Graham to join me. He does so in an ungainly manner, folding his long legs so his knees are near his ears.

"How long has it been going on for?" I ask.

He shrugs. "Ever since I can remember. When Dad's away Uncle Jez turns up."

"Does your dad know?"

"No!"

"That's strange. Your dad doesn't strike me as a stupid man."

"He doesn't want to know. He doesn't like fighting. And she's good at telling lies." The venom in his voice startles me.

"How old are you Graham?"

"Twenty-four."

It hits me that Graham's not unlike a boy with Special Needs that I had tutored to resit his English GCSE. He was poor at English but a scientific genius. I remember how he used to run his fingers along the seam in his jeans all the time, the way Graham's running his hand along the pattern of his ill-fitting, black cord trousers.

"Haven't you ever thought of leaving home?"

"I did once, to go to university. But I was no good at it. I hated it. So I dropped out."

"What did you study?"

"Maths. She says there'll always be jobs for good maths teachers."

"What would you have liked to study?"

"I don't know. I like maths, it makes sense. But doing it at Uni was crap."

"What do you want to do?"

He shrugs. "I don't know. There's not much point in doing anything."

I look at his petulant face and thank God for my lovely Allie. She may have an illegitimate child, a stroppy attitude and a married lover, but at least she's doing something with her life.

"You said you're an artist, Mrs Alder?" That's the first hint of interest I've seen Graham show in anything except his parental problems.

"Call me Honey. To be honest I'm only a sort of artist." I'd said it to see how much garbage Terry's friends would swallow. "I made some textile pictures and they came out better than I expected, so my sister persuaded me to get them framed and put them up in her shop. They're part of the Open Studio displays that are going on in Hampshire for the next two weeks."

"I'd like to see them."

"I expect you could drop in to see them sometime. Do you drive?"

"Yes, but I haven't driven since I passed my test. She won't let me use the car. I'll ask Dad for a lift."

"That's fine. They're on show whenever the shop's open, which is most days. Even tomorrow. Jackie does good trade on Easter Sunday after church."

"It would be better if you'd go with me. You could tell me about all the deeper meanings."

I think that explanation could be very short. "Do you like art, Graham?" Perhaps the kid's a frustrated genius.

"Not particularly, but I'd like to see yours."

I hear Allie's voice amongst the staider tones of the other guests and clamber to my feet. "Come on, Graham. I'll introduce you to my daughter. She's around your age."

"I don't like girls of my age; they're silly and frivolous."

His priggishness appals me but I smile and say, "That's what they're meant to be."

Chapter 8

To my relief, my frivolous Allie has introduced a new sparkle into our middle-aged gathering. She and Ross are making outstanding efforts to be sociable and I'm grateful to them both. When everyone's occupied I draw Edward to one side and signal Jackie to follow me to the kitchen.

"Jackie, Edward's in a lot of pain with his back and needs the help of a first-class masseuse."

"And as he can't have that, he'll have to make do with me?"

"That's not what I meant." One thing Jackie and I have in common is we both do a nice line in putting ourselves down.

"You look like a first-class lady in every way to me," says Edward. It's a smarmy chat-up line and yet it sounds genuine.

Jackie blushes. A wild rose pink engulfs her neck and face. The vivid colour suits her, softening her usual severity and making her look younger than fifty-five. She's still a handsome woman, slim and shapely, with only a hint of grey in her dark hair, but I wish she'd wear some kinder colours than navy-blue or charcoal grey.

"I'd be pleased to help," she says.

I fish in my pocket and hold up the key she'd given me a few minutes ago. "Take him to the study. There's an old sofa in there. Just chuck any rubbish on the floor."

"Are you sure you don't mind? It's a terrible mess in there."

"I don't mind you and Edward. You've known what I'm like for over fifty years and I don't think he's the judgmental type."

Jackie raids my en suite for massage oils and mixes them into a fragrant cocktail, while I conduct Edward through to the study, clear off the sofa and tell him to undo his trousers and lie down. He seems shy, so I leave him to it.

Back in the dining room the conversation has taken a bizarrely religious turn. Apparently Nicola requires a suitably High Anglican Church to worship on Easter Day and Mum has supplied her with details of her village church.

"That's settled then," says Nicola. "Edward, Graham and I will go there tomorrow." She smiles graciously at my mother. "And afterwards we can give you a lift home if you require one."

"Thank you," says Mum, "but I won't be there. I'll be here."

"But it's Easter Day." Nicola sounds scandalised.

"I'll be watching our little one opening his Easter eggs." There's a distinct note of mischief in Mum's voice, "If God begrudges me spending a day of celebration with my great-grandson, then He's not the good Father he's cracked up to be."

I spend most of the evening talking to Graham. He's a funny, prickly, ungracious sort of boy, with a shy, sly manner that slides away from eye contact. In some ways he's incredibly young for his age, in others extremely old-fashioned. I feel sorry for him, stuck in this party of his elders, but when Allie and Ross do try to speak to him he stares at them as if they're a different species. He seems happiest talking to me and so I go with it. I'm the hostess and he's no more boring than the rest of Terry's guests. Although I'm not sure why I'm putting in so much effort when Terry isn't really doing his part. A couple of times I register he isn't in the room, which surprises me. I thought he'd have gone all out to play host in my house.

Mindful of my duties, I do try to chat to Deirdre. It's a hopeless struggle. It's not that she doesn't answer, but all her responses are monosyllabic and she never raises her eyes to look at me. I don't get the feeling of shyness I get with Graham, more an unwillingness to get involved. When Jez hurls some rough remark at her, she doesn't flare back at him and yet I don't get the feeling she's afraid. I guess she's been bullied into indifference.

It's only when they're due to leave that Nicola notices her husband's absence, and even then she reacts with annoyance rather than concern.

"He's lying down. His back was hurting," I say.

"You ought to ask Jackie to give him a massage," says Mum, and I'm not sure how innocent the suggestion is.

"I don't believe in all that touchy-feely stuff," snaps Nicola. "Alternative therapists are charlatans."

"I'll fetch him." As I slip away, Mum moves in with a new Biblical offensive about what Nicola would have said to Jesus when he healed by the laying on of hands.

I tap on the study door and call quietly, "It's me."

Jackie opens up and I think she looks happy. As a rule she seems closed in, especially in the company of men. A small warning light flickers in my mind.

"How's the patient doing?" I ask.

"He's feeling a bit better."

"A lot better," Edward confirms. "Jackie, thank you. Can I pay you? I mean you're a professional therapist and..."

"No, really, it was a pleasure."

He smiles at her and moves past us to go and join the others.

"He's a nice man," says Jackie.

"Yes," I agree. The 'Oh God, what have I done,' feeling is getting stronger all the time. Jackie and I have our disagreements but I don't want her to be hurt.

By the time I get back with them Terry has reappeared and I leave it to him to see his friends out to their car.

"Goodnight," says Allie, blowing a kiss to her Nanna as she disappears upstairs. Ross had already retreated some time ago. I didn't blame him, I'd have liked to run away as well.

"That was fun," says Mum.

I look at her with mock severity. "You're very bad. Winding Nicola up about God."

"It won't do her any harm. Of course, it won't do her any good either. She's the sort who's got her mind set in concrete."

Jackie wanders through, wearing her coat and carrying her bag.

"Jack, it's possible the church-going gang may turn up in your shop tomorrow," I warn her. "Graham says he wants to see my bits of stuff."

"No problem. It's better if I show them rather than you. You always talk them down."

"Not with Nicola. I'm not daft enough to let her get the upper hand."

"I'm glad to hear it. I've got to go. I'm sorry, I've left you the clearing up."

"That's fine. I'll leave it until the morning. Thanks for all you've done."

She hugs us and leaves, and my mum goes up to her room, the one that used to be Simon's, which even now we only use on the rare occasions when the house is full. I'm glad I didn't have to put Matt in there. Mum swears she doesn't mind but I know he'd have found it hard to cope with the memories, especially in his present state.

Allie passes her grandmother on the stairs. She comes down and puts the kettle on. "Honestly Mum, your friends!"

"They're not mine."

She ignores my protest. "Talk about a set of total drearies."

"They're not my friends. Edward's the only one I even slightly like."

"The fat guy with the bad back? I suppose he was okay, but does he have to dress like something out of a Forties' gangster film?"

"The black suit was due to family pressure. And he's not really fat, just well-padded." Actually I'm pleased Allie can talk to me about weight problems without the embarrassment my own obesity had caused.

"I should think the poor guy needs to comfort eat. His wife's like the worst-nightmare caricature of a Headmistress."

"She's head of Maths and RE at a posh girls' school."

We both laugh.

"And as for the son. A hundred-per-cent geek. Thank God he's got a crush on you, so he doesn't fancy me."

"Don't be silly. Of course he hasn't got a crush on me."

"Mum it was blatant! 'Honey this' and 'Honey that' all evening, and he couldn't take his eyes off you. He's probably got some sort of Oedipus complex."

"Then he can keep it unfulfilled. If I ever set up a toy boy it will be someone with some pretensions towards sex appeal. I thought you'd gone to bed. Why are you making tea at this time of night?"

"I looked in on Dad and he said he fancied a cup. That's okay, isn't it? I mean it won't make him sick again?"

"Of course it's okay. Thank you darling."

"I'm shattered. I'll help you clear up tomorrow." She heads off as Terry returns.

I've got my goodnight speech to Terry planned, but I don't get a chance to utter it. He swoops on me and kisses me. His hands are all over me and his mouth is seeking mine. It's the full octopus experience with additional leech effects.

At last he breaks off to say, "You were fabulous tonight. They're all so impressed. They think you're wonderful."

"What, even Jez?" If I keep talking I might prevent a resumption of the grope and slobber game.

"For the first time ever, Jez is jealous of me." The gloating in his voice makes him sound like an adolescent, not a man of fifty-four. "I've locked up. Let's go to bed." His hands are up my top, tracing along my back and fiddling with my bra. Fortunately it's a front opening model and defies his attempts.

I take a deep breath, realise he's interpreted it as a sigh of passion, and launch hastily into speech, "I'm sorry, Terry. Somehow it doesn't feel right, sleeping with you tonight. Not with my mum and Matt here."

He looks sulky. "I think I deserve better than that, Honey."

I'm tempted to throw his lie about us being engaged into the mix. But if I do it will be because I'm bored with him and his dreary friends and want an excuse to get out here and now. I try his own argument. "Don't I deserve some consideration? It may be illogical but it's the way I feel and I think you should respect it."

That presses the right buttons. "Of course. You're right. I'm sorry Honey... But there's no need for Jez and the others to know, is there?"

"Of course not. You can sleep in the study and, if you're up first in the morning, no-one need ever know."

That's it. The end. Even friendship has drowned in hypocrisy. I put the final seal on it when he tries to kiss me again. "No, please, Terry, you mustn't tempt me."

God, what a cow! I've never played the game like this before.

I supply him with pillow and duvet and send him to sleep in the untidy study.

I go up to my room and get ready for bed, then I curse my own stupidity, I'd planned to check on Matt before I undressed. Recently I've gone back to sleeping naked and I don't want to resurrect the serviceable nightdress and fleecy dressing gown that marked my darkest and dowdiest times. I take out my new silk nightdress and put it on.

I creep along to Matt's room and ease the door open.

His bedside light is on and his eyes are open, staring like he's seeing nightmares that waking won't dispel. His face is set and rigid.

"Matt, what's wrong?"

"I am crazy. There's something really wrong with my mind."

"What's happened?" I run to him and hold him. I can feel him trembling.

"She was here again. She stood in the doorway and said, 'Now that was a silly, naughty boy. You deserved to be hurt. Haven't you done enough harm already?' Then she turned and walked away again."

"You were asleep... dreaming."

"No. I wasn't. I was awake. I wasn't thinking about her or anything bad. I was thinking about you and Allie and how kind you'd been to me."

There's nothing I can say. The outer doors and windows are all locked. My mum is sleeping next door and Allie and Ross are two doors along. "When was this?" I ask.

"Just a few minutes ago."

Someone could have come up the stairs while I was in my bedroom. I'm not sure if it's worse to think of Matt being crazy or that there's a lunatic concealed in my house.

"Hold on a moment." I go and check the bathroom and my mother's room. The former is empty and, in the latter, Mum is snoring peacefully.

As I approach Allie's door, it opens and Ross appears, dressed in boxers.

"Honey, is something wrong?"

"Just checking. I thought I heard someone moving round." I feel embarrassed. We're both so scantily dressed.

"Do you want me to go round and check the rest of the house?"

"No, that's fine, thanks." I smell a sweet, flowery scent and ask sharply, "Can you smell something?"

Ross looks startled. He holds out his hands. "It's probably this. It's a new baby massage oil. Your sister recommended it. She said it helps babies sleep."

"I see." Perhaps Matt caught a whiff of the scent and it triggered this new delusion.

I wish Ross goodnight and go back to Matt, who says with gloomy satisfaction, "You see, I'm going mad."

"It was a dream. An after-effect of the concussion. Try to sleep."

"I can't. I'm scared to."

His tone is matter-of-fact but I feel like I've been shredded. Matt has never said he's afraid of anything.

In my next move there's neither thought nor reasoning, just plain old-fashioned instinct. I slide into bed beside him and hold him.

Chapter 9 Easter Sunday

I can get into weirder messes than any woman I know. I wake early on Easter morning and remember I'm in bed with my ex-husband, while my lover, who claims he's my fiancé, is sleeping downstairs on the sofa. Of course Matt and I didn't make love last night; I just held him and soothed him until he went to sleep.

The next week stretches out before me like a nightmare journey balancing on a tightrope. I wish I could tell Terry I know about his lie. Then we could pretend to be engaged and make a game of it. But I don't think Terry's capable of that, certainly not with these people who'd sussed him out in a similar ploy before. At the same time, I don't want to encourage him to think his pretend engagement is for real. I'm still tempted to use the engagement lie to pick a quarrel and walk away, but that would be cheap now the first real anger is past. And I don't want to give Nicola and Jez the satisfaction of seeing Terry and I split up.

I have a bigger problem than Terry and his friends. What the hell is going on with Matt? I don't believe in ghosts, especially the sort who could have stepped straight out of Blithe Spirit or Oscar Wilde's Canterville. Even more I don't believe in a ghost who follows Matt from house to house.

So we're left with the alternatives of mental illness or malicious trickery. I wonder if the checks they did at A&E would show up anything like a brain tumour? Or is someone deliberately trying to harm Matt? Despite his denials, I still suspect it's connected to a girl he's slept with. Perhaps not all the women in his life had been as clued into the game as he'd thought.

But how could an outsider have got into my house last night, undetected?

A new thought hits me. Terry has access to many women willing to do anything for cash. A social worker deals with all sorts and Terry can be ruthless when he wants to be. Under the terms of the will Matt made when we divorced, although Allie is his chief beneficiary, I'd be a wealthy woman if he died. Does Terry really think I'd marry him? The answer is simple. Of course he believes it. He's already told his friends that we're engaged. But surely he's not capable of staging anything that's so bizarre? I remember his university charade and know he is. And he'd certainly been notable by his absence when Matt was having his weird visions last night.

My thoughts are whirling, like a hamster in a wheel, running and running without getting anywhere. And that's without considering the major cause of embarrassment who's lying beside me in the spare room double bed.

I roll over, very gently, so I'm facing Matt. He's a better colour, although still too pale, but even asleep the frown lines aren't smoothed out of his face. I can't fool myself that this is the point where we pick up and start again. We've moved too far apart for that. We've hurt each other too badly and we're both too tired. I can't live with a man who once loved me passionately, then saw me gross and wrecked. With Matt I'd always see that image reflected in the recesses of his memory. Basically, we've got too much history to be lovers any more. This isn't the way back, but at least it's a gentler way of moving apart than we managed when we divorced.

Even after seven years he's so familiar. Not my only lover, but the only man I've ever loved. I know the intimate smell of his body, despite the taint of sickness. I know the smoothness of his skin, although the fuzz of dark hairs on his chest are greyer now. I know the brown mole just above his left nipple. As Matt stirs I realise the mole isn't there.

"What happened to your mole?" I demand.

His blue eyes are still misty with sleep and squinting with the lingering headache, now they look blank with astonishment. "What?"

"The mole on your chest, it's gone."

"It was getting bigger and the doctor thought it might be dodgy, so I had it removed." He must register my horror. "It's okay. It was three years ago and, when they examined it, it was nothing bad."

"I didn't know." Now I look properly, I can see a small scar.

"There was no reason for you to know. Thanks for looking after me last night."

I force myself away from the fear of malignant moles and the hurt that he hadn't told me about it. "You're welcome. Did you sleep okay?"

"Not bad. I woke up a few times but I drifted off again."

"How do you feel? And you're not going anywhere today even if you claim you're up to running a half-marathon."

His grin acknowledges he's been sussed and stifles the lie before it passes his lips. "I'd be hard put to manage a ten metre crawl. I feel more with it than yesterday, but I've still got a headache and a lousy stiff neck. And I'm thirsty."

I pour him a drink of water from the jug beside the bed. "I'll go down and make some tea in a minute."

I'm putting off the evil moment. The chances are Terry will hear me in the kitchen and get up, and I don't want to talk to him.

I might as well spend the time in a useful manner. Thanks to Jackie this house is well equipped on the aromatherapy front. I fetch lavender oil from my en suite and massage the sore muscles at the back of his neck.

"If you do that I'll go back to sleep," he warns.

"Good. It's the best thing for you." His low chuckle surprises me. "What's so funny about that?"

"Nothing. It's just I'd forgotten how good it felt, being bossed by you."

"Aren't any of your girlfriends bossy?" Some deep-rooted hurt drags the words out of me before I can control them.

There's a moment's silence, then he says, "Not in the same way you are."

"I'm sorry, that was out of order."

"No, it was totally justified."

A moment ago we'd been close together, now we're a million miles apart.

"How did the boyfriend take to being sent home last night?" The mockery is back in his voice, underlaid by a hint of savagery.

"He didn't go home."

He turns to look at me, with an unwise jerk that makes him wince. "You mean he's sleeping next door?"

"No, downstairs, on the sofa in the study." I know I sound defiant.

"New treat 'em rough policy, Honey?"

I feel tears prickling my eyes but Matt has turned to lie face downwards and doesn't see.

"I had lessons from an expert." My voice is as taunting as anything Matt could achieve.

"In that case, I can only apologise." His voice is muffled by the pillow. "Please, can we stop this fight? My head is killing me."

There's a knock on the door and I jump. For a moment I think it must be Terry, intending to assert his lover's rights and I contemplate hiding in the wardrobe. I abandon the idea. For one thing it doesn't go with my new hard image. For another, I can't count on Matt supporting me in the game, not after what I've just said to him.

There's another knock and then the door inches open. "Dad, are you awake?"

I find my voice. "Yes, come in, Allie. I'm in here as well."

Allie slides in and shuts the door behind her before she says, "I wondered where you were. Your bedroom door's open and I thought maybe Dad was worse."

"No, I'm okay." Matt's voice is husky but he rolls over and smiles at her.

I see Allie's clear gaze take in my scarlet clinging nightdress but all she says is, "That colour really suits you now you've changed your hair."

"I ought to dress. Then I'll make a pot of tea. Matt, could you manage some toast or cereal?"

"Toast please."

"I'll make it," offers Allie. "I'm going to get Ross a coffee anyway. He's seeing to Ben."

"Fine," I say. "I'll be down in a few minutes."

To my surprise, Allie follows me into my room. I brace myself for aggro but she says, "Are you okay, Mum?"

"Fine."

"Where's Terry?"

"Downstairs, sleeping on the study sofa. Allie, your Dad and I didn't do anything last night. He was having bad dreams and he needed someone with him."

"Would Terry be okay with that?"

"Probably not. Look love, I don't want to muck things up for Terry when his friends are around but, like I told you yesterday, Terry and I haven't got a long-term future."

"What about you and Dad?"

I use the phrase I'd thought earlier on. "All your Dad and I have got is a long history. But it's okay, we're both getting over it and learning to move on."

"I see. I guess there's things no-one can forgive. I'd better make that tea."

I shower and dress at top speed, but I take time to make sure I look good. I owe it to myself not to let things slide again. As I gel my newly-darkened hair into a spiky style, I try to imagine me with a series of young-to-middle-aged lovers and an exciting new life. I don't believe it, but exploring the possibilities brings colour to my cheeks and a sparkle to my eyes.

In the corridor I encounter Allie, carrying a tray. "If you take Dad's stuff, I'll give Ross his coffee. He's hell until he's had it."

"Of course. Thanks for doing it."

"I've put an extra mug and plate on the tray for you. St Terry the Martyr is sulking enough to put anyone off their breakfast."

"I'm sorry love. There's no reason he should muck up your Easter. I suppose I'd better go down and sort him out."

Allie laughs. "I'd leave him to it. He's enjoying a lovely wallow in being hard done by. I've taken Nanna a cup of tea. If you wait till she's downstairs he won't get a chance to moan."

"You're a star." My hug almost upends the tray.

"I want you to be happy, Mum."

She passes me the tray, takes Ross' mug and heads off along the corridor.

Opening Matt's door while holding the tray proves challenging. "Sorry, I've slopped milk onto your toast."

"That's fine. It'll soften it up for the poor invalid." Matt hauls himself into a sitting position.

I put the tray down and arrange the pillows for him. The one he's been lying on is distinctly soggy. At first I think it's fever, but there's no sign of sweat on his face. His eyes are red and puffy. But Matt never cries. He didn't shed a tear when Simon was first diagnosed, and when Simon died he acted as if he was carved out of granite.

"Whatever you say, you're not okay, are you?"

"As well as can be expected in the circumstances."

I pour the tea and he manages two mugs and half a slice of toast. It's clear it hurts him to chew.

"I've got some painkillers for you."

"All contributions gratefully received." He leans back, eyes shut.

"That settles it. You're staying in bed until I'm satisfied you're well."

"That could be a problem. I'm desperate for a pee."

"I'll get you a bottle."

He opens his heavy eyes to glare at me. "No you bloody won't."

I know when not to push it. "Okay, I'll help you to the loo."

He growls at me but when he's on his feet he's obviously too giddy to put up much resistance. As soon as we step into the corridor I realise the bathroom's occupied.

"Mum must be in there. You'll have to use mine." As I steer him through my bedroom, I know I can't leave him in the en suite. It's obvious he's woozy, and we've already played the concussion game.

"I'm okay. Please. Leave me." He sways and grabs hold of the cistern for support. I realise he's a lot more embarrassed than I am.

One hand on his elbow, the other resting gently on his back, I murmur soothingly, "It's okay love. It's no big deal. It's me." As he pees, I think, if he's as shy as this, it's going to severely limit my forays into the world. No way is he going to allow his mother-in-law or daughter to help him to the loo.

"What the fuck are you doing?" The violent words from the doorway make us jump. I tighten my grip on Matt's arm and steady him as I turn to glare at the intruder.

"Terry, don't be such a bloody fool." The look on his face is so vicious that I have to fight back or he'll intimidate me.

He's clearly astonished by my anger and I continue in a quieter tone, "Matt needed a pee but he's very shaky and I didn't want him to fall again."

I see Terry glance back into my bedroom and take in the immaculate bed and then at me, fully dressed and ready for the day. "I'm sorry, Honey. Here, let me help."

"No, we can manage." Again I see that clamped down, tight faced anger that makes me shiver, but he steps out of the way and I get Matt back to his room and into bed.

"I promised to meet Nicola and Edward at your sister's shop after Church. Are you coming? We'll have lunch somewhere."

"I'm afraid not. I'm going to do the Easter Egg experience with Ben."

He looks disgruntled but not particularly surprised. He must know when it comes to Ben I'm not going to give way.

"Okay. I'd better get moving. I need to go home and shave and change. It would be much easier if you weren't so absurdly over-protective about your space." For months Terry has been systematically trying to leave clothes and personal possessions at my house and I've been firmly handing them back to him.

Before I realise what's happening he's got his arms round me, kissing me in the engulfing way I dislike even when we're on our own. It's worse when it's in front of an audience, especially this audience. I break free, gasping for breath, and restrain the impulse to slap him.

I'm not sure if he knows I'm annoyed or if he's offended by my unresponsiveness. He leaves with a brief, "I'll see you later, Honey."

Left alone with Matt, I feel embarrassed. I look at him but there's no emotion visible on his pale face. When he speaks it's quite irrelevant to what's been happening. "I haven't got anything here for Ben. I've got him a set of train books and I was going to put some money with them, but everything's at my house."

"I'll get them when I go round for my car," I promise.

"Thanks." He smiles at me. "It may be a bit late but at least it'll be on the right day. At Christmas, I didn't see him open his presents at all."

There are some things Matt doesn't deserve to lose. I go into my room and get the Easter boxes out of my wardrobe. One is a plain cardboard box with eggs for Allie, Mum and Jackie and a bag of small chocolate eggs for Ben's egg hunt. I've decorated the other box with bright paper and it holds a big egg, a mug and bowl, two books, a wind-up train and a set of cars. This is Ben's Easter treasure trove.

I write the label and take the box through to Matt's room. "You can share my pressies for Ben. And we can have the egg hunt in here if you feel up to it."

"Are you sure?" Matt's a rich man but it's clear I'm offering him something he can't buy in any store.

"Certain." I twist the label to show him: 'To Ben, with love, from Grandma and Grandad.' "For Ben and Allie's sake, as well as our own, there's no reason we can't be friends."

He stares at me, as if trying to read my mind, which could prove challenging when it's totally confused. "Thank you. I'd like to have Ben's egg hunt in here."

Chapter 10

"What are you doing?" asks Allie.

I think the answer to that is obvious. We're lurking on Matt's doorstep while I ransack my bag. "Searching for the code to turn off Dad's alarm." I'd been right when I'd thought my bag was a secure hiding place.

"Mum, you're hopeless."

"I know." But she shouldn't be surprised, I always have been and she's known me all her life.

"Is it the code he sent you before Christmas?"

I nod, still rummaging. She takes the key and, ignoring my protests, opens the door, locates the security box and taps in a series of numbers.

"How did you do that?"

She smiles at me. "I memorised it when it came through."

"But how? I put it straight into my bag."

"No you didn't. You left it on the kitchen table while you were getting ready for work and I knew you'd lose it and I didn't want him to be mad with you."

She's right about my carelessness but wrong about her dad. "Thank you, but he doesn't get mad with me about stuff like that." Allie and Simon inherited Matt's memory for numbers, but I'm a word person and numbers worry me.

I go upstairs, get out a small suitcase and put together essentials for Matt. It takes a while because I don't know where he keeps anything or much about his lifestyle nowadays. The first things I gather are the bits he'd specified: his mobile, his wallet, his keys and his sleeping pills. I spot a bottle of whisky and a glass in his bedside cupboard and shut the door quickly before Allie notices it.

She prowls Matt's bedroom, restless and ill at ease. "Do you think I'm too hard on him?"

"It's not about being too hard or too soft. We were all so screwed up by Simon's death that we spent all our energy surviving. We don't know each other any more."

When Allie looks stubborn she becomes a smaller, younger, fairer, feminine version of Matt. At this moment there's no doubting her parentage. "I always knew you loved me, but he didn't love us enough to stick with it. He went off screwing all those tarts and made you even more sick than you were."

I look back into the bleak grey cavern of the years after Simon's death. "Honestly Allie, I don't think he made me worse."

"He could have made you better." All her lost childhood is in those simple words; the belief that Mummy and Daddy can make everything all right.

"When it comes to mental illness, basically the only person who can heal you is yourself. And your Dad was desolate too."

"Funny way of showing it, screwing around." The words and tone remind me of my sister. Jackie spent a lot of time with Allie in her formative years.

If I'm going to make packing look even halfway neat I have to concentrate. I finish folding Matt's shirt and place it in the suitcase before I say, "Unfortunately, Allie, I don't think you're in a position to criticise anyone for screwing around."

She flushes. "Ross and I are different!"

"Really? In what way?"

"His wife's a bitch! It wasn't his fault. They weren't right for each other."

"It's a pity he didn't find out before they spent eight years together and had three children." I've said these things to Allie before, but in a gentle, muted way because I was scared of alienating her. I've never spoken as forcefully as this.

"She trapped him into marriage. It wasn't his fault he fell in love with me."

I lose my temper. "Face the facts, Allie. Ross wasn't so overwhelmingly in love with you that he'd risk his career by sleeping with you while you were still his student. How calculating is that? To groom a girl until it's safe for him to screw her without risking everything. And Ross stayed nice and comfy, living with his wife, until she found out about your relationship and threw him out."

My words hurt, it's obvious in her blanched face and furious eyes. "You're wrong! He does love me. We're going to get married as soon as his divorce comes through."

I bite back the temptation to say they won't live together in my house. One thing I've learned is to not burn bridges when the people you love are on the other side.

"Let's not talk about it now. I wonder where your dad keeps his shaver?"

The words are clumsy and the tone constrained. Allie glares at me and then flounces out of the bedroom. I hear her storm downstairs and, after a few moments, I hear the front door open. My car's here, so if she abandons me it's not a problem. All I've got to do is work out how to reset the alarm.

"Oh! Is Matt here?" It's a female voice, ostentatiously posh. I wronged Allie when I thought she was running out on me.

"No." Allie's response is curt.

"Well, where is he? I've been trying to contact him since yesterday. I didn't give up my Easter weekend for him to treat me like this."

There's a short pause, then Allie's voice, sweetly feminine and deliberately provocative, "He's staying over at my place. He been in bed all weekend and he hasn't surfaced for long enough to take any calls."

For a moment I'm paralysed by the blatant deceit in the literally true words. Then I rush out of the bedroom and start down the stairs.

"Well, when he does surface, kindly tell him Claudia needs to speak to him." The cut glass tones hold several inches of ice.

"Whatever."

The front door is slammed before I reach the hall. "Allie, how dare you!"

"It serves him right."

"I'm ashamed of you." I go back upstairs to finish Matt's packing.

There are no photos on display anywhere in the house but there are four albums in his bedside cabinet. I'd spotted them in the hunt for his sleeping pills. I'm curious enough to get them out and peep inside. After a confused moment I realise the photos are duplicates of ones that I possess. When Matt moved out he must have taken copies and reconstructed his memories. On the first page there's me and Matt at Uni; a posh photo when we were dressed up for a ball. It's followed by snapshots of other happy times. I'd forgotten how long my hair had been, how bright my colours and how short my skirts.

I dip into the books at random. They seem to be in chronological order, starting when we got together. Book three ends with the last pictures of Simon and the last few pages are blank. Book four is made up of photos supplied by me. They are all of Ben, from newborn until now.

As I slide them back I spot a thin leather album that I recognise. Matt's father still has most of his family photographs but Matt has a few of his mother's family. I turn the stiff pages, remembering my shy, gentle mother-in-law, who has been dead for many years. Near the front of the book I spot a picture I don't remember ever seeing before. It's of an elderly, stern-faced woman with stiffly permed hair. In every detail she resembles the intruder that Matt described. On her hip she balances a child, a toddler, so like Simon at that age that I'm certain it's Matt. She's wearing an apron over her old-fashioned blouse and skirt and on her feet are fur-trimmed slippers. It's a black-and-white photo but I feel sure the fur is pink.

Chapter 11

I hear Allie coming and push the four albums chronicling our lives back into the cupboard, but, without any conscious reason, I slip the old album into my bag.

"Are you ready yet?" She sounds cautious, as if she's expecting me to bite.

"I think so." I pick up the last few items: Matt's iPhone, the Easter present he'd bought for Ben, and his bedside reading, a book about cracking the Enigma Code.

"There's lots of messages on his answer phone," says Allie.

"Okay, I'll check them out."

The messages are all from Michelle, his office manager, referring to various imminent jobs. In the events industry, the Easter weekend is a maximum busy time.

"No problem. I'll remind him to phone Michelle. Can you set the alarm?"

"Of course. Mum, I'm sorry. I was out of order with that woman."

"Yes, you were. But it was bad luck, her arriving after I'd wound you up."

"It wasn't just that. You didn't see her. She was a total upmarket cow and so bloody arrogant. She looked at me like I was a slut long before I said anything to her. I hated the thought of Dad being with a blonde bitch like that." Suddenly she sounds like a naughty child fearful of reprimand, "Will I have to tell him what I've done?"

"One of us will. It's better than him getting her version, isn't it?"

"I suppose so." She sounds profoundly unconvinced.

My house is remarkably peaceful and full of delicious cooking smells.

"You shouldn't have," I say to Mum, when I find her in the kitchen.

"I can still cook a dinner and enjoy doing it. I like your kitchen, plenty of room to move around. The chicken and roast potatoes are almost done so I'll put the veg on. You go up and check on Matt, make sure he's still all right with the little one."

"Ben's with Dad? Where's Ross?" demands Allie.

"Gone off to see his other boys. He said he'd got Easter Eggs for them and he had to do it this morning because his wife said she was taking them out this afternoon."

Allie looks dismayed. "I told him he ought to try and see the boys, but I didn't mean you and Dad to get lumbered with Ben."

"It's not a problem. Honey, while you're up there, try to find out if Matt's really happy with chicken or whether he just said that because he didn't want to be a bother."

As we go upstairs, Allie's still fretting. "If I'd known, I'd have taken Ben with me." She selects a suitable scapegoat. "It's typical of Ross' wife to makes things difficult."

I bite back my scathing answer. Allie and I have already fought too much today.

Ben is sitting in the circle of Matt's arm, looking at a storybook and contributing his own narrative. My heart lurches as the sight takes me back to another time.

Matt smiles and says, "Good timing. One of us fellows is in need of an urgent nappy change."

"Dare I ask which?" I struggle to regain flippancy.

"Not funny. I'm still all of a dither when I think of the boyfriend's scowl this morning. I thought I was going to end up bruised and bleeding two days in a row."

"You were safe enough. Terry's not the violent kind." Which is polite parlance for 'Terry hasn't got the balls.' And yet, as I say it, I know it's not true. Terry is capable of doing harm as long as he thinks he can get away with it.

Allie picks up Ben and says, "I'll go and change him. I'll be back in a minute, Mum." The look she gives me reveals how deeply she's dreading telling her dad about her run in with his latest bit of stuff. She disappears along the corridor.

"What's up with Allie?" asks Matt.

"What do you mean?"

"Talk about looking guilty. She's not pregnant again is she?"

"No, nothing like that. Just a misunderstanding. She'll tell you later."

I've made a resolution to stop acting as family negotiator. The idiot who stands in No Man's Land waving a peace flag tends to get bombarded from both sides.

"There were lots of calls on your answer phone, Matt. Mainly from your office."

"I must get in touch. They'll be wondering where the hell I've got to. I should have called Michelle yesterday but I felt too rough."

"Before you get too deeply immersed in work, are you really okay with chicken for dinner? It's no problem to do you fish or an omelette."

"No, it's fine. I still eat white meat."

I pass him his phone and leave him to his business calls, while I nip downstairs to relay the information to the cook, who's sharing the wine between the white sauce and her glass. I wish I wasn't driving again today, a few glasses of wine would go down very well.

As I start back upstairs, I hear Matt shouting. Oh God! I guess Allie's confessed and he's taken the Claudia quarrel in the worst possible way. I run up the stairs, my heart thumping in rhythm with my feet. At the top I see Allie standing in the doorway of her room. She looks startled but not upset.

I go into Matt's room. He's sitting upright in bed, yelling down the phone. I hear, "For Christ's sake!" The iPhone whizzes past my ear and crashes against the wall.

Allie rushes forward, in full protective mode, but I signal her out of the room. I close the door and pick up the phone. "What was that about?"

His face is bleached white, except for the scarlet flares of colour on his cheeks. He's panting but he manages to gasp, "Sorry. I didn't mean to throw that at you."

"I know." Matt's got an excellent aim and, if he'd meant to hit me, he'd have done so.

I cross the room and sit on the edge of his bed. "What's wrong?"

"I've just sacked half my bloody staff."

"Any good reason or a sudden whim?" He glares at me, so I switch to a coaxing tone, "Tell me."

"I phoned through to Michelle to tell her what had happened and where I was and, before I could speak, I got this bloody earful about neglecting the firm and going off screwing sluts and how loyalty worked both ways. She wouldn't listen to a bloody word I said." He pushes his hands against his eyes and I know his headache's bad.

Michelle has been with the firm since Matt had enough money to employ permanent staff and, for the last few years, she's been his second-in-command. She's a big, loud, kind-hearted woman, in her sixties; not significantly older than us now we're all middle-aged, but she's always played the older and wiser game.

"Michelle has always been the forceful kind, but it's not like her to turn on you."

He shrugs. "We've got some big deals on at the moment and they've made her a lot of work. I was all set to apologise about not getting you to phone her yesterday, but I couldn't get a word in. So I told her I'd sell the bloody firm and she and Claudia and Patrick and the rest could take their chances with a new boss."

"Claudia?" Nasty prickles run down my spine.

"She's our rep for the posh end of the market. There's a big dance tomorrow she's been organising, and Michelle says she's been trying to get hold of me."

I can't keep up my non-involvement; this is escalating into a nasty mess.

"I'll phone Michelle and sort things out. You lie there quietly and calm down."

"I'm sorry. I don't usually lose my temper like that."

"You don't usually have concussion. I'll use the landline, your phone's distinctly dead."

I go into my room, look up the number and sit down on the bed to dial through.

"Good afternoon. Alder Experience. Michelle Brandel speaking."

"Hi Michelle. It's Honey Alder."

"Honey, hello. What can I do for you?" She sounds both warmer and more cautious.

"Matt had a serious fall yesterday. He's got a bad concussion."

"But I was just talking to him. Why didn't he say?"

"I don't think you gave him a chance."

There's a brief silence, then, "I suppose not. How badly hurt is he?"

"Bad enough. Too sick to be left alone. He's staying at my house."

"But Claudia said..." her voice trails away.

"Let me guess. Claudia said she went round to his house and encountered a blonde bit of stuff young enough to be his daughter."

"Oh God! Don't tell me it was his daughter?"

"We'd gone round to get some things for him. And Allie thought Claudia was a blonde bit of stuff, also young enough to be his daughter."

"Only if he'd fathered her before he left school. Anyway, Matt doesn't shit on his own doorstep."

Very elegantly put. I know I shouldn't ask for more information but I find myself saying, "So whose doorstep is he performing on at the moment?"

"None that I know of."

I find this surprising. Michelle might decide not to share it, but she's been clued up on every detail of Matt's life for the last thirty years and most of mine as well.

Her next question confirms this. "What does your new bloke think about you nursing Matt?"

"He's no problem. Can you sort things out with Claudia and keep the office going for a few days without Matt?"

"Of course I can." She sounds offended at the implication she can't cope and I feel like asking why she's been making so much fuss about Matt going AWOL.

"If you need Matt you'll have to call him on my home number. His mobile had an unfortunate collision with the wall after you wound him up."

"Yeah, well sorry about that. Not that it takes much to wind him up recently. He's been really touchy. Talk about walking on eggshells when he's around."

I store that information with all the other stuff that's worrying me about Matt. "As soon as he feels better, he'll give you a ring."

"Can't I speak to him now? Just to make my peace."

"Better not. He's pretty wiped."

I hear a movement in the corridor and cut across her arguments. It doesn't matter whether she thinks I'm overprotective or domineering; it's Matt who has to work with her not me. I speed across the room and intercept Allie outside Matt's door.

"I'm just going to see Dad and confess my sins."

"No." I lead her back into my room. "Your dad doesn't need any more stress. He's feeling bad again. And by the way, that woman you insulted was one of your dad's senior employees, not his latest lady friend."

I savour her expression of dismay. I love my daughter but there are times when I enjoy seeing her taken down a peg or two.

"Oh shit!" says Allie.

"Yes," I agree, "That seems to sum it up."

Chapter 12

We have a lovely dinner, Mum, Allie and myself, three generations of women who enjoy each other's company. Our representatives of the weaker sex are asleep upstairs in their beds. We'll microwave their food when they wake up.

"I wish Jackie was here," I say. "What time's she closing?"

"About three," says Mum. "Perhaps she could come over for tea."

"I sort of promised Terry I'd make it over to Fareham this afternoon."

"Is there anyone you want to hear?" asks Mum.

"No, not desperately."

"Then why don't you do what you want?" demands Allie. "Terry has got his dreary friends to keep him company. Please yourself for once."

Put like that it sounds simple and I struggle to explain the problem to Allie.

Mum comes to my rescue, although not in a complimentary way. "Your mum has never pleased herself, Allie. Even when she was a little girl, she'd try to please everyone, and when she grew up she got even worse."

"You make me sound like some sickening plaster saint," I object.

"Not a saint, certainly not a plaster one, just someone who's too aware of the demands of others for her own good."

"And Dad always bossed her," says Allie.

"No he didn't!" Mum and I say the same words in unison and Allie stares at us.

"He was the one person who never tried to boss her," says Mum. "I watched out for it, believe me, especially after I'd met his dad."

Allie looks subdued but she can't deny her paternal grandfather is a domineering man. "Grandpa's not as bossy as he used to be, Nanna. Ross and I went up to see him just after Christmas and he's got very frail and forgetful. He doesn't like living in the Old People's Home and he spent a lot of time talking about the old days when Dad and Aunt Sarah were little and Granny was alive."

My mum smiles. "She was a lovely woman, your Granny. So gentle and kind. She was so pleased when you were named for her."

"How come it was okay for Granny Alice to be gentle and kind when it's all wrong for me?" I protest, even though I'd been very fond of my mother-in-law.

"I didn't say it was right for her either. It's the ones who try too hard that end up getting depressed." Mum must see my stricken expression because she continues hastily, "The way Matt's mother did."

That snaps me out of my hurt feelings. "Matt's mum suffered from depression?"

"All the time I knew her."

"I never realised. I knew she was shy and timid but I didn't know it was depression." Although, when I look back, I see so many signs.

"It wasn't something people liked to talk about. And Matt's father would never admit there was a health problem, especially not when it came to mental health. Weak stock, that's what he used to call it. Typical of a farmer."

"Granny Alice's mother killed herself," says Allie.

We both stare at her.

"That's more than I ever knew," says my mum.

"Or me," I say. "Did your grandfather tell you, Allie?"

"No, not really. He was showing us these photo albums and I didn't like it. It was so boring and most of the people in there were dead so long ago that hardly anyone remembered them. Even Grandpa couldn't work out who a lot of them were. Though I liked the ones of your wedding, you looked so pretty, Mum."

I reject the red herring. "Never mind about my wedding. How did you find out about Granny Alice's mother?"

"There was this photo of Granny Alice, only she was quite young, and she'd got a little boy with her. It was weird because the boy looked so like Simon, but it was Dad. It was obvious that part of the photo had been cut away and I asked why and Grandpa said something about bad blood. I was upset. I thought he was talking about Simon. When we were leaving, this lady called us over. She'd heard us talking and she'd realised what I was thinking. She'd been at school with Granny Alice and she said Grandpa didn't like talking about it because Granny's mother had killed herself."

I feel as though I've stepped into a lift and the floor's disintegrated, sucking me down the empty shaft. All these years I've assumed Matt was so much stronger than I am, but he's got this dark heritage and I'm scared it's catching up with him.

The phone rings. I answer it and Terry says, "Honey, we're at your sister's flower shop. Nicola and I are about to head back to Fareham, so you can join us there."

"I was thinking of coming over later. I wanted to invite Jackie for tea. She hasn't had much of an Easter holiday."

"Oh right." To my surprise he doesn't sound annoyed. "That might work out quite well. Edward and Graham seem keen to stay here a bit longer and do a few more studios in the Art Trail. They could come over with Jackie and have tea with you and then bring you over for the concert."

I think that Terry's got a bloody cheek, organising my life, but it's not worth complaining when his arrangement suits me very well. "That's fine."

"It will be a relief to separate them for a while. Edward and Nicola have done nothing but fight all day. I don't know what's got into Edward."

"Perhaps he's fed up with being ordered around by a bossy woman."

There's the sound of sharply in-drawn breath and then silence in which I suspect Terry is waiting for God to strike me down. The Almighty is slow with the thunderbolts and he says, "It's not like that. Nicola's wonderful. The cleverest woman I've ever met. With a brain like hers it's not surprising she's got strong opinions."

I would have substituted 'brain' with 'ego' but I don't say so.

"You don't like Nicola, do you? She's noticed your hostility. You don't have to be jealous of her. She's no threat to our relationship."

That's so insulting it takes my breath away. "I promise you I'm not in the least jealous of her. The good thing with a friendship like ours, Terry, is we don't have to like each other's friends."

"But we're in a lot more than just a friendship, aren't we, Honey?"

Actually, I think we're in a lot less than friendship. "I'll see you later." I ring off.

Life's not fair. I've always known it but it's driven home more forcibly when I see my sister and Edward. Their conversation is casual and yet they sound as if they've been friends for years. She's still dressed with her customary primness and he's in his grey, Church-going suit, although, in his wife's absence, he's removed his tie. The difference about them isn't their clothes, it's the glow in Jackie's eyes and Edward's surprisingly attractive smile.

Mum spots it straight away. I can tell by the quiet, assessing look she gives Edward and the way she invites him to sit down and talk to her while we get tea.

He obeys. Jackie, quite matter-of-factly, arranges cushions behind his back for maximum comfort, before she accompanies me to the kitchen. We cut bread and slice salad without speaking. Not that we could say much if we wanted to. Graham has followed us and we're battered into submission by his monologue on the studios he's visited today.

The kitchen siege is relieved by Allie and Ross. They appear from upstairs with Ben, who's just woken up, eager to start the Easter egg experience once again.

Ross demonstrates his swift comprehension as he takes in our long-suffering faces. "Are you going on the Art Trail again tomorrow, Graham?" he asks.

"I'd like to. It depends whether anyone will give me a lift."

"It's a far more authentic experience if you use Public Transport. Come with me and I'll help you check out the times of buses."

"Right. That's a good idea. My parents don't have any feeling for art."

Yesterday Graham displayed an equal lack of interest in art. A smattering of knowledge is a truly scary thing. Allie chimes in, advising Graham to stick to studios in the Fareham area rather than risk public transport on a Bank Holiday. It's clear they plan to keep Graham at a distance from our village as he tracks down his art.

Clamping down on my laughter, I cut tomatoes into water-lily shapes. From the corner of my eye I can see Jackie buttering bread for all she's worth, while Allie has buried her face in Ben's downy hair. None of us dare to look at each other but, as Ross and Graham leave, I risk a glance. Ross' acting training is serving him well and there's no amusement visible but, behind Graham's back, he winks at me.

"Okay, I admit it," I say to Allie. "Ross is a good actor."

She glows at this small tribute. "He's brilliant. You should see him rehearsing the kids at college; he can switch from one role to another and be really convincing."

"I never said he wasn't talented."

"It's not just that, Mum. He's really interested in people. He spent ages talking to the old dears in Grandpa's nursing home. I couldn't take it, the smell and everything. When I'd spoken to that old lady, Ross told me to take Ben and wait outside."

Perhaps there's more kindness in Ross than I'd realised. I hope so. Allie goes into the living room and Jackie abandons the buttering and turns to face me. All the laughter has drained from her face. "What's wrong?" I ask.

"Nothing."

"Tell that to someone who's not your older sister. It's Edward, isn't it?"

She nods.

"You like him don't you?"

"Yes."

"I like him too. I think he's a decent guy."

"But he's married."

"Well no-one's perfect," I say, in the words of a classic film.

She rubs a hand across her wet eyes and leaves a smear of butter on her nose. "I can't break up his marriage."

"From what I've seen, his marriage is already irreparable."

She stares at me. "It would be totally hypocritical. Think of the things I said about Matt when he was cheating on you."

For the first time it hits me that my relationship with Jackie had been another casualty of Simon's death. I tear off a piece of kitchen towel and wipe the butter from her face. I like it when my self-possessed sister becomes as gauche as me.

"I don't think you pushed me into confronting Matt out of vindictiveness, did you?"

"Of course not! I liked Matt and I'd never deliberately hurt you." She pauses and I watch as she takes out her motives and examines them. "At least, I didn't think I was being vindictive. But, after Barry left me, I hated all men and didn't trust any of them."

"Jackie, the stupidest people are the ones who never change their minds. But don't jump into something you'll regret. You've only known Edward for a few hours."

"That's what I told him."

I almost drop the lettuce. "You mean he's made some sort of proposition?"

Jackie's usually pale face is fiery red. "It wasn't like you're making it sound. The others had gone on the village Art Trail, but he stayed at the shop. We were talking while I worked. I got a thorn in my finger and he removed it for me. And he kissed it better. Then he apologised. And I said it was all right. And so he kissed me on the lips. Then he apologised again. He said he was sorry, he'd never done anything like that before, but I was special, he'd known that straight away."

"What did you say?" I'm torn between nausea and curiosity.

"Nothing. The others came back and we had to pretend nothing had happened."

A giggle escapes before I can capture it. "I'm sorry, Jackie, but that story has more sugar in it than this Easter cake."

She looks offended. "I'd thought you'd understand about romance."

"Afraid not." Matt and I had always been non-starters when it came to the sugar-coated stuff. Perhaps we'd have survived better if we'd had a padding of romantic fluff.

I can't forget the picture of the old woman in Matt's album, with her fur-trimmed slippers and her work-worn hands. Surely it must be a photo of his long-dead grandmother. "Jackie, do you believe in ghosts?"

"Of course." She sounds surprised that I have to ask. "Don't you?"

"I don't know." Yesterday I'd have answered with an unequivocal 'No', but I prefer being haunted by a ghostly grandmother to the thought that Matt's going mad.

Chapter 13

Mum likes Edward. To anyone who knows her that's obvious. It's not ultimate proof he's a decent guy, but she's right about people a lot more often than she's wrong.

Still Jackie can sort out her own love life. I've got problems of my own, fending off the advances of a twenty-four-year-old adolescent who wishes to interrogate me about my 'art.' He's got me trapped in my armchair, while he sits on a dining chair that he's pulled in close beside me. He's got no concept of personal space and his art knowledge is culled from the advertising handouts in the church hall.

Occasionally I contemplate escape. I wriggle my bum forward on the squashy chair, trying to position myself to get up. Every time he says, "Please let me," and fetches me more tea, sandwiches or cake. Edward is talking to Jackie and Mum and they seem oblivious to my torture, but I know Allie and Ross think it's hilarious.

The door opens. "Matt!" I jump to my feet, scattering sandwiches and art brochures and almost capsizing Graham.

"Now I've got a change of clothes, I thought I might as well get up." Despite his nonchalance he's uncharacteristically meek when I take his arm and steer him to my chair.

"You're an idiot. If you needed something you should have yelled."

"Just wanted some company. It's not much fun up there by myself."

"I'd have kept you company if you'd asked." I pour him a cup of tea and sit on the arm of the chair to steady it for him.

He takes a few sips then grins at my mum. "Hiya Daisy."

"Don't you 'Hiya Daisy' me. You should be tucked up safely in bed."

"Like I said, I'd have stayed in bed if I'd had some company." The mischievous glance he flicks at me invests the words with a lecherous sub-text and I giggle. Graham sees the by-play and glowers at Matt.

"This is Edward," I say. "He was at University with Terry. And this is Graham, Edward's son. This is Matt, my husband."

Graham says aggressively, "Don't you mean ex-husband?"

"True," says Matt, "but, as you see, far from estranged." He turns to Edward. "Honey said you were down here for the folk festival?"

"Yes. I enjoyed last night, but to be honest I'm skiving as many of the minor acts as I can. I've got a bad back and those seats play it up. Jackie, did you think any more about coming along tonight?"

"It would be fun but surely they won't have a seat this late in the day?"

"They'll probably have a few tickets for the dance floor. It should be better down there anyway." He says a general, "Excuse me," gets out his mobile and rings through. Within a minute he's fixed up a ticket for Jackie.

Graham has picked up all the art brochures and is assembling them lovingly into their appointed order once again. "We were discussing Honey's art," he informs Matt.

"Honey's what?" He turns to me, "Your art?"

"It's one of the major attractions of the Hampshire Art Trail," chips in Graham.

"Really?" Matt is still staring at me.

"It's not even a minor attraction." I feel my face grow hot.

"But you are exhibiting some art? I know you've always had a good eye for art but I didn't realise you could actually do it."

"It's silly. Not proper art at all. I went on a weekend watercolour course." I shove a self-mocking note into my voice, "I thought it was time I discovered the new me."

"And you discovered the new you was an artist?" I don't blame Matt for sounding incredulous.

"Not exactly. My pictures were wishy-washy, and that's putting it politely. But when I looked at them I had a crazy idea, so I came home and knitted them."

The silence that follows this statement is broken by Matt's laughter and I grin in response.

"They're superb, primitive depictions of colour and texture," says Graham hotly.

"No, they're not," I say, "they're a bit of fun."

"Actually they're very attractive," says Edward quietly.

I smile at him. "Thank you. I'll settle for that."

"Sorry Honey, I didn't mean to insult your work," says Matt.

"You didn't. I enjoyed doing them and it's sweet of Jackie to put them up in her shop. It's fun to be part of the Art Trail but I don't expect any great public response."

"I'd have bought them all if I'd been allowed," says Graham, glowering at his father.

"If you had any money, you mean," he replies.

"I'd like to see them," murmurs Matt to me.

Still sitting on the arm of his chair, I bend closer to reply, "Maybe, by the end of the week, you'll be fit enough to go over there. If not I'll have to give you a Private View when I get them back." I rescue his empty cup and lean across to put it on the side table. "Do you want anything to eat?"

"No, thanks. To be honest, I came down for a cigarette. Thanks for packing them."

"That's okay. I'll tell Allie to take Ben upstairs and you can smoke in here." He's obviously still shaky and I break one of my strictest rules.

"No way! I'll smoke outside."

"Then I'm coming out with you." It's remarkable how, despite our lowered voices, Matt and I can get more stubbornness per square inch into our conversation than anybody else.

I lead the way outside and settle him in a chair on the terrace. I love all of my house but this is probably my favourite spot of all. It's a proper terrace, miniature but worthy of a National Trust House. Its low enclosing wall is supported by carved stone pedestals and the shallow steps lead down to a modest lawn surrounded by shrubbery. Matt and I had created it over twenty years ago, laughing at our dreams of grandeur as we worked.

After Matt has lit up, he asks, "Any more word from my office?"

"Just what I told you when you woke up. Michelle's sorting everything."

"What about Claudia's dance tomorrow?"

"Michelle says she's coping but there's something I ought to tell you." I confess our daughter's sins, finishing up with, "Michelle's set Claudia straight and I've made Allie squirm, so there's no need for you to bring on your headache by yelling at anyone."

"You can't bring on something that's already there."

I move behind him and gently run my fingers across his head. With a sigh he leans back to rest against me.

"Are you angry with Allie?" I ask.

"No. When you've made your bed you can't blame people for thinking you're lying in it with every blonde who comes knocking on your door."

"There's been quite a few redheads and brunettes as well."

"I know. I really screwed up, didn't I?" I'm seeking for a suitable response when he says, "That's enough of my moaning. How's your job going?"

I move to sit on the terrace wall opposite to him, my back to the garden. "It's okay. Any form of teaching is more curriculum tracking than spreading enlightenment these days. And we've got a new Head of Department who's changing all the paperwork whether it needs it or not. They all do that, it's like an animal marking its territory."

"If you need more money to quit work then say so. You must know you can have it any time you want."

"I don't need more money." I'd returned to work to reclaim my identity. "Some parts of the job are still fun. I took my A-level groups to Stratford last month and that was great. Ross helped organise it and brought some of his drama students along."

"I'm glad it's not all aggro between you and Ross."

"If he and Allie are going to stick together, I've got to try and like him but I admit I find it hard to trust him."

"Aye, still I guess you're right, you've got to get on with him."

"You too," I point out. "Having you here at Easter has made me realise I'd like it if you were here for more of our celebrations: Easter, Christmas, birthdays. You're part of this family. Ross' father buggered off years ago, so Ben needs his remaining Grandad. If you've got time, that is. I know you're busy." The sub-text to this is, 'I know you've got lots of women to wine and dine and screw.'

"I can think of nothing I'd like better. Thank you. About Ross, where did he come from before he worked at your college?"

"The Midlands, I think. Somewhere near Birmingham." I scour my brain and tell him the little I know about Ross.

"Are you all right, Honey?" Graham appears and moves in close. I feel like I'm part of some magnet game. I'll have to check for homing devices when I change.

"I'm fine. Why shouldn't I be?"

"I just thought... I don't want anyone to take advantage of you."

"Jolly good. I'll mention that if I meet anyone who wants to. Weren't you looking on the website for art exhibitions?"

The sulky look doesn't lift. "Ross wanted to use his laptop to do some work."

"Well you can use mine, I'll..."

"Honey!"

I break off and stare at Matt. His face is ashen. "I saw her! There!" His trembling hand points towards the end of the garden.

I turn and stare at the shrubbery, then I run down the steps and across the lawn. There's no sign of anyone lurking in the bushes or skulking behind the trees.

"What's going on?" Graham has followed me into the undergrowth, while Matt is still making his shaky way across the lawn.

"Matt thought he saw someone. Did you see anything?" Unlike me, he'd been facing the same way as Matt.

"No." He considers the wall that confines the large back garden. "That's a high wall for anyone to climb."

"Yes." With that in mind, I go across to check the small side gate, built into the wall in the corner by the garage. It's bolted but the small door into the garage isn't locked. Nervously I open it and peer inside but there's no-one there, just the usual clutter of car repair tools and gardening stuff.

I return to the shrubbery where Graham is searching for 'clues'. His large feet churn the earth and I think there's no hope of finding any other footprints now.

"There's something over there." Matt points to an object deep in the shrubbery.

I see the glint of gold and pick it up. Graham is approaching, clearly curious. Some instinct of privacy makes me say, "It's just a chocolate paper," and pocket it.

Chapter 14

Back in the house I make the excuse of getting changed and scurry upstairs to my bedroom to examine my find in private. It's certainly not paper. It's a slender, wristwatch, made for a lady. I like old-fashioned jewellery and I'd guess this was made in the 1940s or '50s. It's made of gold but it's modest. I'd rate it as a working woman's luxury rather than a rich woman's toy. I brush a few crumbs of mud off and it gleams as good as new. I'll check with Mum, Jackie and Allie, but I'm pretty sure it doesn't belong to any of them and they're the only other women who've had opportunity to lurk in my shrubbery.

Which brings us back to ghosts. Despite what I said to Jackie, I don't believe in them. Certainly not a ghost who wears a wristwatch and drops it as they waft out of sight.

It was Matt who'd spotted the watch. I consider the possibility I'd rejected before. Could Matt have lied? That still seems unlikely. But if he's really imagining these things, he could have become desperate enough to plant some evidence to prove he's not going mad.

I think it through all the time I'm dressing for the evening concert and, before I go downstairs, I slip the watch into my skirt pocket. I don't want any ghost, corporeal or ethereal, slipping into my room to reclaim its property.

We make it to Fareham a few minutes before the first performer takes to the stage. Terry is clearly delighted to include Jackie in the party. He speaks to her in a jokey manner and I think he's trying to show his friends he's an integral part of our family. Jackie's answering smile contains more than a hint of gritted teeth.

"If that bloke of yours calls me Jack once more, I'm going to swing for him," she hisses in my ear.

"Go for it. A good left hook should easily take him out. But you let me call you Jack, and you haven't hit me for it, at least not since you were ten."

"That's different. Older sisters are privileged."

The lower half of the hall has been cleared of seats, ready for dancing to the folk rock band that tops this year's bill. Because of her late booking, Jackie has to stand, although the rest of us still have our seats reserved. As I take my place, I glance down the hall at my sister. Since her divorce most of her hobbies have been solitary but that doesn't mean she likes being alone in a crowd. I get up but Edward's before me, edging his way out and saying casually, "I'll stand. The sound's better down there."

"Stand? But you're always complaining that standing hurts you even more than sitting!" snaps Nicola. "I suppose you'll moan all night about your back."

"Well, if I do, it's not going to make any difference to you, is it?" Edward reaches the end of the row, smiles at me, and goes down the steps.

Terry pulls a wry face. "You see what I mean? They've been like that all weekend," he tells me quietly.

"What did he mean about whether he was in pain not effecting her?" I ask, matching my volume to his.

"Separate rooms. Haven't slept together for years."

"Oh?"

"You can't blame Nicky. She said it was destroying her health and work, the way he wouldn't let her get any sleep."

"Really? There must be a wild side to Edward I haven't seen."

Terry looks at me sharply, to see if I'm really as thick as I'm pretending, then he grins. "I didn't mean sex, you know that. From what Nicky said there hasn't been anything between them in that department for years."

"I see."

As with many tattle-mongers, Terry seems to repent of his gossip as soon as he's broadcast it. "You won't tell Edward I mentioned it, will you? Nicky only told me because I'm such an old friend. She knew I'd give her good advice."

That doesn't make his gossiping any better. "No, I wouldn't dream of telling Edward. What advice did you give Nicola?"

He hesitates and I say, "It's too late for the secrets of the confessional now, Terry."

"I suppose so. Anyway, telling you doesn't matter, does it?"

It would be nice to think he meant I was so trustworthy, but I suspect he thinks I'm negligible. "No, it doesn't matter at all. What did you say?"

"I think she's sacrificed herself enough. If she gets out now, it's not too late to start a new relationship."

I have a sparkling moment when I think he's going to tell me that he and Nicola have discovered they're in love.

"After all, I found you when I was beginning to think it was too late," he continues, then lapses into silence as the performers are introduced.

The concert starts off well but it would be better without Terry's hand resting ostentatiously on my knee. Perhaps I'm wrong to postpone chucking him. It seems like he's getting in deeper and deeper. I don't believe he's in love with me but I think he's talking himself into it. He wants it to be like this and so it's going to be. Three songs in and his hand is travelling; now it's trying to burrow under my skirt.

I murmur, "I'm going down the front," and abandon him.

There's an interval between the first act and the major band. Nicola has obviously taken umbrage. Instead of coming to join Edward, Jackie and me, she grips Terry's arm and steers him towards the bar. Deirdre trails behind them but Jez darts off to talk to somebody.

"So that's showed you," comments Edward.

I look at their retreating backs and laugh. There's triumph in Nicola's manner. She's showing me she can still call my boyfriend to heel.

Graham's lingering in his seat. I go up to him. "Are you okay?"

"Yes." He sounds miserable.

"You can always go back to your hotel if you're bored."

"No. Mum wouldn't like that."

It amazes me that everyone runs scared of Nicola but I have more sympathy for Graham than for anyone else. He's her child, indoctrinated into obedience all his life.

"I'm going to get a drink but if you do decide to leave, find me and let me know. I'll make up some excuse to save you grief."

His colour deepens, turning his sallow face dusky red and, for a moment, he actually looks at me. "Thank you. You're the sweetest, most wonderful woman in the world."

"I really don't think so." I move hastily away in pursuit of Jackie and Edward.

I find them lingering by a clothes' stall. Edward's fingering some softly coloured, delicate, silk scarves. "These are pretty, aren't they?" he says as I approach.

"Lovely," I agree.

He unhooks a scarf in a medley of blues and pale greens and drapes it around Jackie's neck. It transforms her, softening her sharp defensiveness with its sea shades. "Do you like it? May I buy it for you?" he says.

"Thank you." The softness in her tone says everything. Her lips tremble. "Excuse me." She hands the scarf back to him and hurries away.

"Have I upset her?" Edward's eyes follow her anxiously.

"She's confused." This needs explaining and Jackie certainly won't. "When her husband left, it knocked her confidence. And, as she's been on the receiving end, she's got scruples about involvement with married men."

"Excuse me," interrupts the stall holder, "Do you want that scarf or not?"

"Yes," says Edward, "but if you wait a minute I'll be getting something else." Turning back to the rack he picks out a more vivid scarf in tones of pink that range from seashell to sunset. "I thought this would suit you, Honey."

"There's no need to buy me a present."

"I'd like to. You've been so kind to me." He corrects himself, "No, kind's the wrong word. You've been lovely to me. Made me feel like... like less of a bloody failure."

I wait until he's paid and we've moved away from the stall before I say, "You're not a failure, Edward."

"Not in business maybe, but in relationships."

"I think, like Jackie, you've lost confidence."

"You're probably right. I'm going outside. I need a smoke."

I knot my new scarf around my neck and accompany him.

When we're clear of the crowds, he says, "I wouldn't ask Jackie to get involved with me, not the way things are."

"Why not?"

He looks startled at my bluntness. "Because I'm scared she'd say no and I'd spoil everything."

"I think you're probably right. I don't think Jackie would feel comfortable in a relationship with a man who's still living with his wife."

He's not stupid. I see him analysing what I've said, including the small print. We seem to have come a long way in the twenty-four hours since I first met him.

"Do you think Jackie's all right?" he says at last.

"I'll go and find her."

It doesn't take the abilities of Sherlock Holmes to discover Jackie. It's just a question of waiting until the ladies' cloakroom is empty and then addressing the only locked cubicle. "Jack, it's only me out here, so please unlock that door."

The bolt clicks open and she appears. "How did you know I was in there?"

"Genetic heritage. When in doubt lock yourself in the loo. I do the same."

"I bet most women do."

"Okay, so deny me even that bit of originality. For God's sake, splash some cold water on your face."

She obeys and, after she's dried her face, I do some quick make up repairs to tone down her puffy eyes and red nose. I step back to survey my handiwork. "God I'm good! Now you look like you've got a touch of hay fever, not like you're coming down with Bubonic Plague."

"Is Edward all right?" she asks as I steer her back into the foyer, alert to avoid our Festival companions.

"As well as can be expected. But I don't think he's going to offer to buy you any more presents for a while."

"It came over me how perfect it would be if he wasn't married."

"It's not just people who aren't perfect, situations aren't either. But, if it's any comfort, you're not a home-wrecker." I tell her what Terry had said about separate rooms. After all I'd only promised not to tell Edward that I knew, not Jackie. I finish up with my glimpse of Nicola playing footsie with Jez during the concert yesterday.

Jackie looks disgusted. "But he's gross. I know Edward's a bit overweight but Jez..." She shudders.

"It's that nasty little beard," I agree.

"And the hair. And he smells."

"I think that's the tee-shirt. He said it's his Festival tee-shirt so he wears it all week."

"But couldn't he wash it overnight?"

"Or at least between festivals. I guess he thinks that might destroy some of the subtle ambience of the Isle of Wight in the Sixties or whenever it was. Not to mention it's probably held together by the mud of thirty Cropredys."

Jackie laughs but her eyes are on the sliding outer doors, watching for Edward's return. "Honey, ignore what I've been saying. It's all nonsense."

She means she's the sensible sister who never believed in love at first sight.

"Did you know going all out for a guy used to be called throwing your cap over the windmill?" I share a piece of information I find interesting.

Jackie looks at me as if I'm crazy and I think Matt is the only person I know who not only accepts my habit of quotation but travels along with me.

"You mean like you have with Terry?" she says sarcastically and walks away to join the others before I can reply. I guess that's as well. She wouldn't be happy if I told her the simple truth, the cap I threw over the windmill for Matt has never been retrieved.

In the concert hall, a lot of black-clad, middle-aged groovers have beamed down to occupy the dance floor. Most of them have season tickets suspended around their necks, which perch tenuously on their wobbling beer guts.

Jez is in his element, exchanging boisterous greetings and pretentious criticisms of the acts that are, in his view, less than cutting edge. Summoned by his clicking fingers, Deirdre follows him meekly.

Graham approaches me, stumbling down the steps in his eagerness. "Are you going to sit with me, Honey?"

"I'm not sure." All the others are down in the dance space.

"Please Honey," begs Graham.

"It'll be noisy up there," warns Edward.

The venomous look Graham gives him startles me and I thank God that, even at the worst, Allie has never looked at her dad with such hatred.

"I'll give it a try, Graham. But if it's too loud I'm moving."

"I'll look after you." He escorts me up the steps. "My parents are so old-fashioned."

"They're younger than me."

"No they're not. You're timeless." It's the sort of cheesy compliment that deserves loud mockery, but the intensity in Graham's voice sends a cold tremor down my spine.

Halfway through the first number I realise I should have known better than to put myself through this. One legacy of my depressive illness is an over-sensitivity to sound. My stupidity hits me within seconds of the band striking up but it's already too late to get up and leave. The seating is vibrating and the volume pounds inside my head, like I'm being hammered by padded fists. I stare blankly at the cavorting distant figures on the stage and remember it's possible for noise to make you physically sick.

And I can't escape. There's not enough of me left to let me move. I can't speak. I can't scream. I can't even summon the will power to put my hands over my ears. All I can do is endure. My breathing is instinctively shallow, as if sucking in breath would allow more access to the noise.

Graham's arms encircle me, forcing me to stand. He half-carries, half-leads me down the steps, past the crowd and out of the concert hall.

A theatre steward rises from her chair. "Is everything all right?"

"She felt faint. I'll look after her."

I hate making an exhibition of myself, so I let him lead me through the theatre foyer and out into the cool darkness of the car park. Reaction sets in. I'm shaking so violently I can hardly walk and tears are streaming down my face.

I expect him to stop in the car park, but he doesn't, he hustles me across the road, along the pavement and inside a wide wooden gate. We're amongst the tombstones before I realise he's taken me into a churchyard. His arms are still round me. Over his shoulder, I get a glimpse of the church. It's solid and dark against the skyline but its windows are golden arcs of light and I can hear singing. The religious are celebrating Easter. Still shaken by my folk-rock bombardment, I wish I could join them in a gentle, traditional worship.

Graham's grip tightens and, before I can protest, he kisses me. His lips are wet and warm. I try to jerk away but he's got one of his hands behind my neck, pinioning me. He forces his tongue into my mouth and I gag with disgust. My instinct is to slap him. Or to wrench free and tell him what I think. My hand is half raised when an emotion even more primitive than anger takes control. I'm afraid.

Chapter 15

I tell myself there's no need to be frightened. He's just a boy with a stupid crush. But his hands are large and strong and his kiss is desperate. And he's not a child. He's a man and a creepy one at that. He stops kissing and I turn my head enough to free my mouth. I say quietly, "Graham, please don't do this." My only hope is to talk him down. "Please stop. You don't want to do anything I don't like."

"But you want me to. You want this as much as me." Even through my fear I can hear the confusion in his voice. He sounds much younger than his actual age and size.

"No, I don't, Graham. I'm sorry if I made you think I did."

"You bloody pricktease!"

He releases me and punches a gravestone. I flinch at how much that must hurt but I can't stop him, I have to save myself.

I've got no chance of running. He could easily outpace me and, in his shame and frustration, he could be violent and then panic. My retreat has to be even more careful than before. "I'm going now, Graham." With false confidence I turn and walk out of the churchyard. He follows me. I suspect he doesn't know what else to do.

It's a relief to get back to the lighted streets. But what do I do now? Was the whole incident as serious as I thought? Am I over-reacting? The mental paralysis induced by the noisy music makes this probable.

"I'm sorry," he says. His anger's gone but the bewilderment's still clear.

"Let's go and have a drink somewhere," I say.

He follows me to a nearby pub. I select a suitable corner table. It's private enough for us to talk but not isolated enough to encourage his advances.

"What do you want to drink?" I ask.

"I ought to... I mean I'm the man..."

"I'll get these. What would you like?"

"Could I have a whisky?"

"Of course." Again I remind myself he's in his twenties, not a teenager.

I get him a double and a large red wine for me and sit down opposite him. He looks white and tired. "Would it help to talk about it, Graham?"

"I don't know." He won't meet my eyes. There's a slight groove around the edge of the table and he's running his right index finger along it, back and fore. His knuckles are grazed and swollen. As I suspected, the gravestone got the better of their fight.

"You're unhappy, aren't you?" Sometimes one has to start with the obvious.

"Yes."

"How long have you been unhappy?"

He shrugs. "Always. It just keeps getting worse. I always get things wrong... with people I mean."

"I'm sorry if I led you on. I didn't mean to." I don't think I did but it won't hurt me to take the blame.

"Perhaps you didn't. I'm sorry I called you that. I'm not good at understanding people. I thought you fancied me. This afternoon you seemed like you were... different... sort of lit up. Terry said you were hot, a real goer. And you were so nice to me. I thought you liked me."

"I do like you. But I don't fancy you. I'm a grandmother. I don't make love to young men in their twenties." I move onto the bit of his speech that's making me tingle with indignation. "Did Terry talk about our sex life to you?"

"To everyone. On Saturday when we arrived. He was cross because you hadn't turned up and he said you only ran after your ex-husband to make him, Terry I mean, jealous. And Jez said why did he put up with it. And Terry said because you were so good in bed." The words jerk out, like a child who wants to make amends. Or maybe to stir things amongst the grown-ups.

"Terry was boasting, Graham. I'm not particularly hot in bed. And nothing I've ever done for Matt has been to make Terry jealous."

"Dad said that Terry and Jez were sleazy bastards."

"Sleazy, sad bastards. Graham, have you told your dad how you feel? Maybe he could help."

"I couldn't. You don't understand."

"Then tell me."

"I can't talk to Dad. Mother would know we'd got a secret and force him to tell her. Please don't let her know what I did. She says..." He stops tracing the table edge and his hands clench into fists.

"What does she say, Graham?" I take a calculated chance and reach across the table to place my hand over his.

"She says I'm crazy... not like normal boys."

I choose my words with wincing care. "Graham, I don't think you're crazy but you've got mixed up somewhere along the way. You need help to sort it out, before you frighten another woman like you did me."

"I frightened you?"

"Of course you did."

"I'm sorry. You didn't seem frightened. You've been so kind to me." He takes a deep breath, "Would you help me? Please. Tell me what to do."

"I'll try, as long as you promise not to get the idea that I fancy you. Okay?"

"I promise." He sounds like a small child.

"All right. I'll do my best, but I need time to consider." I check my watch. It's earlier than I thought. I'm not going to wait for Jackie to drive me home. She's bound to fuss and bombard me with questions. So would Terry and his friends. I'm tired of being polite to people I don't like and I want to go home. I get out my mobile. "I'm going to phone for a taxi. Why don't you go back to your hotel?"

He can't disguise his eagerness to leave, although, to his credit, he says, "Are you sure you don't mind being left alone in a pub?"

"Of course not."

He leaves and I ring for a taxi. It's a Bank Holiday so I'm not surprised when they say it could take at least half an hour. While I'm waiting I text Jackie to tell her the music was too loud for me but I'm okay. Then I ring home and Allie tells me they're all doing fine.

There are three guys sitting at the bar, middle-aged and smartly dressed. One of them keeps looking towards me and smiling. Deep in my thoughts it takes me a while to realise he's about to make a move. I don't return his smile. I've had more than my share of excitement for one evening. I wonder if I look available. Perhaps my close encounter in the Churchyard is somehow visible. I stand up and head into the Ladies. When I check the mirror I think I don't look particularly sexy. My hair's tangled and my make up smudged. Automatically, I make repairs.

As I walk back to my seat, the guy at the bar slides from his stool and starts towards me. I realise I've played it wrong and he thinks I've been prettying up for him.

"Good evening. May I buy you a drink?"

"No thank you." I draw on skills I haven't used for years and the smile I give him makes it clear he's totally struck out. It works and he retreats back to the bar where his mates greet him with mocking grins.

Allie once mentioned she uses her iPhone as a barrier to avoid stray pick-ups, but I'm old-fashioned. I rummage in my bag and produce a slender paperback, open it and keep my eyes fixed on the page. Cakes and Ale makes an efficient barrier. There are few things that act as a greater put-off to most guys than a woman reading a minor classic in a bar.

In the taxi I try to think what to do about Graham. Years of teaching have given me strange odds and ends of information and I think I know the problem, which doesn't mean I can get Graham or his parents to accept my advice or ask for professional help.

When we reach my house, the gates across the drive are closed, so I tell the driver to stop in the road, pay him off and use the small pedestrian gate. As I walk towards the house I hear a faint, metallic clicking. The security lights have activated and I locate the sound. The side gate that leads to the back garden is swinging open and shut. It had been locked this afternoon. I'm sure of that because I'd checked it after Matt had seen his 'ghost.' For a moment I feel frightened and then I remember that Allie had offered to mow the lawn and the grass that edges the drive. Trust my little scatterbrain to forget to lock the gate when she put the lawnmower back in the garage.

Groping in my bag for my keyring I go across to shut it. The bolt's pulled half across, which explains why it hadn't latched itself as it swung back and fore. I step inside and fiddle with it, cursing the lack of light in this secluded corner.

I hear a rustle behind me and say, "Who's there?" Before I can turn, my scarf is jerked back, the knot hard against my throat, choking me.

Chapter 16

I raise my hands and grab desperately at my scarf. The pressure eases slightly and I kick backwards, hit something solid and gouge downwards with my heel. The grip on my scarf jerks then loosens. I stumble and fall backwards. I land on my bottom, prickled by a tangle of spiky plants and banging my back on something hard. I hear the gate creak but by the time I can look around there's no-one in sight.

"Is someone out there?" Matt's voice, coming from the back of the house. He switches on the lights and I see him standing on the terrace, looking round.

"Over here." To my dismay, my voice comes as a croak.

"Honey?" He hurries to help me up.

"I'm all right." I clamber to my feet.

"Are you sure you're not hurt?" He puts an arm round me. "You're shaking."

"Someone grabbed me."

"What!" He swings his torch round the unlit part of the garden, then goes through the side gate into the front drive. "There's no-one there."

"There was someone. They grabbed my scarf and pulled it tight."

"Jesus! I'll kill the bastard! Did you see who it was?"

"No. I didn't see them... or hear them... just felt them choking me. They must have gone through the side gate. I heard it banging and came to lock it up."

While I explain, Matt is peering round the quiet garden, still hunting for my attacker. "Honey, are you sure you didn't just snag your scarf on this branch?" He plays his light over the tree that stands just within the gate. It's undeniably spiky and I've been planning for some time to have it pruned. His voice is apologetic. "I'm not doubting you, but all my carry on must have upset your nerves."

I open my mouth to deny I'd imagined it but the words don't come. I don't think it was my imagination but the more I consider it the less sure I feel. The thought of fighting a tree makes me feel a total fool.

"Let's go inside."

One thing I'm sure of, that tree is going to get the pruning of its life.

As we go in through the patio doors my mobile starts to ring. I check the display and wait until the answer service cuts in. I don't bother to listen to the message, instead I text: *HI TERRY. SPEAK TOMORROW. H.*

In the sitting room, Brahms is playing softly.

"Why are you still up?" I ask.

"I was waiting for Cinderella," he replies and leans over to turn down the CD.

"Cinderella wasn't a middle-aged grandma."

"Perhaps the boyfriend sees it differently."

Terry doesn't qualify for Prince Charming in my version of the tale. Maybe he might make it as the frog coachman, but tonight he's nearer to pumpkin status.

"You should be in bed, Matt."

"I couldn't sleep."

"Don't your sleeping pills help?"

"No." His tone warns me not to pursue the matter.

"I'm surprised Mum let you stay down here alone."

"She didn't hear me. She went to bed early and so did Allie. I hate lying in bed thinking, so I came down again. Has he gone straight up?"

It takes a moment to work out what Matt means. "You mean Terry? He isn't here."

On cue the phone rings. As with the mobile I wait for the answer phone. "Honey, it's me. I know you're there, so pick up. I don't know what you're playing at, running off like that. You could consider me occasionally." The tone is irritable with more than a hint of whinge. There's a pause then, "Ring me back. I want to talk to you."

In the silence that follows we both stare at the answer phone. At last Matt says, "Have you had a quarrel?"

"Not yet, but we will if I pick up that phone."

"Would it be tactless to ask what he's done?"

"Yes."

"Honey, what's wrong?"

"Nothing."

"Yes there is. I can see you're shaken up. Was it that fall in the garden? I didn't mean to doubt you. If you say someone grabbed you I'm sure they did. It's just I know how easy it is to let your mind play tricks on you." He frowns. "In fact I thought I heard someone out there just before I heard you fall, but I'm so jumpy I keep meeting trouble before it comes. I never meant to let you in for this. Are you sure you're not hurt?"

"No, I'm not hurt. And I was shaken up anyway."

He takes my hand and tugs me towards him. "Tell me." His voice is so gentle it takes me back to the time when I could tell Matt anything. I sit on the sofa beside him, his arm around me, and tell him about the effect the loud music had on me and about Graham and how scared I'd been when he tried to kiss me and afterwards how sorry I'd felt for him.

To my relief he doesn't condemn the kid. "What are you going to do now?"

"Try to help him."

"Of course you will. That's obvious to anyone who knows you. I meant how are you going to help him?"

"I don't know exactly but tomorrow I thought I might take him to see some of those galleries he was keen on."

"Are you sure that's a good idea?"

I expect his protest. In fact I'd angled for it and as criticisms go it's very mild. Nevertheless I object to him thinking he can tell me what to do. "Mum was saying she fancied seeing a few. I thought she'd make a suitable chaperone."

"I walked into that, didn't I? I apologise for caring about what happens to you."

Again the phone starts ringing. Again I let it go on until the answer phone takes over. Again Terry's voice, angry and peevish, "Honey, pick up. I want to talk to you. I'm going to keep on ringing until you do."

Before I can stop him Matt reaches over and picks up the receiver. "Hello, Matt Alder speaking... Oh hi, Terry. Honey's in bed. I guess she's asleep... No, of course I'm not in her room. I'm downstairs. I suggest you leave it until the morning. She's exhausted. She can't cope with loud music. Perhaps you didn't know that or you'd have looked after her better."

He puts the phone back and grins at me. "He rang off pretty abruptly."

I'm glad I won't have to unplug the phone throughout the night, but irritated by his meddling. "I could have dealt with him. Will you kindly stop interfering with my life?"

"You have with mine," he says, quite reasonably.

"That's different."

"Funny that."

"I haven't been seeing vanishing women and knocking myself unconscious."

"No, you've been having panic attacks in concerts, got groped in a churchyard by a sex-deprived kid and scared yourself silly in your own backyard." He must see by my expression that he's gone too far. "I'm sorry if I interfered between you and the boyfriend, but is it such a crime to want to look after you?"

"I can do that myself." I have to cling to that thought. I can't afford to be dependent any more. "I don't need you to look after me."

Suddenly he's still. His face is shuttered and his voice expressionless, "I see." Without looking at me he reaches out to turn up the volume on the CD player. "I'll switch the lights out when I come upstairs."

As soon as I enter my room I have the feeling somebody's been in there. It's nothing I can explain. I can't even justify it to myself. I'm not the tidiest person in the world but I can't escape the feeling someone's moved my things around; a drawer that's pushed in crooked and that someone's searched through my jewellery box. I don't think there's anything missing but I can't be sure. I call myself a neurotic idiot. Allie probably came in to borrow something. She knows I'm cool with her going through my stuff.

I won't sleep. I know it even before I turn out the light. All the same I give it a try. I lie in the darkness, aching with weariness and tension. Had I imagined the attacker in the garden? The thought that I'd been snagged by a tree and had panicked makes me burn with shame but I can't think who would have tried to strangle me. The only answer seems to be Matt's ghost... or Graham, angry at my rejection and taking his revenge. He'd have had time to get a taxi. I wish I'd phoned his hotel straight after I got home, but I didn't think of it and it's too late now.

I've been in bed an hour and I haven't heard Matt come up yet. I put the light on, get out of bed and pull on leggings and sweatshirt. I need to know he's all right.

I creep downstairs. The patio doors are open and there's no sign of Matt.

Chapter 17

I feel a moment's total panic, mind blank, breath ragged, unable to cope. Then I regain control and tell myself not to be a fool. I pick up Mum's walking stick from where she'd left it leaning against the wall and, thus armed, go to investigate.

Matt's sitting on the patio wall, cigarette in one hand, whisky glass in the other.

"You frightened the life out of me, and you'll catch your death of cold," I say.

"It's as good a way to go as any. Sorry I scared you though."

"How about you hold off death long enough for me to say sorry for being a bitch?"

"You weren't. What you said was true."

"Yes I was. It doesn't matter whether it was true or not."

He shrugs. "I guess the question is, when does fair comment melt into bitchiness?"

"That doesn't matter when you hurt someone."

He stubs out his cigarette. "In that case let's go inside. I don't want you to end up wallowing in guilt that you pushed me over the edge into insanity."

"If we're talking about wallowing, you seem to be doing a fair bit of it yourself. And the only edge I'm likely to push you over is this wall." Despite my light tone I'm worried, this is so unlike Matt.

Back in the living room he goes over to the drinks cabinet to top up his glass. "I owe you a bottle of whisky, Honey."

"Oh God! Matt, how much have you drunk?"

"More than I should have. It's the only way I can wind down."

That's not good. "Didn't you say you're on sleeping pills?"

"Aye, but they don't do much on their own."

That moves the gauge along to very bad. "Please, don't drink any more tonight. It's dangerous when you've had a head injury."

"I might as well have a hangover, my head hurts anyway." Nevertheless, he puts the bottle and glass down.

"I'm going to get you a glass of water, you need to dilute the whisky."

"I see you haven't got over this passion for pouring cold water into me after a good night out," he remarks, when I return from the kitchen.

"You mean I've saved you from innumerable hangovers." I wait until he's drained the pint glass, then continue, "And I don't think either of us has had a good night."

"You're so bloody literal."

"It's a bit late to complain about it now." One of our earliest student squabbles was about whether I was more literal or literary and whether either was a good thing to be.

He's smiling at me, gentle and quizzical. Something in me snaps and all I've kept battened down wells up in a torrent of anger and regret. I run at him, fists pummelling his chest. "You bastard Matt! Why did you do this to us? Why did you screw up everything we had?"

He staggers slightly, then regains his balance. One hand closes over both of mine, stilling their violence. The other arm enfolds me, holding me close. "Honey, I'm sorry, so sorry, about everything."

My anger evaporates, engulfed by despair and loneliness. I sob, my face buried in his neck, regretting everything we've both done.

"Perhaps, if you'd done that seven years ago, it would have all been different." His voice is husky, as if he too is near to tears.

Suddenly I understand. Everyone talks of sexual infidelity as if it's the worst thing you can do in a relationship, but emotional infidelity can be just as cruel. I'd withdrawn into desolation and left Matt to cope alone. Oh God! I'd abandoned him long before he was unfaithful to me in any way. And I hadn't even realised it.

Someone once said that you can turn tragedy into comedy by sitting down. I can't remember who said it and it seems unlikely but I sit down anyway.

Matt follows my example. "I'm sorry about interfering, Honey. I honestly didn't mean to make trouble between you and the boyfriend."

"Will you stop calling him the boyfriend! I find it belittling."

"I'm sorry." Three apologies in one minute. He must be feeling fragile. "You must think I'm a dog in the manger, resenting you having a new relationship when I've totally screwed up ours."

I remember something Matt once said to me. At the time it was a foreign language but now I understand. "What I've got with Terry isn't a relationship, it's just sex."

He stares at me. "But that's what I..."

"The difference is, that I'm not married. And I didn't sleep with anyone until well after the Decree Absolute."

This is pure hypocrisy on my part. The stages of divorce had nothing to do with it. I merely didn't have the interest or energy until the last few months.

"What happens with me and Terry has nothing to do with my relationship with you. At the risk of sounding trite, we were always friends and I'd like it to stay that way."

"Of course we're bloody friends. Why the hell else would you be sorting me out when I knock myself silly? Why do you think I stuck my nose in between you and the boyfr... sorry you and Terry?"

"Natural interferingness," I say. "That's one of the things we always had in common." He scowls at me and I add hastily, "Anyway, I don't think Terry's going to be around much longer. I thought I could stick it out to the end of the week, when his friends finish their holiday, but now I'm not sure I can."

"Can't say I'm sorry. You and he never seemed to be soulmates. It wears off after a while doesn't it?"

"What does?"

"The sort of relationship that's based on sex. I'm pissed off with taking girls clubbing. It's so boring and it's bloody knackering."

"I suppose it must be."

"By that snotty look I gather you met Terry at some upmarket cultural event."

"Well let's say it was one which involved people getting together to talk."

"A cocktail party?"

I giggle. "Not exactly."

"So how did you meet him?"

"Speed-dating."

He sits up with an unwise jerk that makes him wince. "You went speed-dating?"

"Sort of. I went along with one of the other tutors at college. It was a charity event for people between fifty and sixty-five."

"What was it like?" Matt sounds bemused.

"It was fun. I wasn't nervous because I didn't expect anyone to ask me for a date, but it was interesting, listening to people talking about themselves. They upped the time to ten minutes each but that still wasn't enough."

"And Terry put you down for a date?"

I allow pride to creep into my voice, "Actually eight people did but I'd only put two down on my list. The others were sweet but much too elderly. I'm not quite ready for day time TV and furry slippers yet."

I see him flinch at the last thoughtless remark and say, "I'm sorry. Have you been seeing the woman in pink slippers any more?"

"I'm not sure. There's this sort of image at the corner of my eye. But I expect it's my imagination and I can't turn my head fast enough to be sure. Go on about the speed-dating. Why did you choose Terry over the other guy?"

"I didn't. I chose the other one. We were together for five weeks and then I found out he wasn't a widower, the way he'd claimed. His wife was very much alive and living in their marital home in Bognor Regis."

"Oh Honey Bear, you do pick them, don't you?" There's sympathy in his voice, as if he knows how much it had hurt when my first foray into the world had ended so farcically.

"It was okay. Terry was still interested. Whatever happens between us now, I have to be grateful for the way he helped me regain my confidence."

"Is he divorced too?"

"No. He says he never found the right woman for a long-term relationship... until now." I pull a rueful face.

"Awkward for you," says Matt.

We sit in silence until he says, "I tried speed dating once."

"Really?" I'd thought Matt just clicked his fingers and the girls fell in line.

"Claudia suggested it. She does it a lot."

My suspicions of Claudia rekindle but I ask, "Was it fun?"

His harsh crack of laughter holds no hint of mirth. "No way! All these women, at least fifteen years younger than me. And all of them with one thought in their heads, 'Just how rich are you?'"

"Surely not?"

"A lot of them even asked me outright. And one said she didn't want to waste her time with anyone who wasn't worth it. It was a fiasco."

I ache for him and take refuge in a piece of irrelevant information. "Did you know fiasco comes from an Italian word? It referred to glass-blowing. A fiasco was when a piece of glass was over blown and burst."

There's a moment's puzzled silence. "Thanks for that," says Matt.

"Be grateful. None of your speed-daters told you anything as ludicrous as that."

"I doubt if any of them could spell fiasco, let alone tell me its origin. There was nothing to talk about. I don't think any of them had ever been to a classical concert in their lives."

"I hate to break it to you, but most people go speed dating for sex not culture."

"Honey, if I got some tickets for next season's Proms, would you come with me? No strings attached. Just as a favour. It's bloody lonely going by myself."

"I'd like that." I'm not as crazy about classical music as Matt, but I enjoy it and the Proms are always fun.

"We could go to Stratford. Take in a few plays."

"I'll see if they're showing Much Ado About Nothing," I say.

"Beatrice and Benedick?" It's clear he's not sure whether my reference to Shakespeare's most passionate squabblers is a good sign or a bad.

"I was thinking of Balthasar's song."

During the years he was my property, I'd educated my Physics graduate well. To help me inspire my students when I'd started teaching English Literature, he'd set several of my favourite sixteenth and seventeenth century poems to music, preferably for a lute but okay for a guitar.

He understands what I mean and his face tightens with pain, but nevertheless, he sings softly,

"'Sigh no more, ladies, sigh no more.
Men were deceivers ever.
One foot on sea, one foot on shore,
To one thing faithful never.'

Oh Honey Bear, I wish I could say it wasn't true. It's no good saying I'm sorry, but I am."

I can't reassure him. There's nothing left to say.

Chapter 18 Monday

The ringing phone jerks me from deep sleep. Dazed, I focus on the clock: eight-fifteen. Rage floods through me. It had better not be Terry. Before nine on a Bank Holiday is pushing his luck too far. As I reach out to the phone, it stops ringing. My first thought is the caller has realised the time and given up, then I spot the engaged light, which means someone has answered it downstairs.

I pick up and hear my mother's placid voice, "If Honey hasn't answered I presume she's still asleep. Would you like me to ask her to call you later?"

Then Terry, "Can't you wake her? I want to speak to her."

I cut in. "You've already woken me. And kindly don't speak to my mother in that tone. Is what you've got to say a matter of life or death?"

"Well no, but..."

"In that case I'll phone you when I've showered and had my breakfast. And if you ring again before then there'll be trouble."

I slam the phone down, roll over and try, in vain, to regain sleep.

There's a knock on my door and Mum comes in carrying a tray of tea and toast. "Breakfast in bed," she says.

"You're spoiling me." I sit up and note with pleasure there are two cups beside the teapot. "You're going to stay and keep me company?"

"I will if you like, although I actually brought the other cup up for Matt." I misinterpret this and feel heat flood my face before she continues, "I peeped into his room and he's still fast asleep."

"He was up when I got in last night and we talked for quite a while. He's having problems with insomnia."

She settles on the edge of the bed and pours the tea. "I'm not surprised. It's the quiet, deep ones who take things hard. What's going on between you and Terry?"

"Whatever there was between us is grinding to a dismal halt."

She gives me a shrewd look and seems satisfied I'm not heart-broken.

"Do you fancy going to a few of the Open Studios today, Mum?"

"I'd love it, if you'd like to, but I'm sure that's not what Terry has in mind."

"I wasn't inviting Terry. Although I may ask Graham if that's okay with you."

"Of course, if you want to."

"He's having a hard time at the moment and he's pretty mixed up. We had a long talk yesterday evening and I made it clear I'm happy to be an adopted aunt to him."

"I'm willing to be an adopted grandmother then. You'd better phone him before Terry bulldozes him into whatever he's got planned."

I wait until I've finished my tea and toast, then I look up the hotel number and ring through. Graham's joyful acceptance rings down the line, "Thank you. They've been nagging me to go to the dockyard. I hate history. All over breakfast they were talking about these boring ships."

I'm fond of our naval heritage, especially the Victory, but I've heard the same complaints from Allie, who has no feeling for the past.

"Terry got there early, didn't he?" I ask.

"He booked a room and stayed here. Last night was awful. The car wasn't where Mum said she'd left it and they thought it was stolen and they called the police and then they found it parked in another car park not very far away. Mum's keys were missing and she blamed me and said I'd taken it to drive you home. She came to my room and made me come out and look for it. But when the police found it, Mum's keys were still in it and the policeman lectured Mum about being careless and she was furious. She said she never makes mistakes and someone had stolen her keys... either me or Deirdre."

"Deirdre! Is that based on the most unlikely person being guilty?"

"She disappeared off somewhere. Apparently, when the lights went up at the end of the concert she wasn't there. It could just as easily have been Terry, apparently he didn't stay for the end of the concert and wasn't around till later. But Mum wanted to blame Deirdre. She hates her because Jez married her."

"It sounds a mess." I'm thoroughly confused by all the people who weren't where they were supposed to be and suspicions prickle through my mind that it's connected with the attack on me.

"It was awful." He returns to his main concern, "Mum's going to be cross when I tell her I'm not going with them. She's furious with Dad. He said he was busy today and wasn't going with them."

I wonder what Edward has got planned and whether it involves my sister. Despite my preoccupation, I hear the nervousness in Graham's voice.

"I'll tell Terry and he can break the glad news," I say. "I've got to phone him anyway."

"He's cross about you leaving without seeing him last night."

I laugh. "That doesn't matter. Graham, do you know whose car they're taking?"

"Terry's. He's got a Social Services' sticker, so it's less likely to get clamped."

"In that case, get hold of your dad in private and ask if he can give you a lift over to my house. If he can't, it doesn't matter, just phone and we'll come and get you."

Reluctantly I move on to my next call. As soon as I hear Terry's voice the term 'high dudgeon' flies into my mind. I know in its other meaning, a dudgeon is the hilt of a dagger, but I've never found out where it comes from when it means a sulky strop. I'm preoccupied with considering dudgeons and miss the first few sentences of Terry's diatribe, but I assume it's in the same vein as the bit I listen to.

I break in to say, "I'm busy today. I'm taking Mum to some of the Open Studios."

"Oh Honey, really! I expected you to come to the dockyard with us."

"Sorry, no can do. Mum wants to see some of the artwork before she goes home. And I've invited Graham to come with us."

"You're welcome to him, the sulky little git, but you could have made an effort to come out with us today. I took the weekend off to spend with you and I've hardly seen you. I expect, if your ex demands your presence, you'll give up on the concert this evening as well. It was a waste of my money getting you a season ticket, you've hardly been to any of the concerts."

I'd been under the impression the season ticket for the Folk Festival was a present for the birthday I'd celebrated a few weeks ago.

"I'll see you later, Terry." As soon as I put the phone down I get out my chequebook. This is one debt I can pay off without delay.

The art tour gets off to a shaky start when Allie hears our plans. "Can I come with you Mum?"

I don't think that's an amazingly good idea. It's one thing putting myself on the line to help Graham. Now I know the score, I'm sure I can keep the situation under control. It's quite another matter to expose my daughter to any type of risk.

"Since when have you been interested in art?"

"Since it's that or stay here and work on my essay. Oh go on, Mum. Ross is out all day and even Dad's going over to his house."

"The least said about that the better." I glance towards the living room, where I've installed Matt with his breakfast. I'm not convinced he's well enough to spend the day at his place sorting out business, but at least I've persuaded him to let one of us drive him and he has agreed to come back here tonight.

"Why don't you want me to come with you and Nanna?" asks Allie.

"Graham's going through a difficult stage at the moment and he's very insecure."

"I promise to be good. Please Mummy, let me come." She knows I've never been able to resist that soft teasing blandishment.

"As long as you behave. Don't give Graham any reason to think you're flirting with him but, at the same time, don't be unkind. The poor boy's very sensitive."

"I know. I told Ross off for laughing at him the other day. You'd think, being a teacher, Ross would understand how hard it is for people like Graham."

"I'm not sure Ross would care about how people like Graham feel." As a personal tutor I often have to deal with students who take Drama as well as English and I've heard that Ross teaches by humiliation, although this technique is reserved for the less cool boys and unattractive girls.

To my surprise Allie agrees, "I know. He can be vile to guys if he doesn't like them. Oliver used to hate his guts."

"But Oliver didn't take drama?"

"No, but Ross would come and sit with us sometimes in the cafeteria."

"Do you ever see Oliver nowadays?" Oliver Prestwick and his sister Kayla had been Allie's best friends throughout school and college. Kayla still comes round quite often but Allie and Oliver have drifted apart.

"He offered to take me to the pictures next week." Allie's tone is non-committal.

"Are you going?"

"I'd like to but Kayla's working and Ross says he's not going to baby-sit so I can go out with another guy."

"What's wrong with me as a babysitter?"

"Nothing. But you're so busy."

"I'm happy to babysit so you can keep up with your friends. As long as you don't mind Ross being pissed off with you."

"Oliver's one of my best friends. I don't want to lose him." She breaks off to exclaim, "Ben, what have you done with your nappy?"

With a triumphant crow of laughter, Ben toddles bare-arsed towards the living room. By the time we gather up a clean nappy and pursue him he's coaxed himself onto Matt's lap and is sharing his buttered toast.

"You can't trust him. He'll probably wee all over you," warns Allie.

"I don't mind. I like spending time with him. He's growing up so fast."

"I've told your dad I want him to have more contact on birthdays and Christmas and other times like that." I give Allie a no-nonsense look.

She smiles. "That's great." She captures Ben and fastens his new nappy in place, but then she returns him to Matt's lap.

"I'll drive you over to your house if you like, Dad." She grins at me. "As long as Mum promises not to go off to look at art without me."

Matt picks up the implications of this far faster than I like. "You mean you're going on this art business as well?" And then to me, "Are you sure that's a good idea?"

"Don't you start!" exclaims Allie. "I've already been through this with Mum. You don't have to worry. I can do the big sister thing, you know."

There's a brief, tense silence. I see Matt wince at the term 'big sister'. Before I can react, Allie swoops on him and hugs him fiercely. "It's no good brooding, Dad. Ouch!" She moves back hastily as Ben, objecting to being squashed, bites her.

"I'll go and change. Ready in five minutes, Dad."

"What do you make of that?" asks Matt as she departs.

"I think one of you is growing up. Have you got anything to eat at your place?"

"I've got a freezer and a microwave."

"Not good enough." I fill a small flask with hot soup, as well as the giant flask I'm preparing for our lunch, and wrap two buttered rolls. As I load the carrier bag, I say, "I've put in milk for your tea or coffee and painkillers in case your head gets worse and chocolate cake in case you need an energy burst."

"I'm going back to my living place, not camping out in the wilderness."

I ignore his protest. "Don't try to do any housework. I've already cleaned up the blood in your bedroom. I'll leave my mobile on. Phone me if you need me. Don't hesitate. I'll come over straight away."

He reaches across and touches my cheek. "Aye Mum." He uses the words he'd said two days ago, but this time neither of us flinches.

I go up to my room to pick up the large bag I carry on expeditions such as this. As I swing it onto my shoulder I think it feels heavier than usual; a bit of a pain to carry round all day. I empty it onto the bed and work out what I can jettison. Allie will be taking Ben's changing bag so I don't need all the items connected with his care. Nor do I need the photograph album I'd borrowed from Matt's house. In fact I need to return it to him. I don't know what got into me to take it in the first place. But I won't give it to him now, when he's about to go back to his house. I don't want to start him brooding again.

Before I return the album, I want another look at the photograph I'm sure is Matt's grandmother. Absurd to think of it as a clue and yet I'm sure it's significant. I go through quickly and don't find it, so I lay the album on the bed and go through again more thoroughly. On this second try, I find the page, towards the front of the book, where I thought it was. The four, old-fashioned photo corners are still in place but the photograph has gone.

Chapter 19

Graham fits into our family expedition better than I expected. This is mainly due to my mum. Her grandmotherly kindness cushions his insecurity and her leisurely manner allows him time to think before he speaks. Allie is good as well, cheerful and friendly, and not challenging in any way. It helps that, although he shares the back seat of my car with Allie, they are separated by Ben's baby seat. Ben's in a sociable mood and sets out to woo this potential new admirer by handing Graham all his toys for inspection and comment. Graham responds diffidently, but it's clear he's pleased.

With Allie's help I've planned a route that takes in five promising art venues. The first stop is our local community centre, a reconstituted village school. Lots of amateur local artists are exhibiting in its rooms. We're there for quite a while. We're not delayed by admiration of the art; quantity rather than quality seems to be the order of the day. We're held up by the number of people that greet me and want to chat. The Old Guard of the village has turned out in force.

At last I manage to extricate myself and dart from room to room, attempting to locate my companions, who've abandoned me. A voice says, "Hello, Honey. Nice to see you. I saw Allie and Ben a few minutes ago, they're looking very well."

"Hi Tom." I smile at my doctor and we chat for a few minutes about our respective families. Towards the end of our conversation he says, "Matt's firm did the DVDs for my grandson's playschool a month or so ago. He still gives a good rate to anyone in the village. Do you see anything of him nowadays?"

"Quite a bit this weekend. He had a fall and knocked himself out, so he's been staying with us while he gets over it. I think his nerves have been bad lately." I know Tom's not Matt's doctor any more but perhaps he can give me some general guidance towards helping him.

"That doesn't surprise me. He's the sort of chap who represses things."

"I don't think he's sleeping. Could that contribute to him imagining things?"

"Quite possibly. He had a lot of sleep problems for the last few months of Simon's life." His swift look checks how I'm taking this.

"I don't remember much about that time. I was at the hospital so much. Matt's on sleeping pills. Has he had them all this time?"

Tom looks grim. "I might have known. I suspected he switched doctor because I was against him carrying on with medication that wasn't doing him any good." He scowls at me. "What do you think you're up to, Honey Alder? Leading me on to talk about an ex-patient. Do you want to get me struck off?"

From what I've read about the British Medical Association that seems unlikely. After all they didn't even remove a medical mass murderer like Harold Shipman.

"I won't snitch. I still need you. You're the only GP who'd put up with me."

I see Allie waving at me across the room and beat a hasty retreat before he can suggest it's time for some blood tests or other unpleasant medical revenge.

We move on through the other venues. The standard of art is mixed and none of it is good enough to fully distract my mind from thoughts about last night.

Had I imagined the attack upon me? Common sense says yes, but all my instincts say no. If so, was it connected with the missing photograph? If someone had crept up behind me to half-throttle me with my scarf, who could it have been? Not Matt. He'd come out through the terrace windows and wouldn't have had time to run in at the front door and through the house. And Matt wouldn't hurt me, I'm sure of that.

Assuming it was in some way personal, that left Terry and his friends. According to Graham's rambling account, Terry and Deirdre were unaccounted for. Terry was the more likely culprit, after all, I'd seriously pissed him off. To the best of my knowledge, I'd never done any harm to Deirdre. Or maybe it was Graham all along. It's possible he is more disturbed than I'd thought. He'd know what time I was heading back. Was he subtle enough to double bluff like that? Anyway, Graham wasn't the only one to know I was on my way home. I'd texted Jackie and told her and she could have mentioned it to anyone. Terry, Graham, Deirdre, any of them could have pinched Nicola's car and driven it to my house, but in that case Graham was the least likely because, when we parted, he'd have had no opportunity to steal his mother's keys.

Terry has to be my prime suspect. But where does the vanishing photograph come in? Unless Matt had found out I'd taken the album and removed the picture. But why should he? He could have reclaimed the whole album, it was his property, and he could have destroyed the photo at any time he chose.

At this point I see my mother's eyes on me and know she's spotted my preoccupation. I smile brightly and turn my mind back to art.

At lunchtime we spend a delightful hour eating our picnic in the park. I get a ball out of the car and we play with it while Nanna guards the picnic basket. Then Allie and Graham take Ben to the playground. I watch Graham waving to Allie and Ben as they go down the slide and think it's the first time I've seen him look happy. I scrutinise anxiously for any signs of infatuation.

"Don't worry," says Mum. "Allie's out of his league and he's well aware of it."

"And I'm not? Thanks a lot."

Her answering smile is loving but her words puzzle me, "If you light up the way you did yesterday afternoon, you can't blame a naive young man for misinterpreting."

Before I can demand an explanation my mobile rings. I grab it out of my bag and check the display. It's Terry not Matt. "Hello Honey, how's it going?"

"Fine. Are you having fun?"

"Yes, of course. I thought I'd come over and meet you. Where are you?"

I give the location of the park and promise to stay near the gallery until he arrives. I wonder what's going on. It's only two-thirty, so either Terry's abandoned his friends or they must have done the dockyard in record time.

Ben forcefully rejects the idea of leaving the park for the gallery and so we divide into two pairs. First of all my mum and Graham go inside, then Allie and me. I take more than my fair share of time, but I have good reason. It's there I fall in love.

The wall-hanging triptych depicts Summer Sunrise, Rainbow at Midday and Sunset after Rain. Its singing jewel colours entice me and I want to look at it forever. At last, reluctantly, I turn away. Three thousand pounds is not a lot for such a beautiful work but, with all the demands on me, it's more than I can casually spend.

"Do you really like that, Mum?" asks Allie, appearing beside me.

"I adore it. I think that artist is going to be a major player in the next few years. Unfortunately, I haven't got that sort of money to spare."

"And if you did, you'd spend it on me and Ben."

It's not a wrench to turn my gaze from the triptych when I can look at my lovely girl. "You matter more than all the artwork in the world. If I never saw another picture, heard another concert or read another book, it would be less of a loss than wasting a moment I could spend with you and Ben."

She hugs me. "I do love you, Mum."

I go round the rest of the exhibition then return for a last covetous look at my favourite. A small red sticker proclaims it has been sold. I feel sad but, at the same time, relieved I don't have to struggle between my conscience and my desire.

"Are you ready to go home, Honey?" Terry comes up behind me and puts his arms around me.

"Yes. I was just having a final covet." I nod towards the picture.

His glance skims over it then he peers over my shoulder at the catalogue. "These artists know how to charge all right. It can't have taken more than a few days."

I'm tempted to quote Whistler's response to a similar complaint. It's the lifetime of knowledge one pays for, not to mention the genius involved, but I just say, "It's sold, so someone thinks it's worth it."

He shrugs. "Some people have more money than sense."

So that's it. The end comes so naturally that I don't see it until it's there.

I'd always known Terry was careful with money, what I hadn't processed was that he's also stingy with his emotions. He doesn't give anything unconditionally.

I sort through my handbag and find the cheque. Silently I hand it to him.

"What's this for?"

"It's for my festival ticket. This way it's my money that's wasted not yours."

He flushes and thrusts it back towards me. "I didn't mean that."

"No, please take it, Terry. I'd feel better if you did. I'm sorry but it's not going to work." I hadn't planned to end it like this but the time feels right.

"Not work? What do you mean?"

"Our relationship. It was good fun for a while but I guess we're both too old and set in our ways to make allowances for each other."

The skin around his tight-set mouth goes white and I realise his temper's only just under control. "It's your bloody ex-husband! He comes wheedling round with all his money and suddenly I'm not good enough for you."

At this moment it's easy to believe Terry had crept up behind me and twisted my scarf around my throat. I make a conscious effort not to back away. "That's not true."

"Of course it's true. I'm just a poor bloody social worker not a top businessman. A man with money, that's all you women want."

I can't let him get away with this. "When I married Matt we had less than a hundred pounds between us and lived in a rented bedsit."

The ice in my voice seems to cool him down. "I'm sorry but I hate it when your ex thinks he can toss you down and pick you up as if you're a toy."

"This is nothing to do with Matt." That's not entirely true. Matt and I may have no future, but this weekend has made me remember how good real love can be.

Terry's face clears. "In that case we can sort things out. You're just tired and stressed. Please Honey, give it a few more days. I'm sure we can get things together."

"You mean until your friends leave?"

"I don't want to spoil their visit."

From all I've seen of Nicola and Jez, it would make their trip perfect to have someone to gloat over, which is why I say, "Okay. I'll play along until they go."

As we turn to leave, I see Deirdre approaching us. "Is everyone here?" I ask Terry.

"No, just Deirdre and me. Nicola's tired so Jez took her back to the hotel."

"That was noble of him."

Terry ignores my sarcasm but Deirdre raises her eyes and fleetingly her gaze meets mine. The malicious amusement in her expression is unmistakable. She looks down again, her face as vapid as her comment, "That's pretty," as she looks at the glorious triptych.

With the arrival of Terry the zest seems to have gone out of the day and we head back to the car park. Graham sidles next to me. "Please, can I go back with you?"

"Why do you want to, Graham?"

"I don't want to go back to the hotel and them."

I feel sorry for him. "Of course you can come home with us."

Inevitably, when he hears this, Terry insists on coming back with us, but Deirdre says she'll call a taxi to take her back to the hotel.

Fortunately Terry's not a skilled lanes driver. I put my foot down and leave him well behind.

I pull up on my drive and say, "Move along quickly please." As soon as all my passengers are clear, I start off again before Terry arrives and decides to come with me to pick up Matt.

I have the key and security code with me but it seems more respectful to ring the doorbell now Matt's on his feet. I ring twice, and the second time I keep my finger on the bell for quite some time. The chime is pealing but Matt doesn't come.

I use my key and this time remember to type in the security code. Then, calling his name, I search for Matt. He's not downstairs, although a whisky bottle and glass on the side table by his chair reveal how he has spent his afternoon. With a horrible feeling of having been here and done this, I go upstairs.

Again he's in his bedroom. Again on the floor. But this time he isn't unconscious and there's no visible sign of any wound. He's kneeling beside his bed, breathing fast, the duvet clutched convulsively in his clenched fists.

"Matt! What's wrong?" I kneel beside him.

No answer.

I touch his cheek and turn his head, forcing him to face me. "What's wrong?"

At first nothing, then he registers me. "Honey. Make her go away."

"Who go away?" There is no-one and nothing untoward in the room.

"The dead woman... on the bed."

Chapter 20

I feel fear trickling up and down my spine. "Matt, there's no-one there."

He stares at me, then wrenches his gaze away and turns it towards the bed.

"Matt, can you still see her?" I slip my hand into my pocket and clutch my mobile phone, ready to dial 999.

"No. There's no-one there. I could have sworn..." His voice trails away.

"Let's go downstairs." I take his arm and urge him to stand.

Safely down and in the living room, I say, "Tell me what happened."

He takes a few moments to sort his thoughts but when he replies he's lucid and controlled. "I was sitting in here reading some papers. I was feeling tired and I was glad you'd phoned to say you were on your way. Then I heard someone calling me... a woman's voice... it came from upstairs. I went up to find out what the hell was going on."

"You shouldn't have gone up there. Not after last time."

"I guess you're right but the funny thing is, this time, I was more angry than scared."

"What was she calling?"

"At first just my name. 'Matthew, Matthew', over and over, very insistently. Then, as I got nearer, it changed and she was saying, 'You let me die. Why didn't you call for help?' I went into the bedroom and she was lying there, on my bed. Fully dressed, still wearing those pink slippers. But I knew she was dead."

I hug him tighter. "What happened then?"

"I don't know." His voice crumbles and he struggles for control. "The next thing I remember was kneeling on the floor and you came and found me. I guess this definitely proves I'm going mad."

"Stay here a minute." There's something I half saw and didn't properly process niggling at my mind.

I go back up to Matt's bedroom. I think there's a hint of flowery perfume in the air. I'm certain there's a faint indenting on the pillow, like someone has lay their head there, and one grey hair on the pillowcase. Glad I'm still holding my handbag, I use my tweezers to pick it up and place it in a spare envelope. I haven't the foggiest idea how I'm going to use it to solve what's going on, but it's the sort of thing they do in CSI.

Downstairs I discover Matt in the act of topping up his whisky glass. I cross the room at speed and wrench it out of his hand. "You've had enough."

"I'm not drunk!"

"You shouldn't drink at all with a head injury. I'm sorry, Matt. I worry about you."

To my surprise he bursts out laughing. "Honey, you've been using that line to get your own way with me for the past forty years."

That's sad but true. Not only have I been using the line but I've been worrying about him all that time.

I sit down beside him. "Matt, if this woman is a creation of your imagination, who do you think she is? Is she someone from your past?"

"I don't know! She seems familiar and yet unfamiliar." He grapples in the maze of words and says impatiently, "I swear I can't remember meeting her in the last few years. I spent some time today trying to sort out whether she was an actress from one of the video sequences we've set up but it doesn't tie in with anything we've done."

"I wonder why you thought that?"

"What do you mean?"

"There must be some reason you thought she was an actress. Perhaps it all felt unreal." I'd had the same feeling when Deirdre suddenly seemed different in the park this afternoon.

"You're bloody right it felt unreal. But it still doesn't make any form of sense. As far as I know, I've never screwed up any actresses although, before you say it, I may have screwed a few."

I won't let him see how much those mocking words hurt me. "I'm sure if you had screwed them there'd have been no complaints."

"I'm sorry, Honey, that was a lousy thing to say."

"Then why say it?"

He shrugs. "I suppose I was letting you know I despise myself just as much as you despise me."

"I don't despise you. Come on. Let's go home for tea."

Obediently he hauls himself upright, staggers and sits down again as his balance fails. I say, "Please promise me you won't drink any more, at least for a few days."

He shuts his eyes. Then he opens them and smiles at me. "I promise."

By the time we get in Mum and Allie have made the tea. The table is laid for six. "Who's not eating?" I ask.

"I'm not," says Allie. "At least I am, but at a safe distance over there with Ben. I'm not trusting him anywhere near your new tea service. In fact I don't trust me near it."

"So how do you think I feel?" It's well established that I'm the clumsy one.

I think how beautiful the tea service looks. It's Art Deco, white china with scenes in black and yellow and it's called Sunset. "It's gorgeous, Matt. Thank you." I explain to the visitors, "Matt got it for my birthday. He saw it in an auction and knew I'd love it."

Terry scowls and I realise I've been tactless. Now I've paid him for my Festival ticket, Terry hasn't given me a birthday gift.

We eat in uncomfortable silence until Matt says, "How were the art studios, Honey? Did you see anything nice?"

I turn to him, grateful for the diversion, although a slight prickling at the back of my neck warns me the question is not as innocent as it seems. I've known Matt for too long not to register the soft sparkle of malice in his tone.

"Most of the stuff was pretty amateurish but there were a few nice landscapes, and a beautiful triptych at the Gallery in the park."

"Would you have liked to own it?"

Again my warning radar tingles. "I'd have loved to but it was a bit above my price-range. Anyway, before we left the gallery, it was sold."

Matt pulls a sheet of paper from his pocket and passes it to me. "I got them to email a confirmation of sale. You can pick it up as soon as the Open Studio event finishes."

"But how...?" I stare at the paper.

"I asked Allie to let me know if there was anything you really liked and she phoned through and said you'd fallen for this big time."

"Thank you," I say, aware of Terry's fury and Matt's amusement at his anger.

"I suppose, if you're filthy rich, you can afford to throw three thousand quid away." Terry's jealousy boils into words.

"That's right," agrees Matt, "but most of the things Honey chooses go up in value. She's got a good eye for a winner... in art I mean."

I wish I could feel angry. I know I should. Matt has no right to use me to score points. But I just feel bruised inside.

As soon as tea is finished, I say, "Excuse me," and leave the room.

I'm halfway up the stairs when Terry catches up with me. "Honey, wait."

Reluctantly, I pause and turn to face him. "I'm sorry if I upset you, Honey. Your ex provoked me. Cocky bastard, flaunting his money like it can buy you back."

I say nothing and he continues, "Please forgive me. Don't let my stupid jealousy destroy our chance of sorting things out."

"Terry, I said I wouldn't publicly split up with you until your friends go back to London. But, as far as I'm concerned, things are already sorted."

He strokes my cheek. "I'm sure I can make you change your mind."

I move away from his touch. "The thing is Terry, I don't want to be made to do anything. Not by you or Matt." I run upstairs to my bedroom and slam the door.

I want to cry but the tears are clogged by something hard inside me. The words of Terry's accusation irritate like gravel in my mind. It's true it's easy for a rich man like Matt to make expensive gestures, but it wasn't always like that. I look at the Clarice Cliff vase on my dressing table. I'd spotted it in a second-hand shop just after we were married, and Matt had bought it for me. It was before Clarice Cliff came back into fashion and it hadn't been expensive, but it still took more money than we had, and meant Matt had to walk to work for weeks.

A knock on the door is followed by Allie's voice saying, "Mum."

"Come in, love."

She looks anxious. "What's wrong, Mum?"

"Men," I say.

"Nothing new then? I could see you were upset. I'm sorry if you didn't want me to tell Dad about you liking the picture. He said he wanted to thank you for looking after him. I didn't know he'd use it to make trouble between you and Terry."

"As far as I'm concerned, Terry can go to hell and fry there."

"What's the problem then?"

"It's about me not being walked over by any bloody man ever again."

"Right." Allie still looks bewildered but not as worried. "Ross is back and he can put Ben to bed. So I'll take Nanna home to save you going out."

"What you mean is you don't want to be left here with all the aggro."

"Well it is your aggro, isn't it? Graham's off in a few minutes. His dad phoned to say he'd pick him up because he wants to talk to him. It sounded very mysterious."

"I'll be down in a few minutes, love." I hug her. "Thanks for cheering me up."

I cleanse off my make-up and wash my face. I feel better for Allie's visit. Whatever else has self-destructed in my life, my girl and I are growing close again.

There's another knock on the door. "Who is it?" If it's Terry I'm going to shove a chair under the handle and tell him I'm too tired to talk to him.

"It's me."

It's strange I can't adopt the exclusion policy when it comes to Matt. "Come in."

Chapter 21

Matt enters. He looks pale and grim-faced. "You left this on the table."

I make no move to accept the sale confirmation paper he holds out. "I'm not sure I want it."

"Why not?" He asks the question gently, with no form of challenge in his voice.

"Because every time I looked at it I'd remember you bought it to spite Terry. That's spoiled it for me."

"Oh God!" He sways and sits down abruptly on the bed. "That's not why I bought it Honey. Please, you've got to believe me."

"You didn't need to buy me a present to thank me for looking after you. I'd have done that for any friend." I'm still hurting and I don't want to let him off the hook.

"I am grateful, but it wasn't because of that."

"Why then?"

He takes a deep breath and lets it out very slowly, then speaks with caution, as if he's inspecting every word before he offers it to me. "I love the way you look when you see something beautiful. The way your eyes light up and there's this tiny smile at the corners of your mouth. I wanted to give you something special because I wanted to make you happy and to see that expression again." He stops but I don't say anything, so he continues, "Then I lost my temper. I wanted to rub his bloody nose in it. He doesn't deserve you. And all that happened was that I insulted you and made you unhappy."

I hear sounds of departure. Looking out of the window I see Graham climbing into his father's car. That's one self-inflicted responsibility out of the way.

I look at my watch. It's only five o'clock. "How do you feel?" I say to Matt.

"Like a total loser."

"Good, you deserve to. But do you feel fit enough for another short drive?"

"Aye. Are you taking me back to my place?"

He looks miserable but I let him stew. He needs to fully realise that being a bastard can have lousy consequences. I slip along the corridor to Mum's room, where she's packing her things ready to go home. "I'm going out for a little while, Mum. Thanks for supporting me through this peculiar weekend."

"You're welcome. Thank you for having me." She gives me a shrewd look and seems satisfied. "Drive carefully." In our family this is shorthand for 'I love you more than anything in the world and couldn't bear it if bad things happened to you.'

I hug her. "Tell Allie I'm fine. Love you, Mum. I'll ring you tomorrow."

"Say goodbye to Matt for me. Are you really angry with him?"

"Furious." But my smile belies my words.

I feel no desire to smile as I go downstairs to find Terry, who's lurking in the hall, presumably waiting for me to reappear. "It's time you went," I say. "I'm going out."

"But, Honey, I..."

"Goodbye, Terry." I open the front door and see him out.

As soon as I'm sure he's gone, I go back to Matt. "Come on."

He follows me downstairs. Luckily no-one spots us as we head out of the front door. When we've been driving for five minutes, he says, "Unless this is the incredibly scenic route you're not taking me home. Where are we going?"

"Wait and see."

"I've got the feeling you're going to drive me into the depths of the countryside and abandon me to walk home, like the time I was an idiot before Sarah's wedding. I give you fair warning I'm going to refuse to get out of the car. And don't smile like that. It scares me when you get that Mona Lisa look."

I admit he's got some reason to be scared. The occasion he's referring to was twenty-six years ago. I had to collect Matt from Portsmouth Station when he'd caught the last train home after his soon-to-be-brother-in-law's stag night. He was drunk, obnoxious and lairy and demanded I stopped every half-mile for him to piss or puke. I got fed up with his aggro and drove off, leaving him to walk the last six miles home. An hour later I repented and drove back to look for him. I found him trudging down our lane, clutching a bunch of bedraggled wild flowers culled from the verges as a peace offering.

"Here we are." I pull up in the almost empty car park.

"Are we?" says Matt. "Why?"

I wait until he gets out of the car to join me, then take his hand to lead him along the path. "The gallery's open until six and I wanted you to see the pictures you'd bought me and give them to me properly, in private."

His pace slackens and he pulls his hand free. Surprised, I turn to stare at him, and see he's tugged off his glasses and is wiping his sleeve impatiently across his eyes.

"I'm sorry. I forgot you're still not well. Let's leave this until you feel okay."

"No way." He puts his glasses on again. "I want to see it now."

It's near closing time and the curator doesn't look delighted to see us enter. I smile at him and say, "We won't be long."

I lead Matt to stand in front of the triptych. "Isn't it beautiful?"

"Beautiful," he agrees. The raptness of his voice surprises me. I turn to look at him and realise he's staring not at the artwork but at me.

Embarrassed and totally out of my depth, I head towards the door. "We ought to go. The man wants to lock up."

"Aye." He smiles at the curator. "Thanks for giving us time to look at it." As he follows me out of the studio he says, "Is the woodland walk still open?"

"Yes but it's muddy going. We did it a few days ago." Going through the woods puts an extra mile on the walk to the car park but Allie, Ben and I love it.

"Shall we go that way?"

"If you feel up to it." Last week the first bluebells had been tentatively in flower, by now, with luck, they could be spectacular.

We go up the pathway that leads into the woods. We're the only people walking there and it's quiet and shaded, filled with the deep-as-time secrets that pervade ancient woodland. The bluebells don't quite form a carpet, the way they did when I was a child, but they put up a brave show. Matt and I don't speak. I'm soothed by the encompassing beauty and the memories of happiness long past and I know he is too.

We're on the last lap, three minutes from the car park when I see the couple lying in a clearing, making love. That annoys me. I'm not a prude, at least I don't think I am, but this is a path used by families with kids, and they're not deep enough in the bushes to be discreet. Not to mention the damage they're doing to the spring flowers. They're old enough to know better, not desperate teenagers. The woman is on top; she's toned and supple but definitely not a kid.

Matt's hand on my arm urges me on. I guess he's picked up on my outrage and wants to avert a scene. Not that I planned to make one. It's not my battle and I've plenty of my own.

The woman pushes upwards on braced arms and laughs down at her lover. I gasp, then try to stifle the sound. Fortunately they're too engrossed in each other to hear me. I make sure Matt's between me and them and, behind his shelter, I peer cautiously at them to confirm what I'd just seen. There's no doubt about it. The woman is Deirdre, but the undeniably fit guy that's under her is definitely not Jez.

Chapter 22

As Matt and I drive back, I worry at the peculiar thing I've just found out. Not that it's that strange that Deirdre has a lover. Good luck to her. Proverbs about sauce and geese flutter through my mind. What's really weird is the difference between the woman I've just seen and the Deirdre I was introduced to at the Folk Festival. Surely no woman would deliberately act as drab and droopy as she pretends to be? Although Jez would have a depressing effect on anyone. I push the thoughts of Deirdre away. It's none of my business and I can't see a connection with what's going on with Matt.

When we get home the house is blessedly peaceful, just Allie, Ross and Ben up in her room. There's a message on the answer phone. "Honey, it's Terry. We're having dinner at the hotel at eight. Please join us."

"Are you going?" asks Matt.

"I don't think so." I'm sick of their sordid little games.

I make coffee and turn on the fire because Matt is shivering. As we sit in the living room, I think there's so much between us there's no room for words. The past cannot be altered or ignored and we're different people to the ones we were before. Matt's vulnerable and self-destructive, more needy than I've ever known him. And I'm both harder and more brittle, more capable of inflicting injury and of being destroyed.

The peace is shattered by the sound of angry voices and clattering footsteps.

Ross yells, "Okay, I'm going!"

"Go then, you lying, cheating bastard."

The front door slams. I hear Ben's wail and Allie's voice, "It's okay, sweetheart, Mummy's here."

Matt looks at me enquiringly. "You going up to see if she's okay?"

"Not at the moment. If she wants me she'll soon tell me." If I go to Allie now, I'll try to make her quarrel with Ross permanent, and it's not my place to do that.

I've decided I'll text Terry and refuse his invitation.

The phone rings. I pick up and a desperate, high-pitched voice says, "Honey, please, you've got to come tonight."

"Graham? Whatever's wrong?"

"This dinner tonight, please come."

"But why?"

"It's going to be terrible!"

That's a great inducement. "Graham, is your dad there?"

"He's at the bar. I'm in the Gents."

Too much information. "Could you go out and give him the phone? I'd like to talk to him."

There's a minute of muffled sound and then Edward says, "Hello?"

"Edward, it's Honey. Graham phoned me. He seems incredibly upset."

"I'm sorry, Honey. I didn't mean him to bother you and I didn't mean to upset him. I seem to have played this wrong." I can hear tension twanging in Edward's voice and I'm sure he's almost as uptight as his son.

"Played what wrong?"

"I spent today flat hunting."

"On a Bank Holiday?"

"It's not a problem with the Internet. I've fixed up a place to rent and I can move in next weekend. When I told Graham, he turned white and bolted into the Gents."

"He probably felt sick." I launch into interfering mode. "I know he's a grown man but he's very insecure. You can't just walk out and leave him with Nicola."

"I know that! What do you take me for? That's why I wanted to see Graham to tell him first. It's a two-bedroomed flat and he's welcome to stay with me."

"I'm sorry. I misunderstood."

"I haven't been much of a parent but I wouldn't walk out on him. Honey, I'm trying to do this properly. I didn't mean to tell anyone but Graham until I've spoken to Nicola, but Graham scuppered that."

"You haven't even told Jackie?"

"No, not yet. I thought I'd tell Nicola after dinner tonight. Then I'll clear out and Graham can come with me if he wants. Terry, Jez and Deirdre can console Nicola. Leaving Nicola is nothing to do with Jackie. Well nothing to do with whether she's interested in me. I'm leaving Nicola anyway. I should have done it long ago."

"I see. Has Graham decided whether he wants to go with you?"

"I'm not sure. The whole thing seemed to overwhelm him."

"Where are you now?"

"Some pub in a place called Havant."

I sigh. "You'd better come back to my house to talk things through."

"Okay. Thank you. We'll be there in half an hour."

I key off and Matt grins at me. "Life with you is turning into more of a soap every time I tune in. Are you going to tell Edward about his son's goings on?"

"That is a very good question and I've got all of half an hour to decide."

In the end it's not my decision because Graham wants to tell it as it is. Matt goes tactfully upstairs and the three of us sit in my fire-lit living room. Graham stumbles through his story, me helping out whenever he gets tied up. Not surprisingly, Edward is appalled at Graham's shamefaced description of what happened in the churchyard.

I intervene. "Let's not make a melodrama out of this. The important thing is to get Graham sorted out." I take a deep breath and plunge into a diagnosis that I'm not qualified to make. "Have you heard of High Functioning Autism, sometimes known as Asperger's Syndrome?"

To my surprise Graham says, "Yes, one of my teachers wanted Mum to send me for assessment but Mum said there was no need. She said it would be too embarrassing for her to have a son who had Special Needs."

Edward looks stunned. "I didn't know. No-one told me." He turns to me, "I've heard about autism, of course, but I don't know much about it."

"People with Higher Functioning Autism are often very clever but they don't do well in social situations and they don't read social signals very well, so they don't always know how people think." I smile at Graham. "Often things don't make a lot of sense." To my relief he smiles back at me.

"But is there any treatment?" asks Edward.

What he wants to know is if there's any cure and the honest answer is 'no'. "There are strategies to teach people how to cope. If I'm right, and I'm not an expert, Graham has been managing well by himself, so with some professional help he'll be able to make a real success of things."

The words 'professional help' obviously set alarm bells ringing in Edward's head. "Are you sure that's a good idea? I mean it's not as if he's disabled or anything."

I think it's exactly as if he's disabled but I've known many parents who find it hard to face such facts.

"If Honey thinks I should see someone that's what I want to do," says Graham. "You don't know what it feels like, always being different, never understanding what's going on."

I see Edward flinch but before he can answer there's a knock on the door and Allie enters. "Sorry to interrupt but could I grab Ben's train boxes? His granddad's going to set it up in the kitchen for him."

She picks up one of the large yellow plastic boxes of Thomas the Tank Engine train set. "I'll be back in a minute for the other one."

"I'll bring it." Graham jumps to his feet.

"Why don't you help set it up?" suggests Edward. "Ben's granddad oughtn't to be doing too much until he's better."

"I'd like that," says Graham. "I always loved Thomas."

I'd be worried about his eagerness if it wasn't obvious the attraction was playing trains rather than Allie.

"Boys and their toys," says Allie, "I can see I'm going to be redundant."

Graham flushes. "I'm sorry, I didn't mean to intrude."

Allie stares at him then laughs. "I was teasing. Come on, let's build the biggest and best railway in all the world."

Edward waits until the door shuts behind them before he says, "Honey, do you think he'll ever be... normal."

Personally I've never been too sure what normal is, or that it's the best thing to strive for, but I know what Edward means.

"I really don't know how to answer that, Edward." I pick my words with agonising care. "I've taught lots of teenagers but I'm not a psychologist. One thing I'm certain of, it's got to be dealt with, not ignored."

In my heart, I fear it's too late. The precious developmental years of childhood are irretrievable. But that's no reason to give up on Graham; he has already grown, even in the last few days.

Edward interprets my hesitation. "All I want for Graham is to have a happy life. Even if I have to put my own personal life on hold, I'll do everything I can."

By his personal life I assume he means his hopes of a relationship with Jackie. I feel sorry for my sister but I approve of Edward's priorities. In my creed one's kids should always come first.

If I'm going to attend this wretched dinner, I'm going to look good. Although I'm aware that Terry will misinterpret any outstanding efforts on my part. I tell Graham and Edward I'll meet them at the hotel and go up to shower and change.

I'm dressed and finishing my make-up, when Matt knocks on my bedroom door and says, "Okay if I use your en suite? Allie's bathing Ben in the bathroom."

"Sure." I'm suspicious about his motives for this intrusion and, when he returns, I point out, "You could have used the downstairs cloakroom."

"True, but that would have entailed walking up again."

Okay, I'll give him that one. "You look knackered."

"Aye, I guess I overdid things." He crosses the room to fasten the necklace I'm struggling with and his fingers linger on my shoulder. "I love your hair like that."

"Thank you." I stand up and move across to my wardrobe to get out my jacket, the silk of my dark brown skirt whispers softly with every step.

Without invitation he sits down on my bed. "Is everything okay with Allie?"

"I think so. Why?" The sharpness of fear echoes in my voice.

"I don't mean her health. I thought maybe she and Ross might not be getting on. Do they often quarrel like that?"

"I don't know. More often than they used to, I guess. I think her infatuation with him is wearing a bit thin. She told me today how her friend, Oliver, can't stand him. But I haven't asked her how she feels. I mean how can she admit she doesn't care about him any more, when, as she sees it, she broke up his marriage? Not to mention she's the mother of his child and has assured everybody he's the one love of her life."

"Pride's a bugger, isn't it?" he says. Then with an abrupt change of direction, "I haven't had a woman in my life for quite some time. Not even a one night stand."

I stare at him but, before I can respond, the door bursts open and a small, damp figure hurtles into the room. "Grandma!"

Matt intercepts him before he reaches me. "Easy Tiger. Grandma's going out. She doesn't need you mucking up her skirt."

"As if it matters," I say, and bend to kiss Ben's wet hair.

"Sorry, Mum," says Allie from the doorway. "He got away while I was emptying the bath of all his toys. Come on, Baby, let's get you dry and dressed."

"Throw the towel over here," says Matt, "I'll dry him while you get his clothes."

When the sweet-smelling, cuddly, angel child is dressed in his sleep-suit he smiles at me beguilingly. "Grandma, story."

"Grandma's got to go out," says Allie, "and Daddy's already gone. You'll have to put up with me." She offers no hint of whether she expects Ross back.

"Or me," offers Matt. "I'd like to read him a story."

"Anything except the Gingerbread Man," I warn.

"I regard that as one of the great performance achievements of my career."

"You traumatised fifteen four-year-olds!"

Towards the end of Allie's fourth birthday party, Matt had completed his do-it-yourself clown act with a rendition of the story of the Gingerbread Man. The room was hushed as he, in his persona of the wolf, balanced a gingerbread man upon his nose. Then, with a snap, he bit the biscuit neatly in half. Eleven of the small visitors had burst into tears. The situation wasn't improved by two-year-old Simon, who took advantage of our preoccupation to raid the tea table, bite the heads off all the surviving gingerbread men and lay a trail of their decapitated bodies around the room.

"We used to have fun, didn't we?" says Allie. She sounds surprised. I know that for her, like us, the happy times have disappeared into a fog of grief and the misery of Simon's suffering. I think it's time we resurrected the good memories, instead of dwelling on the bad, we owe that to Simon as well as to ourselves.

They all head off to Allie's room, in search of books. I check my watch and realise it still says seven-twenty, as it had done quite some time ago. That means the battery's dead. I'm not going into this ordeal without independent means of counting the minutes as they drag past. I wonder if Allie has a watch I can borrow. I doubt it, she usually uses her phone to check the time. I could do that, but in these circumstances it would look too obvious. Then I remember the lady's watch I'd picked up the other day.

It takes a few minutes to find it but I discover it in the pocket of the skirt I'd been wearing yesterday. It's a pretty watch, with a slender, elasticated, gold band and a delicate, round face. I wind it, careful not to turn too hard and break the spring.

Matt comes in as I slip it onto my wrist. "That's pretty," he says. "Did you get it in an antique shop?"

"I'm not sure. I found it the other day." It feels wrong to lie to Matt.

"My mum had one like it in her jewellery box, but she said hers didn't work."

"This one does. At least I think so. It's all right so far. I hope it's reliable."

"My mum's one was stuck just after three. I asked if I could try and fix it for her but she said 'no'. It had sentimental value for her."

"I see." I keep my tone casual but my mind is spinning. I'd just reset this watch and knew that it had previously read seven minutes past three.

Chapter 23

I'm over-dressed for this dinner party but that doesn't worry me. In these circumstances I'd rather be too posh than too casual. Apart from me, only Nicola is smart. She's abandoned the folk club informality and is wearing a navy blue dress with matching jacket. The over-all effect is formidable in a middle-aged, middle-class, stuffy sort of style.

Terry's wearing a suit, but it looks well used and old-fashioned. I suspect it's one he used to wear for work in the days before Social Workers were advised to look user-accessible and dress casually.

Jez and Deirdre are still clad in their manky festival gear, which makes it absurd that Nicola's moaning at Edward for wearing casual trousers and shirt. As for Graham, he's beyond the pale in jeans and jumper. This is clearly an act of defiance aimed at his mother and he turns sulkily away from her complaints. I can see he's dangerously wrought up. If Nicola doesn't back-pedal there could be a hysterical outburst before we reach the coffee and mints.

As we head towards the table, I think this is going to be a delightful meal. Jez is at his most malicious, Nicola at her most prickly, while Edward looks tired and moves like his back's about to seize up. Terry is veering between pushy and petulant, at least in his attitude to me. I shrug free of his attempts to take my arm and make sure Graham's seated between me and Edward. It's not ideal when his mother's opposite but it's the best I can do. I study the menu, then place it to construct a barricade.

We get through the soup without incident but halfway through the roast beef the trouble starts. Jez smiles across the table, revealing a row of discoloured teeth worthy of a rather sleazy wolf. "So what are you planning to do with the rest of your life, Graham?"

Graham's knuckles whiten on his knife and fork. "I haven't decided yet."

"Isn't it time you got your act together? After all you gotta do something. Can't sit on your bloody arse all your life living on mummy and daddy."

Edward intervenes, "Shut up, Jez. That's our business not yours."

"Jez is right," pronounces Nicola. "Graham can't depend on us forever. He seems to think dropping out of University gives him the right to sponge on us. Personally I'm tired of coming home after a hard day's work and finding him sitting around, doing nothing but watch TV. Although that's better than what he was doing before I locked away access to the computers."

"That's enough," says Edward. "Leave it, Nicola. This isn't the time or place."

Nicola stares at him as if she can't believe he's rebuked her publicly. "How dare you? I should have known you'd take Graham's side. It's your fault he's so weak. You didn't even take action when he was downloading disgusting sex-filth on the Internet. You..."

"Stop it!" Graham's screech cuts through Nicola's low-voiced diatribe. He slams to his feet and his chair crashes backwards. "You hypocrite! Who are you to talk about sex-filth when you've been screwing that filthy bastard all my life?" He points a trembling hand towards Jez.

"Be quiet, Graham!"

Nicola's command is strident but he carries on over her.

"As long as I can remember, as soon as Dad was out of the house, he was there, up in your bedroom. I used to sit in the hall, outside your room, and listen to you going at it. All my life you've made me feel like shit. I hate you. I never want to see you again."

He gags on the last words and wipes the back of his hand across his mouth. Then he starts to sob and gasp, struggling to breathe.

I glance at Edward's rigid face and see he's shocked into immobility. All those years and he hadn't known what was obvious to a stranger in the first hour.

I stand up and turn to Graham. He's still hyperventilating and I'm scared he's going to faint and so I coax him to sit down on my chair. I keep my arm round him and tell him he's okay.

"Is this true?" Edward's voice is cold and remote. It's a rhetorical question, a bid for time as he adjusts to the reality. "No, don't bother to lie. God, I've been a bloody fool. But why the hell did you marry me if you wanted Jez?"

"Guess," says Jez. "It wasn't for sex or your looks or your fascinating personality."

"No, it was for my money." Edward sounds remarkably calm. "That's it, isn't it, Nicola? You wanted a respectable businessman for everyday use and a bit of rough for screwing on the side."

Despite the dramatic words, they're all still seated. Terry seems stunned, and Nicola looks as if she's carved from stone. At the other tables, the diners are listening avidly and the waiters are frozen into immobility.

Again it's Jez who launches into taunting speech, "You really didn't see it, Eddie boy? She's been screwing me for over thirty years and you're the last one to know. Haven't you ever wondered who really fathered that weirdo over there? Not that he's anything I'd want to claim."

For the first time I see Edward flinch. He looks at Graham. The fear on Graham's face is blatant. Then Edward smiles at him. "Don't worry, you're my son."

He turns to face Jez. "I may not be much of a dad but I'm the only parent he's got. It's something you wouldn't understand, Jeremy. You're just a big cock and an even bigger mouth." Wincing he stands up. "Nicola, I was intending to leave you anyway. Thank you for making it so much easier. Come on, Graham."

Obediently Graham stumbles to his feet. He seems overwhelmed by the magnitude of the earthquake he's provoked.

Edward glances towards me, "Are you coming, Honey?"

"Not at the moment. I'll see you before I leave." Okay, so I'm nosy. I want to see the outcome of this melodrama.

As I sit down again, Jez says, "Let's get out of here. Everyone's looking at us."

"No." Nicola's mouth is like a steel trap. "I won't be intimidated by a pack of provincial busybodies. I intend to finish my meal."

That suits me. The remains of my dinner has congealed on the plate but I've spotted a particularly delicious strawberry gateau on the dessert trolley.

In the uneasy silence before our puddings come, I notice that Deirdre has disappeared. I wonder what she's up to. After what I'd seen this afternoon in the park, I don't believe she's broken-hearted.

I'm halfway through my gateau when Jez says, "He doesn't mean it, Nicola. He wouldn't leave you. He hasn't got the balls." Despite the reassurance he looks uneasy. I wonder if he thinks Nicola could be more demanding from now on. Not to mention less generous without Edward's money to call upon.

"He loves you too much," says Terry, translating Jez's crudity into politically correct speech.

"That's true," says Nicola, looking marginally less grim.

Her ego may make her indestructible but that doesn't mean I'm not going to launch a few missiles at her.

"Actually what Edward said is true." I smile at her. "He'd already planned to leave you and he's found a temporary flat."

"What? You mean Edward's got another woman?" demands Jez.

I deal with the priority of licking the cream off my spoon before I reply, "No, he just doesn't like living with Nicola."

"You lairy bitch!" Jez leans across the table to shout the insult and I feel the sour heat of his breath in my face. I force myself not to flinch.

When I've looked at him long enough to make my point, I turn to Terry and say, "Are you going to let him talk to me like that?"

That puts him on the spot. The look he gives me borders on dislike but he says, "Please Jez, don't make things any worse. Honey, you can see poor Nicola's upset."

"I can imagine. It's a bit of a pain to get found out after thirty years of infidelity."

"Everyone knows why you're being self-righteous," snaps Nicola. "Terry told me how your ex-husband slept around and how you became a total mess."

Her words glance off without hurting me at all. "Was that when he was telling you how hot I am in bed?" I enquire.

I see him squirm and catch the look he casts at Nicola, half-guilty and half-appealing. Everything clicks neatly into place. "Or was it pillow-talk, last night, when he stayed over at the hotel?"

Their faces confirm it.

Jez sees it too. "You said you had a headache," he splutters, the outraged lover, two-timed in his turn.

Give Nicola her due, when it comes to hypocrisy she wins first prize with insolent ease. I want to laugh. "That's really living on the edge," I say. "Husband and two lovers all in the same hotel, and you fitted in time to go to church."

"Honey," begs Terry, "please, I can explain."

"You don't have to." I stand up. "To be honest, Nicola, I don't care how many middle-aged losers you screw. What I can't forgive is what you've done to your son. You've brought him close to a total breakdown with your bullying. And Terry, the next time you pontificate about the promiscuous women you work with and how they neglect their kids, just remember it happens in your own backyard."

As a final word that would have worked well, but as I reach the dining room door, Terry catches up with me and grabs my arm. "Honey, wait!"

I won't give any of them the satisfaction of seeing me struggle to get free. I stand still and glare down at the offending hand. "Let go of me."

"You've got to listen. I didn't mean to hurt you. Nicola needed comforting. I guess she knew by instinct that Edward was about to walk out on her."

I've always suspected Terry has a selective listening device fitted to his brain. It appears he hasn't processed eighty-per-cent of what's been said.

"I promise it will never happen again," he continues, stumbling over his words in his haste. "I know how much it must hurt you, after what your bastard ex-husband did to you, but I promise you, Honey, I'm nothing like him."

"Excuse me." We're blocking the doorway and an elderly man wants to enter the dining room.

Terry's grasp slackens and I wrench my arm free. "That's the truest thing you've ever said, Terry. You are nothing like Matt." I step aside to let the indignant diner through.

Alone in the hotel lobby I know I should feel humiliated that I'm the sort of woman men are unfaithful to. But I don't feel damaged or bereft, just disgusted at the spite and messiness of it all. Nicola, Jez and Terry deserve each other. In the past few minutes, I've been pretty mischievous myself but they deserve that too. As Mum said the other day, a taste of their own medicine won't do them any harm. Of course, neither will it do them any good, but I wasn't setting out to cure them.

I wonder who to check up on first: Deirdre or Edward and Graham? I check at the desk for room numbers and go up to the second floor. I knock at the door and call, "Deirdre, it's Honey Alder. Are you there?"

No response. I go along the corridor and knock on Edward's door.

"Who's there?"

"Honey."

The key clicks in the lock and Graham opens it. As soon as I'm in the room he shuts the door and locks it once again.

"Welcome to Alcatraz," says Edward.

I think the situation's more like a fort under siege, possibly St Rochelle, but I don't say so. As Matt has often reminded me, there are times and there are places for being literal and literary and this isn't one of them. "Are you two okay?"

"Could be worse. How about you?"

"I'm good. But then I'm not really involved the way you are."

There's a moment's tense silence then Graham says, "We've got to tell her, Dad."

"Tell me what?"

"I was waiting last night to see who went in her room," says Graham. "I always watch. I hate her so much."

It's a terrible statement for anyone to make about his mother. The Elizabethan tragedies have their roots in truth, but I feel relieved that this is still not my problem.

"If you mean Terry and your mother, I've sussed that already."

Edward stares at me. "Don't you mind?"

"Why should I? Apart from it making things even lousier for you."

"Terry said you were engaged. So either you're being incredibly brave or he's been lying his bloody head off again?"

"I'll give you a hint. I'm a total wimp."

"I don't think you're that, but I'm glad you're not hurt."

I sit down on the chair beside the bed. "Have you made any plans yet?"

"Assuming my back's not too bad for me to drive, we're going home tomorrow. Graham will pack for us and we'll store everything in my office. He's promised to do the donkey-work for me. Then we'll find another hotel or a B&B for a few days until my flat's ready. We're going to keep clear of everyone."

Graham shudders. "I don't want to see her. She says I'm weird. She's always saying that." Tension is sharp-edged in his voice again. "Those girls she used to bring home from her school all laughed at me and called me names and she laughed with them."

Edward limps across the room and hugs him. "You're not the weird one. I just wish you'd told me."

"I thought you'd take her side."

"Never!" He sits down again, slowly and painfully.

Graham has a rapt expression on his face, like he's sorting through some new, scarily alien thought. "Dad, Honey's sister does massage treatment, doesn't she?"

"Yes." Edward doesn't meet his eyes.

"And you like her, don't you?"

At this Edward turns to look at him. He replies quietly, "Yes I do. I like her very much. But this isn't the time to ask her if she likes me in the same way."

I hold my breath, waiting for Graham's response. For the first time in his life, this confused and immature twenty-four-year-old has one of his parents devoting all their care and attention just to him. How can he be expected to pass up on that?

"I think she does like you, Dad. She smiles at you a lot."

"It's not that late. Perhaps, if we phoned Jackie, she'd come round and start treating your dad's back," I say.

I see the effort it costs him but he says, "I think that's a good idea."

Edward protests, "I was going to leave it until things were straightened out."

"Sorry," I say unrepentantly.

"No you're not. And nor am I. Except I don't know how to explain it all to her."

He looks like he can't think straight any more. "Would you like me to talk to her?"

"Would you mind?"

"Of course not, I love interfering."

I take Graham's key and go into the next door room to phone. Jackie listens to my involved account of the evening's events and then says, "Honey, are you all right?"

"Of course I'm all right. Why shouldn't I be?"

"All that unpleasantness, I thought it might have upset you. And that business with Terry. It's bound to have left you feeling vulnerable."

I see my hand is shaking but it's from anger not distress. "Jackie, for God's sake get real! I divorced the husband I adored for sleeping round and I survived. Do you really think I care who Terry screws?"

In the silence that follows I can feel the shock waves emanating down the line. At last she says, "I'm sorry."

I'm sure she's crying but I keep my tone hard, "I didn't phone you because I needed comforting. I called because Edward is in agony with his back. If you want to come round here, you can probably do some good. If you don't want to put yourself on the line that's up to you."

"I'll come. Honey, will you stay there and wait for me?"

"Okay. I wanted to check up on Deirdre anyway."

"Oh Honey, you can't look after everyone in the world."

"Whatever."

I put the phone down before she can say anything else. I'm in no mood to explain that I'm not actually worried about Deirdre but I want to know what she's up to.

I don't want to encounter Nicola, Jez or Terry again tonight, so I ease the door of Graham's room open to peep out before I leave.

A young woman is speeding along the corridor. She's slim, with a nice figure and short feathery blonde hair. She's dressed in jeans and a purple jacket, with a small rucksack slung over her shoulder. There's

nothing familiar about her, except for the turn of her head as she looks up at the lights above the lift.
"Deirdre!" I exclaim.

Chapter 24

She jumps and turns to glare at me, then she grins. "Oh shit!"

"I don't understand," I say as I catch up with her.

"You're not meant to. I thought you'd gone. You scared the life out of me when you banged on my door earlier. What did you want?" The chirpy tones are a world away from Deirdre's flat speech.

"To check on you."

"Yeah. Of all of them, you're the only one who would." Her smile lights up her pretty face. "You're a nice woman, Honey Alder."

"No, I'm not. I said 'check on', not 'check you were okay'."

Up until now, I'd been working on the assumption that Deirdre had no motive to harm Matt, but it has just occurred to me that she could be an actress who's got history with him, although I'm sure he doesn't remember her. This persecution could be her crazy way to repay him for some neglect or carelessness.

"I saw you in the woods this afternoon, hours after you were supposed to have taken a taxi home."

"I wanted a bit of time to myself."

"Strange that. You weren't alone when I saw you."

"Oh shit!" she says again.

"What's going on?"

"Not here." She casts a harried look along the corridor.

"Come into Graham's room."

"No thanks. That boy's seriously strange."

"The room's empty. He's next door with his dad."

In the privacy of the room I say, "So tell me about it. Where are you going and why the fancy dress?"

"I'm leaving the old man, ain't I?" She puts on a mock Cockney accent. "And I dressed like this so he wouldn't spot me on the way out."

"And your heart is broken. I may look stupid but I'm not that thick. The fancy dress was that vile wig and those droopy clothes. Who are you and what are you playing at?"

She laughs and runs her fingers through her hair. "Okay, it's a fair cop. I'm Natalie Carmichael. And I'm not playing, I'm working."

"Escort or actress?"

I see a flash of anger in her blue eyes, then she laughs. "Actor. What sort of guy would want an escort who dressed like Deirdre?"

"One as sick as Jez."

She shudders. "Yuck! No this was a legit acting job. He didn't touch me and we didn't sleep in the same room."

"Where did he sleep last night then?" I ask, momentarily side-tracked.

"You know about him and Nicola do you?" It's obvious I've taken her by surprise. "He slept in his car, but boy didn't he whinge about it?"

"So that's why Nicola had to make it up to him this afternoon. Why are you here impersonating Deirdre?"

"For money, of course. Cash up-front. I don't trust Jez one inch."

"But why does Jez want you to impersonate his wife?"

"So that load of losers he's friendly with wouldn't know she'd left him. He's got a mate who's a theatrical agent and Jez went through his books until he found someone who was the right sort. It wasn't a problem. None of them knew Deirdre really well."

"It's still incredible you could get away with it."

"It's what actors do."

"And Jez really paid you just to save his face?"

"Yeah." She grins maliciously. "Jez reckoned they'd rip the shit out of him if they found out she'd buggered off with the plumber who came to sort their drains."

"Quite probably." Although leaving Jez seemed a reasonable move to me, and a good plumber's a rare commodity. "It seems excessive to put on such a pantomime though."

"Jez is that sort. And, from what he said, Nicola would give him hell if she found out. It's funny really. She looks so strait-laced and yet she's a total slut."

I suppose it makes sense. After the grief Jez and Nicola gave Terry when they were students, Jez wouldn't want to leave himself open to mockery.

Nevertheless a bizarre but scary thought is niggling in my mind. "Are you sure Deirdre's still alive?"

She stares at me and then begins to laugh. "You reckon he's done her in? You must be joking. Not Jez. He hasn't got the balls."

"I'm not sure about that. I suspect he's the sort who could lose control."

"Forget about it. In fact forget about everything I've said. I shouldn't have told you. It was part of the agreement that I didn't tell anyone about Deirdre going off."

I make no commitment. I'm sick of keeping secrets for people who don't deserve my loyalty and I'm still not convinced the real Deirdre's okay.

She reads my obstinate silence and shrugs. "So what can he do? Sue me? Why were you hanging round here?"

"Checking Edward and Graham were okay."

"Mother Theresa also ran." Her smile is friendlier than the words. "You haven't got anything going with Edward have you?"

"Just friendship."

"I didn't think it was likely you fancied him. He isn't a patch on your old man."

I feel myself blush. "My ex-old man," I remind her.

"Whatever. Ex or not, you've got to admit he's gorgeous. When I went back to your place, it was the first time all weekend I regretted wearing that Deirdre disguise."

"Yes, he likes blondes," I say, and hate the words the moment they leave my mouth.

She stares at me. "I've got a bloke, that was him you saw me with earlier on. We're okay, but if he looked at me the way your guy does at you... well don't be a bloody silly bitch. And don't get stuck with Terry. No way is that bastard good enough for you."

"One thing I don't get. Why did you keep that hideous wig on this afternoon when you were meeting your boyfriend?"

"It's hell to get on. You need a mirror and plenty of time to make sure it looks convincing. I'm glad to be rid of it. It's hot and itchy and the cheap ones shed hairs all over the place. It's like wearing a moulting cat on your head." She springs to her feet. "Christ! If I don't run I'll miss my train."

"Okay." I reach into my handbag and take out the small camera that I carry in case I want to capture a precious Ben-moment while we're out and about. "Natalie!"

Framed in the doorway, she turns to face me and I take a photo. I think I believe her story, but means of identification may come in useful later on.

Jackie is nervous around Graham. Her brittle politeness charges the atmosphere. It gets through to Graham, although he reads it wrong. "I'll go to my own room."

I prepare to stick my nose in once again but Edward says, "Pack up your stuff and bring it in here. We'll find another hotel. I know you don't want to stay here."

"You can stay at my place," offers Jackie. "I've got two spare rooms."

"Are you sure?" Edward and Graham ask the same question at the same time.

She blushes but manages a smile. "Positive."

Graham walks towards the door, then hesitates. "I don't want to go out there. I'm scared she'll try and talk to me."

"I'll come with you," I offer.

"Thank you." When he smiles like that he's a sweet looking kid.

It only takes five minutes to pack Graham's case. Again I think how old-fashioned his clothes are. His pyjamas would be dreary for a man his father's age.

"It might be an idea to ask your dad for some money and choose new clothes. Something a bit more suitable to twenty-four than sixty-four."

"She bought them." The sourness of his tone makes it clear he's talking about his mother. "She said I'd waste the money if she gave me cash so she ordered stuff from a catalogue. In a way I was glad. I never know what's cool to wear."

"Maybe Allie and I could go out with you and help choose some stuff?"

"I'd like that. Allie's kind. Not like a girl at all."

"What do you mean 'not like a girl'?" I'm too relieved that he doesn't fancy Allie to feel offended by his implication that she's not feminine.

"Like a friend. At least what I guess a friend would be like. I don't know, I haven't got any friends."

"You have now."

"Would Allie mind coming out shopping with me?"

"Graham, whatever Allie seems like to you, I assure you when it comes to shopping she's a hundred-percent girl."

Chapter 25

I'm tired and drive slowly and carefully, especially along the road that circles near the top of Portsdown Hill. To the left of me runs the wire of the naval installations; to the right a dark, steep drop and then the sparkling lights of the city, which in their turn disappear into the sea. I turn into a lay-by for a few minutes to enjoy the peace.

When I get home it's late, but Allie is sitting in the living room, nursing her son.

"What's wrong with Ben?"

"He's teething and he keeps screaming when he lies down in his cot. It's not his fault. It's those big back teeth that really hurt coming through."

"Of course it's not his fault." I bend to plant a gentle kiss on Ben's drowsy head and another on Allie's tired face. "Couldn't you have cuddled him in bed?"

"Ross got angry. He says he needs his sleep."

So Ross is back on the scene. I try not to show my disappointment.

"What are you thinking?" she demands.

"Lots of things."

"Like what?"

I sit down beside her. "Yesterday you were uncomplimentary about me allowing myself to be walked over. And yet you won't tell Ross it's your room, in your home, and if Ben keeps him awake he can stay in his bedsit and not hog your bed."

Her expressive face acknowledges the truth of this but she says, "It's awkward."

"Want to tell me why?"

"Ross has lost everything and it's all my fault."

I resist the temptation to snap, 'Rubbish!'

"I think I'd like that explained in more detail."

"He's lost his wife and family and home."

"It's true he's lost his house and his wife, although I think he could see more of his children if he tried." I see her stricken look. "What's wrong?"

"Nothing."

"Allie, please don't lie to me."

"We had a fight."

"I guessed that. I heard Ross slamming out."

"This morning he said he was going to see his kids but this afternoon his wife phoned, screaming abuse at me because he hadn't turned up. She said the kids were upset. His phone was off. At first I was scared he'd had an accident, but then he turned up and I thought..."

I can guess what she thought. I remember the woman I'd seen shouting at him in Waterlooville, but my suspicions are absurd, she was easily old enough to be his mother. "Did he explain where he'd been?"

"No, at least not then, but later he told me he'd lost his nerve about visiting the boys. His wife's so nasty when he picks them up that he bottled out."

I have to be fair, even to Ross. "That could be true. I know your dad said there were a good few times when it took all his courage to collect you for the weekend." And I'd rate Matt as a far braver man than Ross.

"Really? I never noticed you being horrible to Dad."

"No, not me."

"Oh!" She understands and blushes. "I suppose you think I'm a total hypocrite?"

"Yes, I do rather. But I also think you're playing the martyr." It's time to speak my mind, even though it risks everything we've built up. "I'm sorry Allie, but from what I know of Ross I can't believe he was swept off his feet for love of you."

"That's a horrible thing to say!" She can't raise her voice for fear of waking Ben but her tone is stormy.

"Yes, it is. And I don't mean you aren't loveable and gorgeous and everything a sane man would want. I'm sure Ross wanted you and probably still does. But Ross wouldn't be swept off his feet, because he always looks after Number One."

This time she doesn't protest. It's impossible to read her expression. Her eyes are fixed on Ben and there's a stubborn set to her mouth. "The college bosses are being awful to him. The play he's directing starts at the weekend. He says it's the last one he'll be allowed to work on. There's some big meeting at college next week that he's really uptight about. He says it's to discipline him. It's not fair. We waited until I'd finished college but I feel like it's my fault."

"The meeting has nothing to do with his relationship with you." I'm in the second minefield before I have time to think.

"What then?"

"A young male student is claiming Ross has been victimising him."

"Who is it?"

"His wife's brother."

"Well that proves it's just spite."

"Allie, I'm the boy's Personal Tutor and, from what I've seen, he's fully justified. If half of what he's saying is true, Ross has been making his life a misery. He's made a lot of jibes about stuff he only knows by being his brother-in-law. The boy's got circumstantial evidence and a lot of witnesses to back his claims."

I stop short of telling her that, once the college authorities had started checking properly, they'd discovered Ross' CV was far from accurate.

"And you believe this boy? You're backing him against Ross?"

"I'm doing my job. I can't have him transferred to another tutor this close to A-levels. Allie, please believe I'm not doing anything out of spite."

The fierce look softens. "I know. That's not your style. Why didn't you tell me?"

"I try to keep work and home as separate as I can." I know that sounds stuffy but it needs to be said. I cross to the drinks cabinet and pour myself a glass of wine.

"What have you been doing this evening?" she asks. It's a deliberate change of subject but that doesn't mean she's rejected what I said. Allie's like her dad, the quietly tenacious kind, who likes to think things through before they act.

"Oh I've been doing the usual sort of stuff. Chucking Terry, unmasking Deirdre and setting up your Aunt Jackie with a married man. Do you want a drink?"

"Please. It sounds like I'm going to need it." She waits in simmering silence until I sit down again. "Now tell me all about it."

I tell her everything about Terry and his friends, apart from Graham's attempt on me in the churchyard and the personal stuff he told me afterwards.

"So what happens now?" she asks when I finish.

"Not a lot. The only ones we're likely to see again are Edward and Graham. At least we will if I read the signs right with your Aunt Jackie."

Allie giggles. "How are the mighty fallen! Auntie Jackie in love with a married man. What price the moral high ground now?"

"You're not to rub it in," I warn her.

"Why not? She was so disapproving of me and Ross, much nastier than you were."

"Please don't be unkind to her, sweetheart. I promise you, I've already made her squirm, but I don't want to spoil things for her and Edward. They both deserve more happiness than they've had and so does Graham."

"The best way to help Graham would be to poison his mother."

"I want to help Graham but I won't risk going to prison to do so."

"We'll just have to frame that Jez guy."

"Good plan. I'll reread Agatha Christie and work out which poison to use."

She giggles. "Mum, you are so cool."

We sit in silence for a while, sipping our wine, deep in our own thoughts. Eventually I rouse myself to say, "How's your dad?"

"Exhausted. Reading ten stories to Ben takes its toll."

"Ten!"

"He wanted to and Ben wanted him to. What was I supposed to do?"

I can't argue with that. I'd spend my entire life reading Winnie the Witch stories for the joy of hearing Ben say 'Adacadada' at the relevant points.

"I know Dad's tired but I think he's okay. I made us both supper and we chatted for a bit. I'd forgotten how nice he can be."

"Me too." I think the truth is neither of us let ourselves remember it.

"He was talking about my work experience next year and said he'd find me a job."

To me that seems like good news, but she's frowning. "What's wrong with that? I told you to ask him."

"There's nothing wrong. It's great. All my tutors said no firm would take me on when I've got Ben to look after. The thing is, Dad said I should get a feel for the firm, because if he retired or anything happened to him it would be mine."

"Didn't you know things were left that way?"

"I assumed everything went to you."

"He's made sure I'm well provided for, enough to keep me safe all my life, but most of his assets go to you. It makes sense for death duties."

"I see." She still looks troubled.

"Allie, what's wrong?"

"If Ross finds out, he's going to start nagging at me about how I should ask Dad for enough money to buy a house so that Ross and I can live together."

"Presumably it depends on whether you want that as well."

"I ought to. I know it's time I grew up."

"You are pretty grown up compared to most girls your age. You look after Ben with very little help from Ross and you're on line to get a 2:1."

"I get a lot of help from you though." She won't meet my eyes.

I know Ross has been telling her I'm a clinging, domineering mother who's afraid of being left alone. There's an element of truth in that but there are a lot of other more important things in the mix as well.

"I'll miss you terribly when you and Ben leave home but I want you to be happy and successful. The day you tell me you are certain you want to go and live with Ross, I'll talk to your dad and see what we can do." Although I'll advise Matt to tie any help up in a way that means Ross can't get his greedy hands on it.

"I don't know what I want."

"Oh sweetheart!" I put my arms around her and Ben. We cling together for a few moments, then move apart before we waken Ben.

On his white blanket I see two grey hairs. "Sorry, I seem to be moulting."

"They're not yours. You're not grey any more."

"True." And they're not my mother's, her hair is white not iron grey.

Allie eases the blanket away from Ben's face. "I meant to wash it. Terry was leaning on it the other day and his revolting jumper is covered in fluff."

Trying for casual, I pick the hairs off. When Allie's not looking, I surreptitiously wrap them in a tissue, for comparison with the hair I found on Matt's bed.

Chapter 26 Tuesday

Although it's well after midnight, I compare the hairs I've collected as soon as I get to my room. They match. At least as far as I can tell. And that gets me nowhere. Matt or I could have picked up the hairs at Matt's house and transferred them to Ben's blanket. But I still suspect Terry. I can see how he could do it. His work puts him in touch with plenty of women who'd play any game for the price of a drugs score. Although I've never given him a key to my house, it would be easy enough for him to take my spare and get a copy made, and quite possible to pinch Matt's key from me and copy that as well, and find out the security code when I'd left it in my bag.

It appals me that I can believe he'd come up behind me in the dark and half-throttle me. He's got a nasty temper and he'd be furious that I'd left the concert without him. He's very into 'teaching people lessons.' But why would he persecute Matt? Terry hadn't even met him when the liver-cooking woman first turned up.

Then the answer hits me. So simple I wonder why I didn't spot it straight away. I know Terry likes the lifestyle my money could offer. I've spent most of the past months thwarting his attempts to move in. I'd be an even more attractive prospect with the small fortune I'd inherit if Matt died. That makes me feel sick. I wonder, now I've chucked Terry, will he take 'no' for an answer? I'll get my locks changed as soon possible and when I go shopping I'm going to buy some bolts for all my doors.

The next morning I'm woken just after nine by the beep of my mobile, announcing I've got a text. It's

Jackie, letting me know that she's driving Edward and Graham to their house to pack. I smile at the thought of my workaholic sister so casually shutting her shop for the day and text back, *HAVE A GOOD DAY.*

When I go downstairs, Matt's sitting in the kitchen, dressed in jeans and shirt. He still looks pale and heavy eyed but a lot fitter than before.

"Hi. You want some coffee?" He raises the half-empty percolator.

"Please. You're up early. Are you okay?"

"Aye."

Why don't I believe him? "Have you been seeing that woman again?"

He shrugs. "It's not so much seeing. I keep on smelling her."

That puzzles me. My expression makes Matt grin. "No, you fool, not liver and onions. I keep thinking I smell a flowery scent."

"Oh, I see."

Smell is such a cruelly evocative sense. Seven years ago, for the first few weeks after Matt left, I could hardly believe he'd gone. It wasn't just the way his things kept turning up: his squash racket in the hall cupboard, his guitar music between a pile of old magazines. The house smelled of his presence. Sleepless, in bed, I'd press my face against his pillow. I kept that pillowcase back for quite a while, until my sister sussed me out and took it away from me. Afterwards, furtively, I'd sprinkled it with an aftershave he'd missed when he'd cleared the bathroom cupboard, but, without his chemistry, it wasn't the same.

"You've changed your aftershave," I say.

Not surprisingly, even Matt can't follow my line of thinking. "Not to lily of the valley," he says impatiently.

"I didn't mean that. I was thinking of something else."

This time he gets what I'm thinking. "I'm older, Honey. The same things don't suit me any more. Like I can't wear contact lenses because my eyes get too tired."

Again Matt's passive acceptance frightens me. He's in his fifties but it's like he's resigned to old age

"The glasses are really sexy." I never thought I'd say anything like that to Matt again.

He shrugs. "You reckon?"

"Tell me about this perfume."

"There's nothing to tell." The denial is accompanied by a shudder.

"Matt, please."

"Last night I smelled this flowery scent. I opened my eyes and saw her standing beside my bed. She said, 'You could have saved me. Why didn't you do something? It was your fault that I died.' Then she left again." The handle of his mug gives way under his tense grip and coffee sprays across the breakfast bar. "Sorry."

"No problem." I grab a wad of kitchen towel and mop up. "Did you cut yourself?" I know the coffee is too cool to scald.

"No. Lucky it wasn't your new tea service."

"It still wouldn't have mattered." Graham got one thing right; people matter more to me than things. "There's something I want to ask you." I get out my camera and show him the snap I'd taken of the pretend Deirdre. "Do you know her? Her name may be Natalie."

Matt stares at the picture on the tiny screen. "She looks kind of familiar but no, I don't think I know her." He gives a wry, self-mocking smile. "Not one of my blondes."

"I just wondered." Matt had met Natalie when she was posing as Deirdre, so there's nothing strange in him thinking she looked familiar. "I wanted to tell you about her."

The door opens and I break off what I was going to tell him about the weirdness of it all and my fears for the real Deirdre.

"'Morning." Ross strolls in, carrying Ben.

"Hi. Is Allie still asleep?"

"Yes. She said she wanted to have a lie in. Ben was a bit restless in the night."

"You could say that. They were down here when I got in."

He picks up on the underlying criticism and gives me a lairy look. "Now, I suppose I'll have to wait until she wakes up. Either that or take Ben with me into town."

I know he's fishing but I take the bait. I don't mind babysitting Ben, and Ross will get impatient with him if he whinges when they're out. "I'll look after him."

Ross dumps him on my lap. "Thanks. There's a lot to do before the play opens next weekend. They may call me the director but general dogsbody would be closer to the truth. I've spent half my life in charity shops looking for the clothes."

"You're lucky the students were available and willing to rehearse in the holidays."

"I only choose the keen ones for big parts."

I'm sure when he says 'keen' he means his fans, the kids who think he's wonderful.

"What play is it?" asks Matt.

"It's called 'Dare To Be The Same.' The students put it together themselves from their improvisation sessions. It's a groundbreaking piece of interactive theatre."

"It always is," remarks Matt cynically.

"Well this is. It's got a lot of interactive work, like getting the audience involved through smell and touch as well as looking and hearing. We've got incense burners with really innovative smells."

"What sort of innovative smells?" asks Matt. I wonder if he's making mischief or if he really wants to know.

"The sort of smells that shatter Establishment people's complacency... ordinary cooking smells that blend into the stench of decay and destruction and burning bodies. And some of the props people are weaving strips of fur under the seats so they brush randomly against the audience's legs, like passing rats."

That settles it. This is one student production Allie isn't going to drag me to. I don't know what revolts me more, the thought of synthetic death smells or furry rat things brushing against my legs.

"But what's it about?" persists Matt.

"It addresses the issues of gender and sexual identity." Ross throws a defiant look at me. His comments about his young brother-in-law's sexuality form a large part of the complaints that have been made against him.

"You mean like Twelfth Night?" Matt says this so straight-faced that Ross is clearly uncertain whether he's being mocked. I get up hastily and busy myself with putting Ben in his high-chair.

"Not at all like Twelfth Night," says Ross. "We leave old-fashioned stuff to people like Honey."

"Thank God for that. It's good to know the Bard's in safe hands."

This time Matt's sarcasm gets through and Ross scowls. His hostile expression reminds me of something I'd been meaning to ask him for the last few days. "Ross, who was that woman I saw you with in Waterlooville on Saturday?"

"Woman? I don't know what you mean." Despite his denial he looks decidedly shifty.

"Middle-aged, plump, with blonde hair. She seemed to be having a go at you."

"Oh her! Just a parent who doesn't think I've given her kid a big enough part." Ross stands up and moves towards the door. "I must go. I'm off to Portsmouth. Is there anything you need dropped into your office, Mr Alder?"

"There are some papers you could drop into my office if you don't mind," says Matt. "I'll get them."

Matt and Ross go upstairs and I give Ben his breakfast. Released from his high chair, he takes my hand and determinedly tows me into the sitting room.

"So what's it going to be?" I ask.

As I feared it's trains. I don't object to playing with Ben's immense collection of wooden trains but, when I assemble it, somehow it always curves the wrong way and won't join up. My attempts aren't improved by Ben dismantling it quicker than I can make it up and his vocal outrage when his train is derailed.

I've achieved a somewhat peculiar arrangement when Matt returns.

"What are you doing down there?" he asks.

"Demonstrating my incompetence."

He laughs and squats down beside the track. Three lightening alterations and the whole thing is viable.

"I love being made to feel totally useless," I complain. "And now you've put that bridge in my way I can't get up."

"Why not?"

Does the idiot man think time has stood still for the rest of us? "Because, while your eyes have given up, with me it's my joints. To get up from kneeling I need space and the sofa to hang on to."

He steps nearer and offers his hands. Up you come."

He hauls me upright and holds me until he's sure I'm steady. We move apart and I have to restrain an impulse to reach out to keep him there.

"I'll call a taxi and get out your way." Is it my imagination or is he breathing faster than before?

"Please wait until Allie comes down, then I'll run you home."

"No, it's okay, I'll go now. I need to buy some cigarettes."

"I thought you must be running short so I got you some yesterday. I grab my bag from the sofa and rummage. In my first foray I produce a purple coloured cardboard box. Matt says, "Thanks, but I draw the line at smoking rubbers."

Trying not to look embarrassed, I shove the box of condoms back in my bag and produce the cigarettes.

"Aren't you through the menopause?" asks Matt.

"As a matter of fact I am." I have been for years but I've never confessed this to Terry. I don't need the pressure he'd put on me to have sex without protection.

"I always use them too. Better safe than sorry. I guess Allie wasn't so careful?"

"Yes she was, or so she told me." My guess is Ross was careless when he put it on. From what Allie let slip he's got a macho attitude to using condoms. My gaze embraces Ben. "He's the little soldier who dodged the spermicide."

"Thank God," says Matt. His religious faith is even less existent than mine but I know what he means.

He takes his cigarettes out into the garden and I sit on the sofa to watch Ben play. The sofa has been reupholstered but it's the same one I'd sat on seven years ago when I told Matt I knew he'd been sleeping round and agreed when he offered to move out.

Ben picks up a book and toddles over to me. The story about the Bear Hunt is one of his favourites. I lift him onto my lap and explain that on a bear hunt sometimes there are terrifying objects in the way that people can't go round or over or under. When that happens there's only way to carry on and that's to go straight through.

Chapter 27

Fortified by my donation of cigarettes, Matt is glad to wait for me to drive him home and appreciative when I go in to settle him and make sure he's okay. I make a pot of tea and bring the tray through to where he's sitting, listening to soft music on a CD.

He opens his eyes and smiles at me. "I've said thank you so often I've practically worn it out. I'm sorry I'm not being more proactive. I still feel pretty wiped."

"It's not surprising, with the concussion and stress and everything. You don't have to stay here. You're welcome to come back with me."

"Better not. If you start to lean on someone, soon you find you can't stand on your own two feet."

"I know."

Along with all my other worries, I'm still concerned about the fate of the real Deirdre. "There's something I'd like your advice on, if you don't feel too rough?"

"Of course. What's wrong?"

I don't describe the entire fiasco of last night but I relay what Natalie had told me and explain my fears.

"No problem. He notes down the details about Jez and Deirdre. I'll get my PI. onto tracking her down."

"Your what?"

"PI. Private Investigator."

"Now you're just showing off, Matt."

"No, I'm not. I don't mean he's employed by my firm alone but we've used him a few times when things need checking out."

"I've never met a PI," I say wistfully.

"You'd be disappointed. He's a quiet, well-mannered businessman, and he's totally professional. Not a seedy little gum-shoe like you're imagining."

"Another illusion shattered." I pull a clown's grimace.

"Are you trying to make me laugh?"

"Well I thought a smile might be pleasant."

"You're a manipulative woman, Honey Bear."

"You mean you've only just noticed? Make sure you phone if you need anything."

I hesitate in the doorway, unwilling to add to his stress but needing an answer to the thought that's been worrying me ever since Allie mentioned it. "Matt, what do you remember about your mother's mother?"

He looks surprised. "I don't remember her. She died before I was born."

"Oh, I thought it was her I saw in a family photo album with you as a little boy." I feel embarrassed and dread him going upstairs to look in his album. I'd have to explain I'd taken it and now the photograph in question had disappeared. I can't think what had got into me, poking and prying and removing Matt's property.

Fortunately, I don't have to confess. Matt assumes I'd seen the photo in one of his dad's numerous albums. "I don't know who that could be. Dad's got so many pictures. I guess it must be some friend of my mum's."

That's a reasonable explanation but it doesn't explain why it was in Matt's album, and why he doesn't know anything about it, and why it had disappeared. Unless the photo never actually existed and it's me that's crazy... a plausible explanation.

"I guess you're right," I say.

I drive home in a state of total confusion. I simply don't know what to think. If what's happening isn't connected to the grandmother who killed herself, what can it be about? The really good thing is that, although I accept I may have been mistaken, I really don't think I'm delusional.

As I enter the house I meet Allie coming out.

"Hi Mum. I left you a note. I'm taking Ben to a teddy bears' picnic and then I'm going over to Oliver's flat. But you can come to the picnic if you like."

"No, thanks, love, I've got other plans. But I'm glad I caught you. I've got a couple of questions. I know they don't make much sense but humour me. You know that photo you saw in Grandpa's album when you were visiting him, the one of Dad when he was little, with a bit of the picture cut away. How old do you think Dad was in it?"

"I'm not sure. Three or four, I guess."

"Do you remember the name of the old lady at Grandpa's nursing home, the one that talked about Granny Alice?"

She screws up her face in concentration. "No. I'm sorry. Ross could tell you more than me, he talked to her a lot. I hated being there and the things Grandpa was saying about Simon. I guess I just turned off."

"No problem." I don't blame Allie. Matt's dad acts as though Simon's death was a personal insult rather than a family tragedy. Switching off from his complaints is the only way to survive.

"Is there anything else you can remember about her, love?"

"She was in a wheelchair. I didn't talk to her for more than a minute or two. I took Ben outside." She must see my disappointment. "Is it important? Why do you want to know?"

"I wouldn't mind having a chat to her. I want to know more about Dad's early childhood and Grandpa won't want to talk about it, you know what he's like."

"Mum, is there something really wrong with Dad? Not just the concussion but something scary?"

"I don't know. There may be, but hopefully it can be put right."

"Like with you?"

"Yeah. Like with me. Drive carefully." I wave until they're out of sight.

I need to find out more about Matt's childhood but I'm unwilling to phone the nursing home with so little information. To be honest, I'm unwilling to phone the nursing home at all. I don't like talking to my father-in-law. Instead I look up Ross' mobile number and ring through.

"Hi Honey, what can I do for you?" His voice is friendlier than usual.

"I wanted to ask you something. I'm sorry to bother you."

"You're never a bother. What do you want to know?"

"It was about the last time you went up to visit Allie's grandfather with her."

"Yes?" Is it my imagination or does he sound more guarded?

"You talked about Matt when he was a little boy. About his grandmother."

"Did we? I really don't remember. I'm not being funny, Honey, but you know what Allie's grandpa is like. He keeps rambling on. Most of the time you just say 'yes' and 'no' and hope you've put them in the right places."

"He showed you a photo of Matt and his mother, it had the end cut off." I feel like I'm paddling upstream against a strong current.

"He showed us hundreds of photos, he always does. After a while they blur into one another."

That was true. I too had sunk into a near coma when Matt's dad got out his albums. I try a new approach. "There was an old lady you were talking to. She was in a wheelchair."

"Yes, I remember her." My spirits lift. "At first she seemed quite lucid but actually a lot of the time she was rambling on and on and none of it made sense."

I feel as though the path has crumbled in front of me. "Do you remember that old lady's name?"

"No. Sorry. I'll think about it and come back to you if I remember anything."

"Thank you."

"Anything I can do to help, Honey. After all I'm part of the family."

I key off and sit staring at the phone. I don't know where to go from here.

There was something weird about my talk with Ross, something missing. I try to track it down, then give up. As soon as I stop thinking about it, it hits me. Ross hadn't asked why I wanted to know.

Not giving myself time to chicken out, I pick up the phone and ring the nursing home. The matron is obviously surprised at my call. It's been a long time since I spoke to my father-in-law. Fortunately, I send him letters and small gifts regularly and apparently she doesn't see me as a neglectful ex-daughter-in-law.

My father-in-law views things differently. "What d'you want?" he demands in a crabbed cross voice.

"I wanted to speak to you, Harold."

"You want to talk to me? That's a turn up for the books."

"I need your help because Matt's not well."

"Not well? What's wrong with him? Nothing a bit of hard work won't cure. Always had ideas above himself, he has. And you made him worse. I never thought I'd see my land, Alder land, being farmed by strangers."

"Sarah's hardly a stranger." When Matt declared he didn't want to inherit, the family farm passed to his younger sister and her husband, and they've got children to carry on.

"Not that it would have had much future with that girl of yours. Real little townie she is. And that fancy man of hers, no gumption to him at all. Now Simon, he'd have carried on for me. But bad blood will show itself, no getting away from it."

There was a time when that cruelty would have hurt me intolerably but now all I feel is angry for Matt.

"What sort of bad blood are you talking about?" My voice is so cold and sharp it could cut through tougher substances than an old man's spite.

"Eh? What? What d'you mean?"

"Who brought in this bad blood you're talking about? Was it Granny Alice?" I send a mental apology to the memory of my frail, gentle mother-in-law.

His silence tells me I've struck home and I push my advantage, "Or was it her mother? Matt's grandmother? I've been hearing about her."

"Hearing? What do you mean hearing? Who told you? What the hell do you think you know?"

"The lady in the wheelchair. She was telling Allie's boyfriend all about it." I play the few cards I have in one wild bluff.

I hear him splutter with impotent rage. "She doesn't know anything. I never had time for reporters and that one's worse than most. That Polly Linnell has always been a lying cow."

I've got the name I'd been looking for. Now to get off the phone as quickly and smoothly as possible, before Matt's father drives himself into another stroke.

"I ought to go, Harold. I don't want to tire you."

"Tired? Of course I'm tired. I'm an old man. Not that you care. Not that anybody cares. Why the hell Matt had to marry a southern bitch like you..."

The rant carries on for a while, until he starts coughing. I take the chance to say, "Goodbye Harold," and ring off.

I'm shaking. I take a few deep, steadying breaths, then pick up the phone and dial again. This time, when I get through to the nursing home, I ask for Polly Linnell and the nurse on duty puts me through to her without asking why.

"Hello? Polly Linnell speaking." She's a sprightly sounding lady with a remarkably youthful voice that holds little of her native accent.

"Mrs... Ms Linnell. My name's Honey Alder. Matt Alder's wife."

"It's Miss Linnell, never had the misfortune to be married, but you call me Polly. What can I do for you?"

"I wondered if you could tell me about my husband's mother and grandmother?" I match her bluntness.

"Husband is it? I thought you were divorced?"

"We are but we're still good friends."

"And it's for him you're asking?"

"Yes." Indirectly that's true.

"And what does he remember about her?" Why had Ross said Polly Linnell was senile? She's one of the sharpest people I've ever spoken to.

"He doesn't remember her. He said she died before he was born."

"Oh, I see."

"What do you see?" I wrest the questioning back.

"I gather he's having a kick-back from that time."

"What do you mean kick-back?"

"A reaction. A shock like that was enough to send any child over the edge. I always thought it was a miracle he turned out to be such a nice, well-balanced man."

There's a drumming sound in my ears and my knees begin to shake. I sit down and say, "Please tell me."

"I was working for the local paper at the time. It sounds a terrible thing to say but it was a big break for me, because I'd been at school with Matt's mum, Alice, and she'd talk to me when she wouldn't speak to anyone else."

"Yes?"

"Alice was expecting a baby. To be honest I can't remember if it was Sarah or one of the ones she lost between Matt and Sarah. What I am sure of is that Matt was about four and his mum was very poorly with the baby and had to lie up a lot. Her husband didn't like it. Like many farmers he hadn't got much time for his family, especially a woman he'd categorised as sickly. He thought the world began and ended with his crops and stock. Although, from what Alice said, he was proud of Matt. He was glad to have a son to carry on the farm."

She pauses, perhaps waiting for me to comment. We both know Matt had left for university and had never again lived at home. I wonder if Polly realises that Matt's father blames me for his defection. To him I've always been 'that fancy southern bitch who led my boy astray.'

"Tell me about Granny Alice's mother," I plead.

"She'd always been a nervy woman. Nice, mind, and kind. She thought the world of little Matt and looked after him a lot. She was a good cook, could make the cheapest cuts go a long way. And she always looked ever so clean and smart. But somehow, deep down, she wasn't able to cope. I know Alice suffered with her nerves later on in life and I suppose her mother was the same."

"What happened?" I'm so tense I can barely get out the words.

"It's funny, you asking. I was looking back at my records not that long ago. It happened like this. One night, Alice was taken poorly. So very early the next morning Matt's dad put a note though his ma-in-law's door to say he'd be dropping Matt off a bit later, and to phone him if it wasn't convenient. They were on the phone at the farm, you see, and there was a phone box right outside Alice's mother's house."

It strikes me that Polly's enjoying herself. She's taking pride in the wealth of detail she can remember and she's delighted she can string it together despite her age. I'm sure it hasn't occurred to her she's torturing me.

"Matt's dad never heard it wasn't convenient, so around nine that morning he took the boy down, opened the door with Alice's key and sent him in to find his gran."

"You mean he didn't check, just shoved him in?" I think I know what's coming and my heart is pounding in my throat.

"I know it doesn't sound likely, but we're talking fifty years ago. Anyway that's the sort of man he was. If there was something needed doing on the farm that's all he'd be thinking of. Afterwards he was angry if he thought people were blaming him."

"What happened?"

"As far as anyone can tell, little Matt couldn't find his gran downstairs, so he went upstairs to look for her. He found her lying on her bed. He thought she was asleep and maybe she was poorly like his mammy and he didn't like to wake her. So he knelt down on the bedside rug and waited for her to wake up. He was still waiting hours later when his dad came back for him."

Chapter 28

And, fifty-four years later, Matt claimed he'd seen an old woman lying on his bed and had known she was dead. I'd got it wrong. It was in his mind. I struggle to tie together the child who'd been so bitterly traumatised with my warm, out-going Matt.

On the other end of the phone, Polly waits with courteous patience for me to speak. "He doesn't remember it," I say at last.

"That's not surprising and for all I know it's as well."

"How did his grandmother die?" Please God there was no obvious violence.

"She'd taken an overdose. She'd suffered from depression for years, poor soul. The note his dad put through was still there on the floor. He'd have seen it if he hadn't been in such a hurry to get back to his farm."

I wonder if, in the depths of his soul, Matt's dad feels any guilt?

"Are they sure she was dead when Matt got there? I mean, if he'd been older and able to call for help, could they have saved her?"

This time the silence stretches into eternity. An eternity of hell, the way it must have been for Matt, kneeling beside his grandmother's bed.

At last the old voice says softly, "They said he couldn't have saved her. No-one could. She was too far gone for that."

"But she was still alive when Matt got there?"

"They don't know. It wasn't possible to tell the time of death that accurately and all Matt could tell them was his grandmother was asleep."

"Thank you for telling me, Polly."

"I hope it helps Matt. I was so sorry when Matt's father told me about the death of your little boy. It seems a wicked shame the way bad things happen to good people."

"Thank you."

"Give Matt my regards. That is if you don't think it will stir up bad memories."

"I suspect, if the memories have surfaced this far there's no going back."

"In that case I could send you copies of my press cuttings. Our local rag covered it quite extensively."

"I'd appreciate that. Could you get someone to put them in the post today?"

"Post?" She says the word with such withering scorn I might have been suggesting carrier pigeon. "I haven't bothered with snail mail for years. I'll scan them and send them to you as an attachment if you'll give me your e-mail address."

I supply her with the information, feeling like an idiot. Of course this wonderful lady would have the latest technology at her fingertips, she's that sort of person.

The phone call over, I fight the urge to rush round to Matt's house. I tell myself I'm being absurd. Me knowing this terrible story about his past doesn't make him any more sick and vulnerable than he was an hour ago.

One of my survival strategies is to compromise with my fear. I pick up the phone and call Matt. When he answers, he sounds subdued and weary but not on the brink of nervous collapse. "Just checking you're okay," I say.

"What is this? Do you know something I don't?"

"What do you mean?" I don't want to tell Matt what I've found out over the phone, and not at all until Polly's attachment arrives.

"If I'm about to be sectioned, I'd be grateful if someone would tell me. Michelle's been on the phone, clucking at me. I don't need my office manager bloody humouring me. Have you told her I'm having a nervous breakdown or some crap like that?"

"No. I haven't spoken to Michelle since Sunday when you quarrelled with her."

This brings him up short. "You haven't? Sorry. When she said about me having a nervous collapse I thought you must have tipped her off."

"I wouldn't do that, not without your permission."

"No. I'm sorry. I'm not thinking straight. I guess Michelle must be in a flappy mood. I suppose it's because I haven't taken much time off in the last few years."

"What no exotic holidays?"

"No. There didn't seem much point."

The old Matt had been more fun than anyone I've ever known. It seems like all the zest for life has drained out of him.

"If you like I'll phone Michelle and try to soothe her down."

"If you've got time I'd appreciate it. I hate people fussing over me."

"I'm sorry, I know I'm fussing, but you know what I'm like."

"And I'm sorry, I know I'm snarling, but you know what I'm like."

We both laugh in a phoney, constrained way.

"Would you hate it if I dropped round later to check up on you?"

"No, that would be fine. But Michelle's coming by after work."

"No problem. I'll come to referee. Have you had your locks changed?"

"No. There's no way this woman I keep seeing could have been at your house without the rest of you spotting her. So she must be in my mind and changing the locks won't keep her out."

I'm not convinced by his logic but he sounds irritable. If I say a word wrong we'll end up quarrelling. "I've got my key. If you're tired, go on up to bed. And don't worry about food, I'll bring some supper with me."

"Won't Terry mind you coming round to me?"

"No." I'm tempted to tell him Terry is history, but discussing the complexities of my relationships is another thing I'd rather do face to face. "I may be out and about today, but I'll leave my mobile on. Phone me if there's anything you need."

"I'll be fine. I don't want to interrupt your exciting social life."

"If you think doing an Asda shop is exciting, your life must be as dreary as mine."

I keep my promise and phone through to Michelle. She greets me with relief. "Ross says Matt's in a very bad way," she says.

"How the hell did Ross get in on this?"

"He's concerned about Matt. We all are. He's a nice boy, isn't he?"

Personally, I don't think Ross is a boy or all that nice. "I didn't know you knew him."

I don't, not really, but he came in with Matt's papers. I was listening when you were chatting. I'm glad you get on with him."

"He was with you when I phoned?"

"Yes. In fact he's still here, having a cup of tea with us."

So much for Ross being so desperately busy he couldn't baby-sit his son. At least that explains why he was so nice to me on the phone. He was grandstanding for an audience. "Well make sure no-one gossips to him about Matt's business."

"Of course not." She sounds offended. "I'm going to see Matt later. Someone has to look after him now he's on his own." It's clear I'm cast as the bad guy in this play.

"Fine." Rather than soothing Michelle down, I long to tell her exactly what I think. I'd forgotten how irritating she can be. Resisting the temptation I ring off.

Housework won't do itself. I've experimented extensively and I know this for a fact. After my busy weekend there's the sort of chaos that could easily get out of control and so I set to work. I strip the bed my mother used but leave Matt's in case he needs to come back here tonight. I change my bed and feel no hesitation about removing the pillowcase Terry used. As I dust and hoover, I carry a black bin liner from room to room with me and gather up the bits and pieces Terry has left.

When I've finished the housework, I phone through to his mobile. "It's Honey. We ought to meet."

"Of course, love. Where and when you want. Thank you for phoning. We've got to talk this through."

"Terry, there's nothing to talk through. It's over."

"You don't mean that. It's natural you should be upset but I know we can sort it out. We both want this to work."

I want to ask who he's kidding but I don't because the answer is obvious. He's fooling himself.

"Please, Honey. Let's talk it through face to face."

"Okay. But I can't come all the way to Portsmouth. I've got a lot to do." I've got to face him sometime, so it might as well be today. It occurs to me I'm getting Terry out of the way, just as I had the housework. As if

I'm clearing the decks of trivia before I turn my mind to helping Matt.

"I'll come to you," he says.

"No, not to the house. I'll meet you in the pub. Will four o'clock in The White Boar suit you?" I name a pub a few miles out of my village, where I'm not well known.

"I'd rather talk in private."

"The pub or nothing. Take your choice." He might not be responsible for the strange stuff that's been happening but I don't want to be alone with him.

"Oh very well. Four o'clock then." He slams the phone down on the final word.

As I walk round Asda, I feel a glimmer of pride. There was a time when I couldn't stay in here by myself. I wasn't great in any shop, but this one was the hardest because it has no windows and the claustrophobic, artificial light used to panic me. Compromising with my agoraphobia, I'd trained myself to make a priority list to go round the store, always buying first the items I had to have. Today I realise how far I've come towards recovery. Even after a stressful weekend, I'm able to do a full grocery shop and linger to select a couple of cheap and cheerful tops that should look good with my new hair colour.

Ross drives up just after I get home. He's in time to help me carry my shopping in, which is a bonus. Then he makes us both coffee while I put the stuff away.

"Where is everyone?" he asks.

"Allie and Ben are at a teddy bears' picnic and Matt's gone home."

"Is he well enough? I thought he still looked pretty stressed."

"He wanted to go. I can't keep him here against his will." I can see Ross thinking, 'Nothing new there,' and feel uncomfortable.

"Ross, why did you tell me the lady you'd spoken to at the nursing home was senile? I've talked to her and she's totally on the ball."

He looks annoyed, or maybe he's embarrassed. "I didn't want you to be upset."

"Pardon?"

"You've been so fragile lately and Allie's dad has seemed so odd. We're worried about you. I didn't want you fretting about things."

There's nothing more undermining than being told you're weak.

"Have you been spreading this nonsense about Matt at his office?" I say sharply.

"Of course not, but his office manager was asking me about him. She said he's been acting strangely. Of course, I told her it was nothing to worry about." He changes the subject, "Is Allie due back soon?"

"She said she was going on to Oliver's. I doubt if she'll be back for a while."

I expect Ross to scowl when he hears this. He doesn't like Allie keeping up with her former friends. But this time I've wronged him, he seems quite happy with this news.

"Nice for you to have a bit of space after your busy weekend."

"I wish! The only time in days the house is empty and I'm going out myself."

"Somewhere nice?"

"I'm meeting Terry." This is awkward. I don't want to leave Ross here alone.

"I'd better get moving too," he says. "Are you out all evening?"

"Probably." This isn't true but Ross has shown a growing tendency to linger in the comfort of my house rather than returning to his bedsit.

"Have a nice dinner."

"I will." I plan to cook Matt something at his house.

As soon as Ross leaves I check for e-mails, discover that the attachment from Polly has arrived and print it out. As I study the old newspaper reports, I realise I'm trembling.

The facts are fundamentally as Polly remembered them but there's more detail. One thing hits me so hard that it feels like someone's punched me in the throat: Matt's grandmother had been fully dressed and there's a description of her clothes, the tweed skirt and pastel jumper and the pink fluffy slippers.

Thinking furiously, I phone through to the nursing home again. "Polly, thank you for the newspaper articles, they're very helpful."

"You're welcome. It's strange, I had a few photographs that Alice gave me at that time. I'd have liked to scan them and send you copies. In fact, I was going to offer to post Matt the originals if he'd like to have them, but I can't find them at the moment."

"Why did Alice give you photographs of her mother?" My mother-in-law was the last person I'd expect to feed details of a family tragedy to a reporter, even if she was a friend.

"That husband of hers was destroying all the pictures of her mum that he could lay his hands on. She asked me to keep them safe. That's why I feel so bad that they've gone missing. It's like I've let Alice down."

"I'm sure they'll turn up. There's some more things I need to ask you. I know it will sound crazy, but please humour me. Do you know what sort of perfume Matt's grandmother used?"

"I'm not sure. Probably something light and flowery. But I may just be thinking that because the vicar's sister used to make lily of the valley scent and rose water and sell it at the Church fair."

"I see. Was Matt's grandmother a big woman?"

"Quite tall and she held herself very upright. She could look quite intimidating."

"Polly, this sounds even stranger, but can you think of any reason Matt should associate the smell of cooking liver with his grandmother's death?"

"It's funny you should ask me that. I was talking about it not that long ago to that young man who visited with your daughter. I'm surprised he didn't tell you about it."

"No he didn't tell me." Presumably another thing he'd decided to shield me from.

"That day after Matt's grandmother died, my editor sent me round to the house to check things out. The whole house smelled of liver and onion where she'd cooked it the day before. I remember thinking how awful it must have been for Matt, kneeling by his gran, smelling that claggy smell. Does that make sense to you?"

I hurt so much for Matt that I feel numb inside. "Yes, I'm afraid it does."

Chapter 29

Terry gets up and crosses the pub to meet me. He takes my hand and bends to kiss me. I try to dodge and his lips brush damply across my ear.

"Still angry with me?" he says.

"Let's talk about it when we're sitting down." Half the customers are turning to see what we're playing at.

"I said we should meet somewhere private."

"Think of this as neutral ground." I smile at him in a way that should warn him to run for cover.

I settle at a corner table and watch him as he approaches carrying his pint and my orange juice. I try to remember the good times we had together. I know they'd happened, just as I know there had been friendship between us, but they have dissipated without trace. It's as if the Easter weekend has poisoned everything.

"Thank you for phoning me, Honey. I should have called you but I've been busy."

"Really?" I wonder if he thinks I'm cheap or desperate. "What have you been doing? You don't go back to work until tomorrow, do you?"

"I've been counselling Nicola.

Counselling, that's an interesting word for it."

He flushes. "It's all very well for you to sneer, but she's devastated, and a lot of it's because of your mischief making."

If Nicola hadn't been a promiscuous bitch, there'd have been no mischief to be made. "What did I actually do?" I enquire.

It's clear he finds this hard to answer. "Well... you persuaded Edward to leave."

"No, I didn't. He didn't tell anyone what he was planning until he'd set the thing in motion. All I did was persuade him to get some treatment for his back before he ends up crippled. Was that wrong?"

He doesn't answer, so I move further into the attack. "I didn't tell him about Nicola and Jez, but perhaps, as a friend, you ought to have warned him his wife had been screwing another man throughout their married life."

I know this is hypocritical when I've blamed Jackie for telling me about Matt's infidelity, and if Terry points this out I'll have to accept it.

"It wasn't appropriate. You wouldn't understand." He gives me that smugly humouring look that gnaws into my basic self-image and never fails to wind me up.

Infuriated, I offer the worst provocation I can think of, "I understand your reasons very well. You have to keep Nicola sweet. Otherwise she might not let you creep into bed with her when she feels like a change of pace. Tell me, what's the best thing about that, the sex or rubbing Jez's nose in it?"

I'd always known Terry had a temper and now I see it snarling at me across the pub table. A white mask of a face, with clenched lips and blazing eyes.

"You bitch!" he hisses.

I'm glad I'd insisted on meeting in public.

At this inappropriate moment my mobile rings. I grab it out of my handbag. The display shows 'Jackie: mobile.'

"Jackie? Hi. Everything okay?"

"Actually it's me," says Edward. "Jackie's driving. Everything's fine. I wanted to let you know we're packed up and on our way back."

I respond cautiously, keeping my eyes on Terry, interrupted mid-tantrum and audibly simmering.

"That's good. Thanks for letting me know. Is everything okay?"

"It will be. I saw my solicitor this afternoon and I'm pleased to say Nicola's going to get a nasty shock."

"Really? Hold on a minute." I stand up and take the phone into the Ladies. The reception isn't great but it's the one place that Terry won't dare follow me. "Sorry. I was with Terry and I didn't want him reporting back to Nicola. What did your solicitor say that's made you sound so smug?"

"He confirmed what I suspected. The way my father left things in his will means Nicola won't be able to get much out of the business. Basically it's a question of dividing the house and other assets and I'll be glad to see that place sold."

"How about Graham?"

"He's okay with it. I suggested he went and stayed with my mother for a while until it's sorted out, but he said he'd rather stay round here and help me move into the flat." Edward's voice loses its buoyancy, "He said, as long as it was okay with me and he wouldn't be in the way. How long has he felt like that? Like he's an encumbrance?"

"A long while. It's not going to be easy to alter that mind-set. And should you be talking about him in front of him like this?"

"He's asleep. And if he wasn't it wouldn't matter. He wouldn't mind what I told you. He said you're the best thing that ever happened to him."

"Oh." I make a mental note to back-pedal again with Graham.

"Don't be offended, but he said you were a cross between a best friend and what a mother ought to be."

"I'm not offended," I assure him, much relieved. "Give Jackie my love and tell her to phone me when she's free."

"I will. Honey, when I said about Nicola not getting as much out of the settlement as she expected, I didn't mean to sound smug."

I laugh. "You didn't, not really. Smug is a lot more Terry's line than yours."

"Say hi to him for me." Edward sounds constrained.

"I'm not sure I can fit that into the conversation. 'Bye would be more appropriate."

I hear him chuckle. "Yeah, that works for me."

When I return to Terry, he's regained control of his temper. "Is your sister all right?"

"Yes, fine."

"I'm sorry I called you that, Honey. It was unforgivable."

"No problem."

"I want you to believe that, until last Sunday night, I'd never slept with Nicola."

"I do believe you."

"I don't know why, after all these years, she suddenly turned to me."

By the reverent note in his voice, I guess he sees himself as some faithful knight waiting to serve his lady without hope of a reward. This is going too far into a sea of schmaltz and I proceed to enlighten him, "Because I'd pissed her off."

"What?"

"I'd encouraged her husband to stand up for himself and, what's worse, I'd shown I liked him as a person and I didn't admire her. Even more unforgivable, I'd befriended her despised son. That evening she was furious with me. She'd have done more than screw you in order to get at me."

The pallor is back in Terry's face, and the anger, but it's overlaid by a sort of dread. "It wasn't like that."

I can't be bothered to argue and I don't need his ongoing enmity. "Perhaps not. Look Terry, let's call it a day. We both know it isn't going to work."

"It's been ruined ever since your ex-husband wormed his way back into your life."

"Whatever." I stand up. "I've got your things in the car. I'll go and get them."

As I remove the black plastic bag from the boot he appears from the pub and crosses the car park. His face is stormy and I feel a momentary pang of fear. I remember the advice I'd heard on a cop show recently that if you're being attacked you should yell 'Fire'. If you shout 'Help' nobody responds.

Silently I hand him the bag.

"I don't think there's anything of yours at my place except that CD you lent me," he says.

"Keep it." I smile, trying to take the sting out of the words.

"No. I'll post it back."

We climb into our separate cars. I wait until he turns right, then I turn left. It adds a few miles to my journey but it's preferable to following Terry down the lanes.

I've been driving for five minutes when my mobile rings. I pull over to answer it. A glance at the display tells me the call comes from Home. I snatch it up. "Hello?"

"Mum! It's me." Allie's voice is shrill. "It's Dad. He's going to kill himself."

"What?" A roaring cloud of darkness descends. I fight through it and say, "Calm down and tell me."

"Ben was grumpy so I came home early. There's a message on the answer phone. It's Dad. He said he's going crazy and he can't cope. I didn't know what to do. I tried ringing back but there's no answer. I'm going round there now but I don't know whether to call 999. If he's changed his mind he'll be so angry."

"I'll go. I'm less than five minutes away. You stay where you are. I'll phone."

I hurl the car along the country lanes. My only thought the pounding prayer, 'Please God... please God... please.'

I leave the engine running and half fall out of the car. I up-end my handbag on the driving seat in my frantic hunt for Matt's key.

"Matt?" I scream as I run through the house. "Matt, where are you?"

He's in the sitting room, slouched in an armchair, his eyes closed, his white face still and shuttered. One arm is trailing limply and, on the table beside him, there's an empty whisky glass and a long medicine foil, stripped of its pills, and the photo of the woman and child that had disappeared from the album.

"Matt! Wake up!" I shake him but he groans and slumps away from me.

I've got to get help. I grab the phone and start to dial. A hand grasps my arm and wrenches the phone away. It clatters to the floor. For a moment I stand, shocked into immobility. Then, slowly, stiffly, I turn round.

"Ross!"

In that strange moment my mind feels split in two, the part that accepts this without surprise and the part that still doesn't understand.

"You interfering bitch. Why couldn't you leave anything alone?"

"Matt's ill. You've got to let me call an ambulance." I try to bend to pick up the phone but his grip on my arm prevents me.

"I haven't got to let you do anything." He lifts his other hand and I see he's holding a kitchen knife with a wickedly sharp blade. "It's not the way I'd planned it, but it should work out. I'm brilliant at improvisation, you know."

I lift my eyes to scan his face, it's cold and empty, but, as I watch, a smile twists his lips.

Chapter 30

"Come here." Ross' grip on my wrist tightens. He drags me into the kitchen and forces me to sit on a wooden chair. As he bends over me, I smell the faint scent of spring flowers. He jerks the scarf I'm wearing from my neck and uses it to tie my hands, entwining it with the back slats of the chair.

The taut silk bites into my wrists and the strain on my shoulders makes them ache. But physical pain is nothing to the desperation of my shock and fear and the knowledge that time is slipping away for Matt. I fight down panic. The only weapons I've got to save us both are my sheer stubbornness and wits.

"Matt will die if we don't call help. But I guess that's what you want. Matt didn't imagine things. It was you, playing a game of ghosts." It's strange that I'd suspected Terry but not Ross.

I get the impression he's preening himself. "How did you work it out?"

"You smell of scent. And there's a scrap of pink fluff on the hem of your jeans."

He frowns then picks it off and puts it with finicking care into a carrier bag beside the kitchen door. Behind his head I can see the clock, counting off the seconds of Matt's life. I've got to get Ross talking. Try to find a weak spot I can use.

"Don't bother staring at the time. Ross' sneering voice breaks into my thoughts. "I turned the security alarm off. No-one's coming. Apart from that old bat from his office, and she won't be here for hours."

I force my eyes away from the clock and concentrate on Ross. "It all makes sense when you know it was an inside job. I admit it was clever, using that smokescreen of Matt's grandmother's suicide. I should have guessed. You're the only person with a motive who's also got the skills to get away with it. But why go to all that trouble? It's such a complicated way to kill someone."

"That's because you're not an artist. It was exciting. A challenge. A test of my skills. And this way no-one will investigate his death or look too closely at motives."

"I see. And you're directing a play about cross-dressing. That makes a good cover if anyone spots you looking odd. Did you get your outfit in a charity shop when you were buying stuff for the students?"

He smirks. "Yeah. I even got the college to pay for it. Except for the slippers, I had to buy them new, but I think I'll still make a profit on the deal."

My heart is thumping but I force my voice into casualness, "Tell me, did you think of using the tragedy of Matt's grandmother to kill him as soon as you heard about it?"

"Of course I did, but I hoped he might save me the trouble and really kill himself."

"Not Matt. He'd never do that."

He scowls as if he's the aggrieved party. "You made me hurry things. You've been a bloody nuisance all along, poking and prying, stealing that picture and the watch. I don't let anyone interfere with my props."

"You're a fine one to talk about stealing." I taunt him, even though I know the risk. "That's exactly what you did. Polly Linnell was telling you about Matt's grandmother and you saw the photos and stole them. Where are the rest of them?"

He shrugs. "I used the best one and dumped the others."

"The watch, did that belong to Matt's gran? Did you steal it from Matt's dad?"

"A nice touch, wasn't it? Still pointing to the time it ran down after she died. When I'm a rich woman's husband I'll write my own plays as well as star and direct." He scowls at me. "Then I dropped it and you got hold of it and started flaunting it. And today you asked about that old woman in the nursing home and I knew I had to move fast."

"But why, Ross? It can't be worth it."

He scowls at me. "What do you know? You don't have a clue what it's like to be shit poor. I've been living in a bloody pigsty of a bedsit since my wife threw me out. This is all your fault. And your stupid bitch of a daughter, getting herself pregnant. If you'd let me move in with her it wouldn't have come to this. But no, I wasn't good enough for you. And she's started listening to you. She's forever finding fault with me. And then, to top it all, you encouraged my little shit of a brother-in-law to complain about me. Now even my job's on the line."

Inside I cringe with fear. If he's that deluded, he's capable of doing anything.

I force my tone into cool interest. "I should have realised it was you. You're in prime position to steal my key for this house and to go through my papers and find the security code."

"Stop sounding so bloody righteous! Who do you think you are to look down on me? You loony middle-class cow." He leans close and, beneath the perfume, I can smell the sourness of drink.

Instinctively, I know allowing him to bully me will feed his eagerness to harm. "Don't give me that middle-class crap, Ross. My dad was a factory storeman and my mum worked in a shop and Matt's family were hill farmers. Anything we've got has been worked for but you're just a parasite."

He slaps me. A stinging blow that whips my face around. It hurts and makes my eyes water but I don't care. Time is getting short.

"Always the hero," I say. His fist clenches but he stops before he strikes again. "How did you know Matt's left most of his money to Allie?" I mustn't ease off the pressure.

"She told me, of course."

"She didn't know until two days ago. Not unless she's a better actor than you are."

I see that barb strike home. "That stupid bitch couldn't act a part to save her life!"

"So who told you about Matt's will?"

"No-one had to tell me. I found a letter about it in your desk."

"Of course you went through my private papers. It's the sort of thing a low-life does." His blow rocks my head round but I continue in the same taunting tone, "When Matt came to stay with me, it was easy for you to carry on. You were already inside the house. But wasn't it a risk when people were around?"

He shrugs. "I had to put on the pressure. It was easy enough. Your mother's deaf and Allie sleeps through when I've slipped a little something into her bedtime drink."

"Not that easy. I almost caught you on Sunday. A minute later and I'd have seen you playing at haunting on the patio." I see his hands twitch, like he's reliving choking me. "Have you got a bruise where I kicked you on the leg?"

I'm trying to whip him with my contempt. To make him so mad he can't think straight. I'm past caring about the consequences to myself or Matt. I've got to make sure Allie and Ben are safe. "Go on, Ross, tell me exactly what you've got planned."

"You aren't supposed to be here. You're supposed to be out with your boyfriend."

"Should I apologise for inconveniencing you?"

I expect my sarcasm to push him over the edge but he seems too eager to explain his clever plan, "I knew, with her dad dead, you'd go crazy again, and Allie would have to turn to me because she'd have no-one else. But I like it better this way. Her crazy dad forcing his ex-wife to take an overdose and then topping himself."

"So have you faked a suicide note?" I think I know the answer. Ross likes to exploit his skills.

"A suicide message on your answer phone. Honey, it's Matt." His voice drops into an uncanny imitation of Matt's soft, lilting tones. "I just wanted to say goodbye. I'm losing my mind. Something that happened in my childhood is screwing me up after all these years. I'm so tired and I don't want to go on any more. Not without you. I'm sorry. Give my love to Allie and Ben and make sure you let Allie make her own choices. She's a lot wiser than you think. Goodbye Honey Bear."

"Nice," I say. "Especially the bit about making her own choices."

He smiles. "I thought so."

"And when Allie sees through you, are you going to murder her as well?"

The smile grows crueller. "Maybe. That's something you'll never know, but you can take that fear with you as you die."

I grit my teeth, fighting back tears. "I was wrong about you, Ross. I thought you were a slimy opportunist. I didn't realise you were a crazy sociopath."

I see his fists clench and think I've pushed him into hitting me again but he takes a deep breath and steps away from me. He looks towards the living room. "He can't last much longer. Then I'll deal with you."

I've watched the clock. Seven minutes have passed since Ross hustled me in here. By now it must be too late for Matt. I feel a tide of grey despair sludge through me. But I know it's too late for me as well. Too late for saving anyone but Allie and Ben.

I haul myself back into the fight. "You won't get away with it. They'll find your fingerprints and DNA in the house."

He smirks at me. "That won't matter. I told that old cow of an office manager how I'd dropped round to get the papers from Matt's house."

That's a blow but I keep on battling, "Everyone knows Matt's good at outdoor things. He'd never tie a crap knot around my wrists the way you have. Once they start asking questions they'll get a voice expert on that message and prove it's a fake."

Amazingly, he accepts my totally stupid argument. Swearing under his breath he comes round to untie me, loses patience and slashes through the silk. As soon as I'm free I move, swinging round and raking down his face with my nails.

Chapter 31

I'm braced for him to stab me, but he staggers back, dabbing at his face and staring with disbelief at the blood on his fingertips. "You bitch!"

I circle warily round the kitchen, keeping my distance, playing for time. "Now, when you kill me, you'll have to remove all traces of your skin from under my fingernails. Face it Ross, you're not as good at improvisation as you claimed. Put that knife down. I'm going to phone for an ambulance for Matt and you'd better pray it's not too late."

He doesn't release the knife but I see doubt, fear and anger battling on his face.

The doorbell rings.

For a moment we both freeze. In the silence that follows I feel my heart thumping. Ross waves the knife at me. "Keep quiet."

The doorbell rings again. Then nothing. The visitor's gone. We're back at stalemate.

Then there's a knock on the back door. My heart lurches. Allie's standing outside, Ben balanced on her hip. Ross leaps across to unlock the door.

I screech, "Allie run!" Ignoring the knife I lunge to intercept Ross.

It's no good. He elbows me away and grabs Allie's wrist, hauling her into the room. The momentum sends her sprawling and she screams. As she goes down, Ross grabs Ben and, holding him under one arm, heads out of the door.

Allie scrambles to her feet and we both run after him, round the house and onto the driveway. Ross has still got Ben under one arm, the knife in his other hand, as he backs towards our cars.

"What will you do to get him back unhurt?" he asks.

"Anything," I say. "Ross, put him down." At the moment he's holding the knife well clear of Ben but if he panics he could do something abominable.

"No way. He's my passport out of here."

Allie begs, "Ross, leave Ben and take me."

For a second he hesitates, then he shakes his head. "You'd just give me grief."

"Please Ross, leave Ben and get clear," I say, as I edge slowly forward. "We'll send you money, a lot of money, as long as Ben's all right. Take me if you need a hostage. Tie me up, gag me, anything you like. Everyone knows you're willing to harm me. I'm a better bargaining tool."

"Who are you trying to fool? You won't let me get away with killing Allie's dad."

"What?" I see Allie's face blanch and I grasp her arm in a biting grip.

"We don't know Matt's dead. If we call an ambulance he may still be okay."

"He's dead. He must be with the amount of pills I put in that whisky."

"We don't know for certain."

Ben whimpers and Ross' voice softens, "It's all right, Ben. Just get down on the floor by the back seat and do what Daddy tells you."

He tosses Ben into the back of my car. "I'll let you know where to send the money if you want Ben back. Thanks for leaving the keys. Considerate of you."

He opens the driver's door and twists slightly to brush my handbag contents from the driver's seat. His attention is on Allie and me. He doesn't see Matt come hurtling from the house. He cannons into Ross, sending him sprawling.

It must be a delusion. The sort of thing you make happen by wanting it so much. Even as my brain rejects the evidence of my eyes, I sprint to get Ben. But Allie's already there. She hauls him out of the car.

I divert towards the men struggling on the ground. Ross is on top and he still has the knife. There's blood on Matt's side.

All my fear explodes into anger. Black blazing rage that doesn't pause to consider consequences. I leap at Ross and the knife tinkles onto the drive beneath our feet. I kick at it, sending it scudding a few feet away. Ross scrambles to his feet and grabs my arm. I lash out with my free hand, screaming abuse. He flings me aside but now Matt's on his feet. He lands two hefty punches to Ross' face.

Ross falls against my car. He bends and grabs the knife. Waving it to keep us back, he scrambles into the driving seat. The engine roars as he accelerates away. Matt tries to pursue, but he's staggering and I hear his breath rasping in sharp gasps. I grab his arm, half to steady him, half to restrain. "You can't catch him, Matt."

He bends over, clutching his side. "I can give it a bloody good try."

"Leave it." We've had our share of miracles for one day and I need to check our luck's not running out. "How badly are you hurt?"

"It's nothing. Just a scratch."

I get my arm round Matt and unbutton his shirt. As far as I can tell the wound is superficial, a slash across the ribs rather than a deep puncture, but it's more than a scratch. I select my mobile from the debris on the drive and phone 999.

"What the hell's going on?" Matt demands.

"Hang on a minute." I ask for police and ambulance and then turn back to Matt. "Ross tried to kill you."

I hear Allie moan, a pain-filled protest. She moves slowly nearer to us, cradling Ben as if she'll never let him go. Her little face looks suddenly old and pinched.

Matt staggers back to lean against Allie's car and slides down to sit on the floor. I kneel beside him, strip off my blouse and hold it to Matt's side to staunch the blood.

I explain what's been going on. My voice is remarkably calm until I say, "I thought you were dying. From what Ross said there were enough pills in that whisky to kill you ten times over." Reality kicks in and I start to shake.

"I didn't drink it. Only a few sips. That put me out of it for quite a while. I was still pretty dozy when someone screamed and that jerked me awake. I managed to get on my feet and then I spotted what was going on outside."

"And you took him on, even though you could hardly stand?" whispers Allie.

"No one hurts you, any of you, while I'm in this world," says Matt. "Don't you ever forget that, sweetheart."

His fingers cup Allie's cheek in much the same movement I'd used for Ben and her hand comes up to hold his. For a moment we stay like that, a united family.

"Why didn't you drink the whisky? Did you realise it was drugged?" I ask.

"No, it wasn't that. I was dozing most of the afternoon anyway. I had a headache and I felt pretty crap. I woke up and saw the drink but didn't know where it had come from. I took a few sips, then I remembered and tipped the rest away into a plant Michelle gave me, so I wouldn't be tempted to drink any more."

"Remembered what?" I say.

He leans giddily forward to rest his forehead on my encircling arm. "Remembered I'd promised you I'd cut out the booze."

Chapter 32

"The police didn't believe us." Allie sounds as bewildered and exhausted as I feel.

"I know, love." I can't spare much attention from driving. She's in the back with Ben and I haven't driven her car that frequently. Even this familiar journey home requires all my reserves of energy.

"I wish Dad had been there. They might have listened to him."

"Yes." All the time we'd spent at the police station, I'd been wishing Matt could be there to back us up. If he'd been fit, his quiet authority might have swung matters in our favour, but the doctor had decided to keep him in hospital overnight and, although he'd been interviewed, he was definitely not on his best form.

The police weren't bad but neither were they good. I guess, contrary to detective novels and cop shows, most policemen don't have a lot of imagination. Our story sounded improbable so they preferred the easier option and decided we were lying. Apparently the chaos in Matt's kitchen and the carrier bag of clothes from Ross' masquerade are inadmissible because we couldn't prove we hadn't staged it all. Even Matt's wound could be explained as part of our conspiracy to frame Ross.

It was stupid of me not to realise how thoroughly Ross had laid his groundwork. When the police questioned him at the college, he had directed them towards several mutual colleagues, a few of whom I'd considered as almost friends. Some of them couldn't resist the chance to play a part in a crime drama and had declared that I was a vindictive, interfering woman, who was determined to destroy Ross.

From the information I pieced together from the police, it seems that, after the fight on Matt's drive, Ross had swiftly regained his wits. My stolen car was abandoned in the village car park, where I presume he'd left his own car. Then he'd gone back to college, disposing of the incriminating knife en route. The cops said there was no evidence that Ross had been at Matt's house that day or that my car had been stolen, and was I sure I hadn't left it in the car park?

They found Ross in the college theatre, running the students through their play. I gather he went through the whole scenario of appropriate emotions, starting with astonishment and concern at the cops' arrival and switching into irritated anger when they questioned him. He agreed I'd scratched his face but had convinced them I'd done it earlier at my home because I was unbalanced and obsessively protective of my daughter. My ex-husband was having psychological problems of his own and I'd persuaded him to play along with my spiteful games. I've never disputed that Ross is a good actor. In fact, for a while it seemed to be touch and go whether I'd be the one charged with assault.

One stolid, youngish policewoman told me reproachfully how Ross had cried throughout the interview. I said, 'Of course he did,' which didn't go down well.

Matters weren't improved when Michelle turned up. She'd been directed to the police station by the security guy who'd been summoned by the cops to reset Matt's alarms. Her tearful ramblings about my depression and Matt's mental problems closed the case as far as the police were concerned.

When I protested that they had not investigated properly, the detective in charge explained that they hadn't got enough evidence to take the case any further. He assured me that they would continue their enquiries. I was tempted to say that those who look with their eyes closed rarely find anything but I knew that wouldn't help.

We're hardly through the front door when the phone rings. Nervously, I pick up. I hear my sister's voice and don't know if I feel glad or regretful that I've got to talk about it again. "Hi Jackie."

"Honey, what's wrong?"

I tell her what has happened and think my voice sounds far away.

When I finish, she says, "We'll be straight round."

I wonder who 'we' is, but I feel too tired to ask.

I make a pot of tea for Allie and myself and microwave a jar of food for Ben. By the time she's spooned it into him there's a knock on the door and Jackie and Mum are there. Edward and Graham hover tactfully in the background, next to her car, clearly willing to stay or go, whichever I indicate.

"Come in," I say, and think, 'Let's have a party, why don't we?' which is unfair when they only want to help.

Mum takes one look at Allie and me and says, "Fish and chips."

"Pardon?"

"Comfort food. Good, solid warm stodge. And chocolate chip ice cream to follow. And don't tell me that you're on a diet, my girl."

"I wasn't going to." There are times for watching weight and times for giving in.

"I'll get it," offers Edward.

"No, I'll drive," says Jackie."

They both disappear, which I think is hard on Graham, a socially inept young man catapulted into this maelstrom. My mother has gone to Allie and is hugging her, talking in a soft undertone. I rescue Ben from his high-chair. He takes my hand and tows me into the living room, heading towards the train boxes once again. I feel limp and shaky and my head aches but I can't deny Ben anything tonight.

"Could I help?" asks Graham.

"That could easily save my life," I say and subside gratefully onto the sofa while he crawls around the floor.

Graham's a godsend. He gets out all the train stuff, sets it up magnificently and, under Ben's direction, he pushes trains along the track. He rescues delinquent carriages that come off at the bend and whistles, "Whoo, whoo," so vigorously that Ben is enchanted and even Allie turns round to smile at them.

"Thank you," I say.

"I wish there was more I could do."

"Being a friend is all anyone can do and that's plenty."

"But you've been so good to me and Jackie's nice as well. She's almost as nice as you."

"Thank you, kind sir." I store up this compliment to tease my sister at some later date. I see Graham's looking bewildered and smile at him. "Joking," I say gently.

"I see." Although I'm pretty sure he doesn't.

He looks at Allie, still cradled in her Nanna's arms. "It's so unfair. She's so pretty and so sweet." Before I can answer he turns back to the toy railway. "Ben's so lucky." I assume he means Ben's lucky to have a mother like Allie but he continues wistfully, "They didn't have all these super Thomas trains when I was small."

The fish and chips are washed down by wine and I see colour return to Allie's face. Ben falls asleep, cuddled in her lap, and even then she can't bear to put him down.

After dinner, Edward, with Graham to do the bending, puts bolts on all our outer doors. They're a bit skew-whiff, the result of too much wine, but they will serve to keep out marauders until I can get the locks changed.

Jackie and Edward offer to stay over if we're feeling nervous but I assure them it's okay. With my sane mind I don't believe Ross will come here. He's got away with it by the skin of his teeth and he'd be crazy to try again.

My Mum is staying with us and the knowledge of her presence is comforting.

Mum and I change all the bedding in Allie's room and bundle it into the washing machine. Allie prowls round the house putting Ross' possessions into a black bin bag. We Alder women don't go for originality but at least we're consistent when we're disposing of the debris in our lives.

I'm worried about Matt and so I phone through to the hospital again. The nurse on duty assures me he's 'comfortable.'

It's a few minutes to midnight when I go up and sit on Allie's bed, gently so as not to disturb Ben who is sleeping beside her. "How are you, sweetheart?"

"Confused. Mum, are you too tired or could you tell me everything from the start? I want to understand."

I am too tired but I tell her anyway.

"But how did Ross manage it, Mum? I understand about the clothes and acting out a part, and how Dad was vulnerable to the suggestion because of what happened when he was small. But how did he manage the cooking smells without any food?"

"In the carrier bag he left at your dad's house there were some small incense blocks with very odd fragrances. I think, when the props guy made up the interactive sense smells for the show, Ross must have got him to do some cooked liver smells as well."

"And the police didn't think that was evidence?"

"They accepted Ross' explanation that they were props he'd brought round to show your dad, because he might want to add them to his business provision."

"And they believed him? How stupid can you get?"

"I wasn't incredibly bright myself. I remember him telling your dad and me about the interactive theatre stuff. He even mentioned food smells and the smell of death. I suppose it was his idea of fun, to dangle what he was doing in front of us, when we had no idea what he was thinking."

Allie nods, "Yes, he'd like doing that. It scares me he could have felt like that, so full of spite and envy, and I didn't realise."

"You were busy being a single mum and working for your degree. And I suspect the thing with Ross is he's so good at fooling others because he convinces himself."

She doesn't pursue this. "Mum, how could you bear to sit there, tied to that chair, and talk to him?"

"It seemed the only chance. At first I tried to placate him, then I realised he fed on fear, it flattered his ego. So I provoked him."

"I'd have screamed the place down. Especially thinking Dad was dying."

"I didn't reason it through, just acted on instinct. I knew I'd only get one chance."

"One chance? To escape, you mean?"

I know what I'm going to say is brutal, but I've got to make myself clear, and Allie isn't a child any more. "Oh no. I didn't think I'd got any hope of that. I wanted to mark him and make him mark me. If there'd been a double death, even those moronic cops might have looked twice at the wannabe son-in-law with the scratched face."

"But why...?" Allie's voice fades and I see understanding dawn.

"The only important thing was that you and Ben were safe. And, if you think I was being arbitrary, disposing of your dad's chances of survival, I promise you he'd be furious if he thought I'd hesitated even for a moment."

I take a deep breath and say the thing we should have made clear years ago. "Your dad and I love you and Ben more than anything in the world. If you feel we cared more about Simon and neglected you for him, then we failed you in the most fundamental way. But please believe it was stupidity, not lack of caring."

She looks down at her hands, which are twisting in her lap, and stares at the bare ring finger, as if surprised it no longer bears Ross' pledge. "I didn't think that, not really. But I was so confused and angry. I wanted us to be like other families. The way we used to be. Not stinking of sickness." Her face crumples. "He was my little brother. I didn't want him to die."

I rock her gently as she cries. The tears are pouring down my cheeks as well.

"Afterwards, you sort of went away. I couldn't blame you because you were sick."

"So you blamed your dad for everything?"

She nods and dabs at her eyes with the edge of the duvet. "I shouldn't have upset you like this. I'm sorry."

A spasm of irritation dries my tears. "I'm not sick, and I'm not fragile, and I can cope. And, looking back, I think your dad had a rougher deal than me."

"What do you mean?" That stops her tears as well.

I struggle to explain, "Have you ever read Somerset Maugham's Cakes and Ale?"

She looks surprised at my divergence. "No. It's awfully old, isn't it?"

"God preserve the classics, because your generation won't."

A brief spark of mischief glimmers on Allie's face. "Blame Mrs Thatcher."

"Oh believe me, I do."

"What about this book with the funny name?" says Allie.

With great self-control I refrain from giving her the Shakespeare quote from which the title came but I try to explain. "In the last few pages the central female character explains how, on the night her baby daughter died, she came back from the hospital, left her grieving husband and went out on the town. It wasn't because she didn't care, it was because she couldn't cope with being shut in there with him and their shared grief. She needed to be with someone who didn't know and didn't feel sorry."

"Yes, I guess I ought to read that book. She looks down at Ben, asleep beside her. Ross can't love Ben," she says. "Not when he threatened him like that."

"I think he panicked. I don't believe he'd have hurt Ben." We have to clutch that slender thread of redemption. Ross is Ben's father.

"It still seems incredible he planned to do that to Dad."

"One step at a time, that's all it takes." This time I don't resist quoting the Bard, "'I am in blood stepped in so far that, should I wade no more, returning were as tedious as go o'er.'" I kiss her goodnight. "Ross should have directed more Shakespeare. He might have learned something."

Chapter 33 Wednesday

I sleep badly. My brain tells me there's no need to be afraid but my nerves are quivering. I hate the darkness and so I put my bedside light on and lie there, cold and shaking, trying to read and failing to concentrate.

It's after four when I hear someone moving round. I scramble out of bed and open my door. Peeping out I see Mum, returning from the bathroom.

"I didn't mean to wake you, love."

"You didn't."

She must read what I'm feeling in my face. "How about a cup of cocoa?"

Before I follow her downstairs, I check on Allie and Ben. By the dim light from the hall, I can see her face is blotched and swollen with tears, but they're both asleep.

Mum and I sit close together on the sofa, drinking cocoa and dunking digestive biscuits. I feel my overstrained nerves relax. At last, she rests her hand gently on mine and says, "I've always been very fond of Matt. He's a good man."

"Yes."

We don't say anything else but, when I return to bed, I fall asleep straight away.

I jerk awake at the peal of the phone. Disorientated, I think it's Terry, who makes a habit of early morning reveilles. Then I recall that Terry and I are finished. I snatch up the phone and Matt says, "Honey? Are you okay?"

"I think so. Are you?"

"I'm fine. I don't know why they kept me in here yesterday."

"I think it's because the ambulance men hate the narrow lanes that lead to your house and didn't trust you not to make it a hat-trick in one week."

He ignores my attempt to be funny. "How's Allie?"

"Getting there." She must have heard the phone because she's just opened my door and is looking at me in nervous enquiry. I smile at her. "It's okay. It's your dad."

"Give her my love." Matt's endearment is curt. This is a man on a mission.

"Dad sends his love," I say obediently and she smiles and departs.

"I've made us an appointment with my solicitor," announces Matt.

"Too late to discuss settlements, we're already divorced." It's a stupid thing to say but his curt manner is sending tension prickling through me once again.

"Will you stop being so bloody flippant?"

"As soon as you stop being so bloody overbearing."

That brings him up short. "I'm sorry. I was pretty woozy yesterday but I woke up at some incredibly early hour and realised the cops didn't believe a word we'd said."

"I think they believed our names and addresses after they'd checked them out."

"I don't want the bastard to get away with it and I've got plans about that, but what really matters is making sure Allie and Ben are safe."

"I agree. I'd like to make Ross suffer, but the fact is, he's got away with it."

"Don't be so sure. I phoned my solicitor early this morning."

"You told me that. It must have made you popular."

"With what I pay him he has to pretend he likes it." The humour is back in Matt's voice although it's grimmer than usual. "He's fixed up a meeting at his Portsmouth office between Ross and myself, and you and Allie, if you're both up to it."

"I think it's more a question of whether you're up to it."

"I'm fine."

"Do you think Ross will turn up?"

"He will if he's got any sense."

I daren't ask what he means. "Do you want me to pick you up for this meeting and if so where are you?"

"No, it's okay. I'm still at the hospital. I've got to go home and change. I'll meet you at my solicitor's at eleven-thirty. And, before you start fussing, I'll use taxis. I know I'm not fit to drive."

"I'll be there and I expect Allie will as well. I'll ask Mum to look after Ben. She can come with us and take him to Victoria Park."

"I'll see you then."

As I ring off I feel even more worried about Matt. Things that are hard and brittle shatter too easily.

Matt meets us in the doorway of the solicitor's office. He's pale and moves stiffly, as if his side is sore, but he looks every inch the successful businessman, confident and decisive.

He smiles at us and asks, "Are you both happy to play it my way?"

We murmur assent and Allie adds, "I just want it to be over."

Matt escorts us into his solicitor's office, where Ross is waiting with an anxious-looking, pretty, young woman who glares at us.

"This is my wife," says Ross. "When she heard how I'd been victimised, she agreed to let me come home." He's playing the injured innocent but I've become sensitised to him and his voice and manner have an underlying complacence that sets my teeth on edge. The scratches on his face glare vividly and his jaw looks swollen where Matt punched him. I wonder if he's enhanced his injuries with make-up and feel glad I've not covered the bruise on my cheek.

Matt sees Allie and I into our seats with more formality than he'd usually show.

The solicitor says, "I believe you wished to lead this meeting, Mr Alder?"

"Yes, thank you." He faces Ross. "We don't need to go over the problem that has necessitated this meeting. We all know what happened yesterday." His eyes rest on Ross' wife. "Or most of us do."

"Ross has told me how you tried to stitch him up," she says fiercely.

Matt quells Allie's angry protest with a soft gesture and says quietly, "What he's told you is of no interest to me or my family." He looks directly at Ross, "Yesterday, the police may have swallowed your story, but I can make life very uncomfortable for you. At this moment I've got investigators looking at your past history and others going through my house for evidence. Between them I'm sure they'll find enough. However careful you think you've been, my PI's forensic people will find the slightest scrap or smear you've missed. The police will be informed about anything my investigators uncover, and if they won't take it forward, I'll consider a private prosecution."

Ross licks his lips. All the smugness has dropped from him and he looks cornered. "Allie, tell him he can't do this. For God's sake, I'm Ben's father!"

I see Allie flinch. For a moment I think she'll give way, then her expression hardens. "You tried to hold Ben hostage. You threatened him with a knife. You plotted to kill my mum and dad. You deserve everything you get."

Matt's smile twists the corners of his lips. I know that smile and the sharpening of his intense blue gaze. It's the look he gets when he's about to close a business deal.

"There's no way out, however hard you wriggle and however loudly you lie. You'll be well advised to do exactly what I require of you."

"What do you want?" Like most bullies, Ross is a coward when he's faced down.

"You'll stay away from all of us from now on. You'll make no attempt to contact Allie or Ben. You won't claim any parental rights regarding Ben. Allie has never received any support from you for Ben and she does not wish to do so in the future."

Ross' wife looks startled. "But you told me..."

"Shut up!" snarls Ross.

She whimpers and lapses into silence. I wonder if he's been pleading poverty to her, as he has to Allie.

"All right," says Ross. "I agree. But what about work? I've got to see her there." A flick of his hand indicates that he means me.

"I can cope with that" I say. "You'll just have to try to be professional from now on."

I'm disillusioned by the gullibility and deceit of some of my co-workers but I'm not giving up my job. I owe it to my students not to abandon them close to exam time, and part of me looks forward to facing down my disloyal colleagues.

Matt takes control again, "My solicitor has drawn up the necessary legal documents to make sure you keep away, and to ensure, if anything happens to us, you'll not gain guardianship of Ben. Although I'm sure you won't want him if you can't access the money he'll inherit. As for the rest, we'll see what my investigators turn up. You'll spend some time wondering if you're about to be taken to Court. That's all I've got to say."

He nods to his solicitor. "Thanks for the use of your office. I'll be in touch about the paperwork." He stands up and ushers us outside.

"Thank God that's over." He puts his arm around Allie.

"I'm sorry, Dad. I was so stupid."

"That's okay, sweetheart. We all make mistakes. God knows I've made enough. Are you going to be all right?"

"Yes. Dad, Ben's going to need a male role-model in his life."

"And I'm all there is?"

"I didn't mean that. You're the best there is."

"Thanks love."

I think, with any luck, in a few years Allie will be in a new relationship and hopefully her choice will be better next time round. In the meantime, Matt can fill the gap very happily.

"Give it another year or so and you'll have to show him how to pee standing up," I say.

"Always the romantic, Honey." He pulls a face at me and I know he's remembering the struggle to persuade Simon to direct his wee into the toilet bowl.

"I don't think we were much use in that meeting. You had it all sewn up."

"I'd been thinking it through since the early hours, but you were both great moral supports." His right arm is still cuddling Allie but now his left encircles me.

Allie says, "I'd better go and rescue Nanna in case Ben's out-running her."

"What are you planning to do today, love?" I ask.

"I thought I'd have lunch with Nanna, then maybe hang out with Oliver and Kayla. I might give Graham a ring and see if he'd like to tag along. Kayla's always had a soft spot for geeks."

"Allie, be nice," I warn her.

"I will. I just like to see the way you rise to the defence of the helpless and hopeless. Do you want me to drop you anywhere?"

"No, that's okay, Dad and I will take a taxi."

She kisses us both and runs off in the direction of the park.

"Drive carefully," I call after her. I know she's not feeling as bouncy as she pretends and there'll be many tearful times when she remembers her world has crashed in fragments around her, but I'm certain she's going to be okay.

A middle-aged man is lingering on the pavement. Matt says, "Hi Dave, thanks for coming to meet me."

"Always a pleasure to do business with you, Matt."

"Honey, this is Dave Benson, the Private Investigator I occasionally employ. Dave, this is my wife, Honey."

I shake hands with Dave and note he's a smartly dressed, professional man, just like Matt told me. I also note Matt introduced me as his wife.

Chapter 34

"There's a café along the street," says Dave. "Why don't we sit at one of their outside tables and have a coffee and chat?"

We walk along to the café, sit down and order coffee. At last Dave gets onto business, "I got your instructions. My forensic guys have already gone over your house and I sent a clean up team to tidy things afterwards."

Matt smiles. "That's great. Thanks Dave."

"I'm not sure we've picked up enough evidence in the house for you to win a private prosecution, not against a man as glib as that guy, but we recovered a scrap of material from your rear fence, and there's tracks of a trail bike on the footpath behind the woods. If he sat up in a tree with binoculars, I reckon he could keep an eye on your movements and know when to make his play."

"The material probably came from his shirt," I say. "I saw his sleeve was torn. But by now he'll have got rid of it."

"Seems likely," agrees Dave. "I'll have my people keep an eye on laddie for you, like you ordered, Matt."

"Cheers. I want to make sure he stays clear of my wife, daughter and grandson from now on."

"No problem. I'll have him watched for a couple of weeks, after that we'll go to spot checks three times a week." He hands me a business card. "That's my office number, Mrs Alder. If you or your daughter are worried, ring straight through, any time, day or night, and one of my people will be onto it."

"Thank you." I feel dazed. I hadn't realised Matt had so much clout. Perhaps it's because he's willing to pour a lot of money into protecting us.

"I've started the checks into Ross' background like you asked," continues Dave, "and your instincts about him were right." He must spot my bewilderment because he explains, "Not many people go straight into a major, violent scam like this. It's looking more and more likely Ross has pulled con jobs before. Although the three women we've turned up so far were a lot older than your Allie. You have to feel sorry for them. There was one woman... a lottery winner... must have been sixty if she was a day. Anyway, it's pretty clear he targeted her and took her for most of her winnings."

"But he's always complained he's got no money," I say.

"That sort spend it as soon as it's in their pockets. He thinks he's got a right to everything he wants."

"Yes, I see." Suddenly it all falls into place. I'd always thought Ross was selfish but now I realise it's far more dangerous than that. I always suspected he had Narcissistic tendencies but now I think that he's a psychopath. "I should have realised."

"No reason you should," says Dave. "You're not a psychologist, are you?"

"No." But teachers of experience tend to have encountered most sorts of aberrant behaviour, quite frequently in the staff room as well as the classroom.

"How did he manage to get so much money out of this woman?" asks Matt.

"He pretended he was setting up a theatre company and, if she backed him, she'd double her money, with him thrown in as a bonus on the side."

I think of a woman my age begging for Ross' embraces and shudder.

It's obvious Dave has spotted my disgust. "Matt told me you never liked him but not everyone has your sort of insight, Mrs Alder."

"My instinct's rubbish." I'd suspected just about everyone but Ross of trying to harm Matt. "This woman, did he ever try to hurt her?"

"She told my operative he threatened her when she said she couldn't afford to give him any more money. She denied he actually touched her but I reckon that's what it was... she's in denial. Probably couldn't bear to admit it, not even to herself."

"The police said he hadn't got a record," I say. "Is that why? Because people wouldn't talk?" After my recent experience with the police I'd be the last person in the world to blame any victim for that.

"Yeah. People don't like to admit they've been totally screwed. Sorry, I didn't mean to say that, what I mean..."

"Don't worry. I know what you mean. I hear a lot worse in the classroom every day."

Dave hurries on, apparently eager to cover his embarrassment, "Anyway, domestic violence isn't easy to prove. If she says he hit her, he says she's trying to get back at him because she's an obsessed older woman who resents him for not fancying her. And proving he conned women out of money to back his theatrical career is even harder. There are probably dozens of women out there that he's conned. Most of them creep away, curl up and lick their wounds."

"I think one of them confronted him. I saw her with him in Waterlooville Precinct on Saturday morning. She was screaming at him. She looked like she wanted to claw his eyes out but when he walked away from her I thought she was going to cry."

I wish I'd gone up to her and asked her what was wrong. If she'd told me, perhaps I would have been able to stop Ross' games and saved us all from a lot of trauma.

"What did this woman look like?" asks Dave.

"Short, plump, blonde spiked hair. I'd think she's in her fifties. She had a revealing jumper, very high stiletto heels and a lot of make-up."

"That's a new one. Might be worth tracking her down. You know, of all of them, your Allie's the only one he's left his wife for. Perhaps he did care a bit."

I shake my head. "From what you've said the others were all over child-bearing age. His mistake was getting Allie pregnant and letting his wife find out. But he'd never have stayed around if she hadn't been an heiress." There's something niggling at me. I turn to Matt. "Dave said he'd found this out in the past two days? Does that mean he was considering Ross before last night?"

"Aye. I called him on Sunday and asked him to check Ross out."

I stare at him. "If you thought he was up to something, why the hell didn't you warn me?"

"I didn't. I mean I didn't suspect him of trying to kill me or of planning to drive me mad, but I could see you didn't trust him and I've always respected your instincts. I thought if I was really going crazy, I needed to make sure Allie was okay with a decent bloke who cared about her and Ben. That's why I asked you what you knew about his past."

That silences me. Ever since I realised what Ross was up to, I've been thinking I should have trusted my instincts more. I feel like I've missed all the major moves that happened in this game.

"It wasn't that hard to catch up with Ross once we knew what we were looking for," says Dave. He turns to Matt, "About that other little job. Nothing to it. One of my guys tracked down Deirdre Davis and checked she's okay. Mind you, she nearly died laughing when my chap told her what her old man had done. Said it was typical of him. She asked my guy to thank you for worrying about her."

"Thanks Dave," says Matt. "I'll be in touch."

"Yeah, but next time I hope it isn't because someone's tried to kill you. Nice to meet you, Mrs Alder."

He walks over to his car, gets in and drives away. We finish our coffee and stroll to the station forecourt to pick up a taxi. Neither of us speak. Matt gives the taxi driver his address then says to me, "Sorry. I didn't think. Do you want to be dropped home first?"

"No. I'll come in with you for a little while and talk, if that's okay?"

"Of course."

Now all I have to do is work out what I want to say.

Chapter 35

We drive to Matt's house in silence.

Once inside, he says, "Would you like a cup of coffee? I'm sorry, I should have offered to take you somewhere for lunch."

"That's okay. I'll make the coffee. You sit down." Now the need to fight is over, he looks drained.

Before he sits down he takes off his tie and jacket. Through the fine material of his shirt I can see the dressing on his side.

When I've poured the coffee I sit down opposite him and he says, "Honey, would you tell me about the woman in pink slippers? Why did Ross do that to me and why did it drive me so crazy? You seem to know so much that I don't."

The picture of him and his gran is still lying on the coffee table. I hand it to him and, as gently as I can, I tell him about the dual layers of the story, of his grandmother's death and of Ross' deception. Matt asks for the newspaper articles. I fetch them from my handbag and I watch his shuttered face as he reads them through.

At last he lays them aside. "I still can't remember. Isn't that scary?"

"Very. You'd probably have never known anything about it if it hadn't been for Ross' scheme."

"I wonder if that would have been a good thing or a bad? At least it explains why I've always felt the way I do."

"What sort of way, Matt?"

"The opposite to you, or at least the way you used to be."

I don't think I visibly react but he seems to sense my secret wincing.

"I'm sorry, that was crass. It came out wrong. What I meant was, when I first met you, you amazed me. You were so willing to grasp life and commit yourself emotionally. Then, when I met your mum and dad, I understood. It was because you were so secure in their love you weren't afraid to take risks. You could jump off the highest peak and try to fly because they'd always be there to cushion your crash landing. Emotionally I mean, I'm not talking about money."

"I know." If my mum was still breaking my fall, what did he think he'd done for Allie in the past two days?

"You made me feel different about everything, especially about myself. For the first time in my life, I felt safe."

He'd said the same thing to me on the day he'd asked me to marry him, but then I hadn't understood. Perhaps, if I had, this last decade would have been different for us.

Painstakingly honest, he continues, "When Simon got ill and died it was terrible, a nightmare, but that wasn't what finally took me apart."

"No, it was me deserting you." I know now that emotional withdrawal is as destructive as any physical act.

He looks startled at the bluntness of the term but doesn't deny it. "I felt like nothing once you'd gone away."

"I was grieving. Not just for Simon but for the person I'd been."

I was mourning for the girl who greeted each day as if it was a gift full of glittering pleasures. The woman who has passed through the holocaust has survived as a fearful, anxious creature, terrified of the enemies I cannot see: the germs, the cancer, the blood clots, the accidents. But I'm still capable of love.

Impulsively I run upstairs to fetch his guitar, desolate and abandoned on its stand. "Play for me, like you used to," I beg him.

"It's years since I touched the thing." Nevertheless he turns his attention to tuning it, then gets up to sit on a chair arm to allow free movement.

What he plays takes me by surprise. Tom Paxton's The Honour Of Your Company, a salute to days of innocence and youth. When Matt sings that if ever he was the singer I was the song, he looks directly at me and my heart melts as if I was nineteen again.

I slip my shoe off and flex my toes and he grins and stumbles over the next words. He remembers as clearly as I do that Paxton concert we'd attended together soon after we met. A song about drunken revelry declared the singer's love for the woman who was running a foot up his leg, whoever she was, and I'd teased my toes along Matt's calf.

He abandons the song and says, "You haven't changed. Whenever I was singing in public, I had to make sure you were far enough away."

"You didn't always manage it."

"No. I used to think you were the bionic woman, just when I thought I was out of range you'd manage another stretch."

"Just staking my claim."

"You didn't need to. I was yours from the first time we met."

He seems to realise the contradiction in his words. "I'm sorry about sleeping around, Honey. I couldn't explain it then and I can't now."

"You don't have to. I understand."

The trouble is, what Matt said isn't true. I have changed. And there's one last hurdle. I suspect it's in my mind, but my mind has screwed us up before and it seems likely it will again, unless I exorcise all my ghosts by exposing them to the light.

"Matt, I'm afraid, deep down, you'll always see me as the fat agoraphobic mess I was after Simon's death."

"For God's sake! In the past week you've seen me disorientated and bleeding, throwing up, crying and shaking with fear. Are you going to hold that against me for the rest of my life?"

"For blackmail purposes, quite probably." My voice is too husky for nonchalance.

He bends over the guitar, tears running down his face. Before I can move towards him he pushes himself upright and starts to sing another of the poems he'd put to music for me when we were young and filled with hope.

"'Even such is Time, that takes in trust
Our youth, our joys, our all we have,
And pays us but with earth and dust...'"

I won't let him continue. Raleigh's poem is beautiful but it was reputedly written on the eve of his execution, an acceptance of imminent death. I've got my fighting spirit back. I'm not giving up on life, and I won't let Matt do so either.

I go to him and take away the guitar. I remove his glasses, kiss his wet cheeks and wrap my arms around him.

"Come home with me," I say.

Epilogue

In our bed, as afternoon turns to dusk, I roll free and think our daughter and grandson could be home at any time.

"We ought to get up. It's past tea-time."

Matt smiles up at me. His blue eyes are amused and tender, and, with the empathy between us, I know exactly what he's going to say.

When we first met, the young Physics student had tried to impress the girl who was studying English Literature by using the literary quote he'd looked up. He was so proud of himself because it contained her name. The result had not been what he'd anticipated. In fact I'd thumped him and it was only total abasing on his part that had prevented me from ending our relationship there and then.

Now, as he opens his lips, I clench my hand, but you can't hit a man who's suffering from concussion and a knife wound to his side.

"And is there Honey still for tea?" he enquires.

I surrender. "And breakfast, lunch, dinner and supper too."

About the Author

Carol Westron is a successful short story writer who now writes crime fiction, children's fiction, articles and reviews. She is an expert on the Golden Age of Detective Fiction. Her four contemporary police procedurals and her first Victorian Murder Mystery are all set in the south of England, as is her new stand-alone romantic mystery, This Game of Ghosts.

Printed in Great Britain
by Amazon